CAUGHT IN THE ACT

CAUGHT IN THE ACT

A COLLECTION OF SHORT STORIES

David M.V. Spiller

The Book Guild Ltd

First published in Great Britain in 2017 by
The Book Guild Ltd
9 Priory Business Park
Wistow Road, Kibworth
Leicestershire, LE8 0RX
Freephone: 0800 999 2982
www.bookguild.co.uk
Email: info@bookguild.co.uk
Twitter: @bookguild

Typeset in Minion Pro

Printed and bound in the UK by TJ International, Padstow, Cornwall

ISBN 978 1911320 470

British Library Cataloguing in Publication Data.
A catalogue record for this book is available from the British Library.

Contents

Feeding guinea fowl in the woods

In the dimly lit study, David sat expectantly in a cavernous, winged, fireside chair that had been over-stuffed and upholstered in dark green button-backed leather. His Uncle Ivo, who was sitting sideways on to his desk so that David could watch, was opening the large brown envelope that had arrived in the post that afternoon.

His uncle's hands were shaking as he tore at the paper, and he reminded David of a child greedily opening a present on Christmas day.

"Let's see what we've got here," his uncle said, as a large glossy brochure fell out of the envelope and landed with a dull thump on to the Persian rug. It just missed by an inch, the old Labrador, which was sleeping off the long walk that they had taken that afternoon across the damp fields. The dog woke instantly, and with eyes wide and looking a bit annoyed, it immediately staggered away drunkenly to a place of safety under the small side table and circling as they do, she collapsed back into a deep sleep.

"This is going to be the trip of your life, my boy. We can go wherever you like, for as long as you like. We're free as the air. You're the boss now. We can start planning straight away."

With some difficulty, Uncle Ivo leant forward stiffly and scooped up the fallen brochure and put it carefully on the desk. As he straightened up, he gave a sharp intake of breath and clasping the small of his back with both hands, he gasped, "Damned bloody war wound. I need a tincture. Where's my medicine?" Looking at his watch, he said,

"Time for a drink, old boy. The sun is well and truly over the yard arm."

Getting up stiffly, he moved across the room to a small lacquered cabinet that stood against the oak panelling in the warm glow of the standard lamp. Choosing a large cut-glass tumbler from the tray on top, he poured out a couple of fingers of his favourite single malt and without ceremony, took a welcome gulp.

"That's better." Uncle Ivo had drained the glass. "Excellent medicine, better than going to the damned quack. Who needs them, eh? What'll you have, old boy, same as usual?" He always asked David this, just as if they were at the bar of the officers' mess.

David got out of his chair and walked over to get his drink. As he passed the desk he looked down at the brochure. He couldn't help but notice the picture emblazoned across the cover, of a large three-funnelled cruise liner, steaming through the ocean, and he could clearly make out its name in gold lettering on the bow: *Queen Mary*. He also saw that the name 'Cunard Lines' was emblazoned across the top of the picture. Were they really going this time?

He took his warm ginger beer, and returned to his seat.

"Are we really going on the *Queen Mary*?"

"We can if you want to, old chap. Can't see why not. It's a lovely ship." Uncle Ivo had poured himself another drink and was back in his chair and browsing eagerly through the brochure.

"81,000 tonnes and can do twenty-eight knots. Held the Blue Riband until '52 when those damn Yanks took it off her. She's a beautiful ship. Come and look at this." And he beckoned David over to his side. "Look we can go across the Atlantic to New York. See the Statue of Liberty and the Empire State Building. How would you like to do that?"

"Er, I would love it," David said hesitantly. But then he immediately began to think of the implications. Who would feed his rabbit while he was away? And how long would he be away for? Would his brothers and sister be jealous? What about school?

For it was always the way when staying with his aunt and uncle for a few days; in the evenings they would invariably go into the study and plan a cruise. They had never actually gone on one yet and David doubted that they ever would. But they had planned so many together. It was a good game and you never knew, maybe this time they really would go. In a strange way David enjoyed the sense of anticipation and thinking about the possibility of it all.

"Look, there's a swimming pool, a cinema and a library. And shops! Imagine that! How splendid!"

His uncle then was quiet for a while as he pored over the brochure, studying dates and itineraries, and making pencilled notes in a pad.

David stood and watched. He had been to stay here several times. The study was a small, cosy, wood-panelled room leading off from the large entrance hall and its black-and-white tiled floor. The only light sources in the

3

room were the desk lamp and the standard lamp. The thick heavy curtains were closely drawn to keep out the cold and frosty Norfolk night. The room smelt of log fire, tobacco smoke and damp dog. One wall was lined with books, mostly travel books, and there was a solid block of National Geographic magazines filling an entire shelf. Uncle Ivo was an armchair traveller.

Hanging over the mantelpiece, above the smouldering log fire, there was an iconic oil painting of a Lancaster bomber, flying in a clear blue sky over the famous white cliffs of Dover. If you looked carefully you could see a tractor ploughing a field in the patchworked landscape below and some farm-workers on the ground were waving. On the opposite wall hung a carved RAF crest with the motto "*Per Ardua ad Astra*" painted on it. Beside this, a map of the world, with many countries coloured in pink, was pinned to the wall.

"What do you think? Shall we go first or second class?" He suddenly turned to David and unconsciously twiddled one of the ends of his handlebar moustache. He had turned his head so that his face was only about a foot away from David's. His uncle's eyes looked haunted and suddenly very tired. They were watery grey and slightly blood shot and the drink had made his face red and blotchy. David stared, transfixed by the moustache that suddenly seemed ridiculous and out of place because it was so close up, and he was assailed by wafts of whisky-breath and smoke which spluttered from the pipe clenched between a yellowing set of teeth. David knew that his uncle had been an officer in the RAF during the war, and that something traumatic had happened to him,

4

but no one had ever said what it was. He noticed again the small black and white photograph that stood in a simple frame on the desk just a few inches away. It was a picture of seven or eight seemingly carefree young men who looked like air crew; he had seen pictures like this in his encyclopaedia of the Second World War. They were sitting around in deck chairs or on the grass, smoking and laughing at the camera. One, Uncle Ivo, slightly apart from the others, was staring directly at the camera, a pipe clenched in his gritted teeth. It was a sunny day and he could see their shadows on the ground and behind them he could make out the side wall of a wooden hut with diagonal crosses taped onto each window pane. He could also see a bell fixed to a bracket by the door with a rope hanging from it. The men looked just like any group of young people on holiday somewhere, without a care in the world, having a jolly good time, except for the uniforms, and the tape crosses and the war.

Suddenly his aunt's head popped round the door as she said, "And what are you two planning this time?"

"We're going to America on the *Queen Mary*!" David said.

"Oh for pity's sake, Ivo, what nonsense have you been telling him now?"

"We're planning our trip, old girl. You, me and David are going on a cruise. We haven't confirmed which one it will be yet, we are just doing some preliminary research. We could all do with a break, need to get away, get some sea air and see some sights."

"Anyway, Ivo, supper's ready and then David has got to have a bath and go to bed."

As he lay in bed that night and drifted off to sleep, David wondered about the haunted look in Uncle Ivo's eyes and he decided to ask his aunt about the black and white photograph on the study desk next time they were alone. He could do it tomorrow, when they went to feed the guinea fowl in the woods.

The morning walk and nature trail

The crocodile of twenty or so small boys in grey blazers, shorts and purple caps moved slowly along the pavement beside the busy arterial road. The elderly lady shepherding the children walked heavily and breathlessly behind them, making sure that they all stayed in line. She didn't have to worry. The children were docile and compliant with the instructions they were given, and were always obedient in her presence. They stayed in their pairs together, some were holding hands.

Miss Jefferies walked with a stick and bore an indefinable air of authority. Her hair was fixed back in a loose bun under her olive green felt hat. Under her dark grey coat she wore a tweed suit and an amber bead necklace. She was short and stocky, with a round cheery face. Her overall appearance was typical of a genteel older woman of mature years. Squinting into the distance, she gently called out, "There's a h'arse coming. Boys… caps off!" The boys responded immediately by taking off their caps, facing the passing cortège and bowing their heads as the procession of cars swept by. A blurring flash of shiny black cars, the one in front containing a profusion of flowers, was all he really remembered. At the time he never knew exactly what a "h'arse" was or why they had to take off their caps. Someone had once said that it was to show respect to a dead person. He knew he had to take off his cap and say hello when he met someone who was alive. But he didn't know any dead people.

At the base of the hill there was a copse of large oak trees and when the crocodile got there Miss Jefferies told the boys that they had ten minutes play time. She sat on a bench with her back to the woods and faced the road. Occasionally, she glanced over her shoulder towards the boys who by now had scattered throughout the copse, whooping and shrieking with joy at this short opportunity for freedom. The noise of the traffic drowned out most of the noise the boys made. If she thought she heard a shriek or someone calling she turned round, smiling benevolently, and quietly said, "No silliness now, boys." But no one really heard her.

At the back of the copse the largest oak tree held the greatest fascination for the boys. It had a wide girth and its gnarled trunk could easily hide a group of five or six boys behind it without being seen. The gang that "owned" it "controlled" the whole wood. A tall wiry boy with a shock of curly ginger hair and a face covered in freckles was the undisputed leader of the most successful of the gangs and he and his few followers had run straight to the tree to claim it as of right. Their weapons were sticks picked off the ground or pulled from saplings and they looked about for other boys to harass and dominate. The sticks were either machine guns, in which case you had to make a sort of rattling whooshing sound as you riddled your victim with bullets, or if you were a gladiator or pirate, they became swords and were waved about in a move that looked like practice for slicing someone's head off. If you were an

Apache in the Wild West they were tomahawks and used in a chopping motion with accompanying blood-curdling shrieks. All these actions were supposed to strike fear into any rival claimants to the tree. Once they were warned off, they would be pelted with acorns.

"Who wants to be in my gang?" cried out the ginger-haired gang leader, waving his stick in the air.

"I do," came the reply. David didn't know why he had said this, but suddenly he was committed.

"You've got to piss on the tree then!" said the gang leader, and he and his gang of three others unbuttoned themselves and sprayed the tree, laughing and seeing who could piss the highest.

"Now it's your turn!"

***

Later that day at milk break, the boys and girls were lined up and made to stand in silence. Once settled, they were ushered in to the dining room, which smelt of yesterday's lunch of grey meat, cabbage and potatoes. Ceramic mugs had been set out round the tables and the children had to stand opposite a mug, they couldn't move places and they had to have the mug they ended up adjacent to. The problem was that some of the mugs had dark blemishes inside them embedded in the cracked glaze, and these marks looked just like bogeys. In fact the boys believed they *were* bogeys and the trick was to not end up opposite one of these faulty mugs. As he gazed into his mug his heart sank for he had seen a bogey. He felt immediately sick and nauseous, but there was nothing he could do.

9

The milk lady was coming down the line sloshing milk into each mug. The boys could not leave until they had drunk all their milk. When she had passed he grasped the mug and tipped the cold slimy liquid down his throat trying not to think of anything.

He left the room as quickly as he was allowed and made his way to the nearest lavatory where he locked himself in and tried unsuccessfully to throw up.

Concentration in lessons was a problem. Arithmetic was an even bigger problem. The teacher would explain the process on a chalky blackboard. She would take the children through the intricacies of the day's sums and explain the necessary process for solving them. She would ask if anyone did not understand. When he put his hand up to say he didn't understand, the teacher would sigh, the rest of the class would moan, and they would go through the whole process again, together, *concentrating*. And yet he still didn't understand. The boy wasn't stupid, he just found no interest in the whole subject, it just seemed so abstract, and thus arose his inevitable lack of concentration and daydreaming. When the teacher had started to explain the way to do the sum, the boy had simultaneously noticed that a wasp had landed on the windowsill outside and had become entangled in a cobweb. Keeping his head down so that the teacher could not see which way his eyes were looking, he watched as the wasp struggled to escape. The more it struggled the more it became hopelessly and helplessly enmeshed. A large spider rushed towards the trapped wasp and immediately began to wrap it in cobweb strands, turning it round and round until it was completely trussed up and immobile.

"David!" barked the teacher. "So what is the answer?"

All he could do was to stare blankly at the teacher as his face turned to crimson.

When it actually came to doing the sums, if he wasn't sure of the answer he made it look like all the numbers it could possibly be. He did this by faintly writing with his pencil a six on top of an eight on top of a three and so on hoping that the teacher would give him the benefit of the doubt. But Miss Watson never did. When the class was working silently, he was called up to the teacher's desk. She was marking the tests they had done.

"What's all this!" demanded Miss Watson, stabbing at his work with the sharp point of her pencil.

David stared at the sum, which was a long division with rows and rows of numbers. Where the answer should be was just a blurred and fuzzy mess of squiggles.

"I can't read the answer!" she continued. "Take me through the question," she said. "and explain how you worked it out!"

He felt just like the wasp and wondered at what point it would lose consciousness or whether it stayed conscious in its bindings of cobweb. Entombed and waiting for the spider to bite his head off, did it panic or just calmly await its fate?

He was usually one of the last boys to be picked up at the end of the school day. His mother would invariably arrive in a fluster in an old roadster estate car, and the two dogs; an old English sheepdog and golden cocker spaniel would jump out and rush up to him and cover him with slobber and a warm welcome. His mother would then spend what seemed like an eternity chattering with whichever of the teachers had drawn the short straw to wait with the children, while David rounded up the dogs, putting them back in the car and climbing in himself. Sometimes his mother would be dressed in full hunting gear; jodphurs, white stock with gold stick pin and black hunting jacket, and invariably covered in a light but noticeable splattering of mud. Mercifully she had taken her bowler hat off and left it in the car. He sat in the front passenger seat and willed his mother to end her conversation. Today he managed to catch bits of what she was saying to the bemused teacher whose body language clearly showed that she wanted to get off home, "... lovely day's hunting, plenty of scent and..." and "... and the master fell off his horse, went right over its head and landed in a hedge..." and "... and I'm pleased to say that after all that we didn't catch a thing!"

Old Jack

The old fisherman narrowed his eyes and pulled the brow of his cap down over his forehead to shield himself from the glare of the harsh bright light. With a slight forward movement of his head, he looked hard into the distance towards the flat line of the horizon. The boat was gently rocking on the swell of the current and the old man steadied himself with his legs slightly apart and his knees resting against the engine box; in this way, his body moved at one with the boat. The sea was a granite, dark oily grey and, where it met the horizon, it was darker yet. Thousands of feet overhead, the clouds were large and puffy. They were constantly forming and reforming themselves as they moved across the expansive sky towards the darker banks of clouds that were building up over the distant swell. He pointed towards the horizon with a bent rheumatic index finger.

"Do you see that narrer strip of white light just above the horizon?" he said to the young boy who was standing against the gunwales of the boat and working his string of feathered hooks by hauling it up and down.

"When you see light like that you know the storm is coming. 'E won't be long now. We've probably got about an hour or two before 'e strikes."

David looked up and squinted his eyes as the cold

south-westerly wind made little tears trickle down his face. He could clearly see where the sea and the sky met; there was a small, sharply defined strip of bright white sky, which separated the dark line of the sea from the dense, lowering blue-black clouds above it.

"Tha's the storm," said the old man, as if to emphasise the point. "Now, how are we doing?"

They had set off a couple of hours earlier to catch mackerel, which the fisherman would later sell on the slipway to holidaymakers or to the local hotels and restaurants. They were both using a line of twenty-one hooks, each with a coloured feather attached, to a line fed through the metal hoops of a short, stocky bamboo rod and lowered at least thirty or forty feet into the water. To attract their prey, the rods were rhythmically pulled up and down in order to mimic the movement of a shoal of fish. With luck, it was not unknown to be able to catch twenty-one fish all in one go.

The most David had ever caught at once was seventeen. That was last summer, on a brighter day than this. He had been hauling the line up and down and he had felt the sudden sharp staccato tugs and he had wound it in as quickly as his cold wet fingers would allow. As the catch got nearer to the surface, he looked over the side of the heaving boat and could see the doomed mackerel just like silver shards of light, darting about in the clear green water. Unable to escape, they spiralled in panic, their gullets impaled on individual hooks. He had helped to haul them over the side of the boat and as they landed on the slatted bilge boards, they had flapped about helplessly, gasping and flicking their tails instinctively in a vain attempt to swim away. As each one was unhooked by the fisherman, it was thrown into a big box at the back of the boat and as it flew through the air it continued to swim as if it were briefly free again in the water, before landing on a growing pile of others, impotently flapping and dying to the mournful requiem sound of the gulls wheeling overhead. As he counted each fish, he noticed their wide staring eyes, as if staring in horror at an alien world, and he wondered at their down-turned mouths. They looked just like the mouths of unhappy clowns, forever fixed in a determined sulk. Seventeen fish had been caught and he had felt both elated and excited, yet, at the same time, he could not help but wonder how much pain and fear that each fish actually felt.

Now, suddenly, there was a series of strong tugs on the line. He felt a rush of adrenalin surge through his gut and he started to wind the line in with some difficulty; it seemed so very heavy. Visions of small sharks flashed in his mind, what had he really caught? The difficulty of hauling in now was far greater than that time last year.

As the fish came nearer to the surface, the old fisherman leant over the side and, grabbing the line in his hand, yelled, "Them's bass – sea bass. You've got the lot there!"

As David leant over and peered into the watery depths, he could see the fish darting about. They were a pale golden colour as they caught the watery shafts of late afternoon light, not like the white and silver-grey colouring of mackerel from the year before.

"Them's all sea bass!" repeated the fisherman again and again, not believing his luck. "You must have been through a whole shoal!"

As they were freed from the hooks, the gilded fish went flying one by one through the air into the box in a golden shower of plenty. David noticed that, in complete contrast to the mackerel, their eyes were sadder and their smaller mouths looked just as if they were putting on a grim, brave smile.

For the fisherman, this was the jackpot. Each bass was worth ten times what he could get for a mackerel and it was a highly sought-after commodity for which the hotels would happily pay a premium.

**

Some years later, David returned to the small fishing village where he and his family had spent so many happy summers. He took his wife and two young children for a short break and they stayed in a small hotel overlooking the cove. He asked the hotelier if the fisherman was still alive and he was pleased to hear that he was. The hotelier knew him well. He told David that the old man, who was now quite frail and still living alone in his bungalow just up the hill, walked down every day to have his breakfast in the hotel kitchen.

David went down to the kitchen to meet him the next morning. He had hardly changed; the kindly face, the smile and the gentle Devon burr in his voice were exactly as he remembered. They had a brief chat about "them good ole days". David invited him to come down to the hotel that evening and to join him and his young family for supper. He was so keen for his wife and children to meet him. When the time came, the old man arrived clutching a small, faded colour photograph in a plain wooden frame, which he said he kept on his television set. It was of a young, slim, barefoot boy, about eleven years old, in shorts and sweater, standing on the slipway by the boathouse. With his head tipped to one side, he stood smiling and blinking at the camera in the fading light and the breeze of a gathering storm. His skinny arms were struggling to hold aloft a string of bright golden sea bass…

Clashnessie

Somewhere in the extreme north west

A fresh and vigorous westerly wind is pushing in over the water. Anyone brave enough to be out in it would describe it as feeling like sharp knives pricking into skin. The tide is coming in and reclaiming the wet piles of slimy kelp that lie like grotesque shreds of rotting meat across the sodden strand. From only a small distance this beach, for you have to call it that, looks as if it could be sandy. It looks just like the kind of beach one sees in warmer and sunnier places; the sort to wander across, and to feel its warmth and trickling sand gently between your toes. But here, this is just a cruel visual illusion. Walking on this sodden surface, it feels more like sharp grit, made up from millions of minute shards of hard granite after several millennia of erosion of the surrounding mountains and valleys. You will find no soft trickling sands here, it is more like an abrasive paste suitable for grinding and smoothing metal things. The weather has been trying to bring rain since dawn and there is a noticeable build up of darkening rainclouds in the sky. They move slowly inland and are threatening to scatter their gifts of pure fresh water, recently drawn up from the Atlantic Ocean, at the earliest opportunity. Premature spots of rain blow horizontally across the empty beach and as one would expect, it is completely devoid of any people; for now, the only sounds are the occasional shrieks of gulls and of the wind as it hurls itself across this empty strand.

It is midsummer, the second week in August to be a bit more precise, but this is no sunny Riviera. This is a lonely beach in the far north-west of Scotland, which faces due north. It is enclosed on both sides, but at some distance, by darkening and ragged headlands, lowering themselves slowly into the sea and completely devoid of any signs of human habitation. To the west it is protected from the worst of the weather by the Point of Stoer over which its own eponymous guardian, the celebrated Old Man of Stoer, stands erect; a battle-scarred monolithic obelisk of grey rock, proudly poised. A rudely phallic mace which is ready to challenge the might of the Atlantic storms. Here today, the sun has no real power to speak of; it is successfully smothered by the mounting banks of water-laden clouds. When its rays do manage to break through the gaps for a brief snatched moment, they are pale and watery things, whose feeble promise of warmth is instantly snatched away across the bleak hinterland by the relentlessly biting winds.

At the back of the beach and below the dripping, overhanging crags, a small single-lane road winds its way among the grassy tussocks and outcrops of rock. Some sheep, apparently aimlessly and with little thought, wander about nibbling the very short and tough grass, occasionally shitting where they stand, carelessly leaving scatterings of shiny, nut-brown pellets of dung on the sodden ground. Or they just lay where they please and imperiously watch the world through glassy, blank, unthinking eyes.

At some point in the afternoon, for time counts for little here, a vehicle comes into view from the southern end of the road. It is moving slowly, perhaps not more than twenty miles an hour at most, and it slows down and hesitates as its driver then stops, in the middle of the road, to take in the view of beach and sea and sky. This causes problems for the hapless queue of traffic, which has built up behind this classic campervan. The line of vehicles contains mostly tourists, but one or two are locals on urgent business, and they all have to break sharply. Some of the drivers curse the wretched campervan that they have been forced to crawl behind so impotently all the way from Lochinver, a distance of some six or seven miles. They have trundled over a winding, potholed and seemingly endless road that passes by some of the most stunning coastal scenery in the entire kingdom. They have passed by the spectacular bays of Clachtoll and Achmelvich and the villages of Rhicarn and Stoer; but, sadly, all were unremarked and unnoticed, as behind their steamed up windows, the trapped drivers fume and focus on the backs of the slow-moving vehicles in front of them. All are held up by the infuriating campervan, which leads like a maternal snail with a line of reluctant, complaining children.

An observer would notice that one of the drivers in the queue behind the now stationary van finally loses patience. He angrily pulls out to overtake and drives over the shallow grassy bank where a startled sheep lays idly chewing the cud. A sheep instantly jumps aside, with an

20

unexpected nimbleness and speed, while simultaneously letting loose a shower of shiny brown dung pellets in its fright. There is a scraping sound as the car's low-slung sump meets with an unnoticed rock rising from the ground, but hidden by a clump of marsh weed. The driver is too angry to hear or even care. He drives on, bouncing over the tussocks of grass, through splattering puddles, scattering more shitting sheep. As he passes the offending campervan, he raises his fist with its middle finger extended pointing upwards and he impotently yells several obscenities, it's hard to tell how many, in the direction of the driver of the now immobile vehicle. He finally regains the road with a sickening crunch of undercarriage meeting with more earth and hidden rocks. The driver of the campervan hears nothing of this, for all the windows of both the van and overtaking car are closed. She sees nothing because she is looking at the sea and is deciding where to park. Only a very observant onlooker would notice that, as he drives off up the open road to freedom, gunning the accelerator, the now relieved escapee's car is leaving a small, intermittent, but persistent trail of black sump oil. This will finally cause his engine to seize up and stall, bringing him to a noisy and smokey halt somewhere isolated and remote. This will be on the A838 beside Loch Merkland, just as the sun is setting and the promised rain is falling in generous torrents. He will never make it to his meeting at the Overscaig Hotel, where he was going to measure up and quote for installing a new central heating system.

The two passengers in the campervan have seen the man overtake, they have laughed as the sheep scatter and have worried about the vehicle driving recklessly over the rocky terrain. They have seen the angry driver mouthing something against the steamed-up window and they have noted the clenched fist with the upright middle finger, but something prevents them from commenting. They merely look blankly at each other as the campervan driver says, "I think we'll park over there. There's a small lay-by." Putting it into gear, she aims it in the direction of the small muddy indent in the side of the road that passes as a lay-by, but which is intended as a passing point. Doing this allows the queue of traffic behind to pass by at last. As they do so, some honk their horns, some shout through opened windows. They are all driving too fast and too close to each other in their desire to get away quickly.

"Gosh, they're impatient." says the unwitting driver. Finally the last of the vehicles drives past the campervan; with a feeble "beep" from its horn and with an air of self-importance it begins to speed up along the potholed lane and disappears out of view.

After a few minutes, three figures emerge from the campervan. The driver, a tallish female is slightly stooped, wearing a green anorak, trousers and a knitted bobble hat. She stands hands on hips, and stares out to sea blinking and breathing deeply. Then another female emerges and moves to stand beside her. She too is wearing an anorak, but this one is blue. She is not wearing a hat, but her hair is blowing in the wind and she keeps pushing it out of her face. She is much younger and shorter than her companion. They link arms and talk excitedly, waving and pointing towards the sea.

The other passenger gets out of the vehicle; he seems reluctant to leave the warmth of the van at first. Foolishly he wears no coat, just a thick jumper and jeans. He doesn't go to be with his two female companions, but runs in the opposite direction, across the road and up the slight incline of the grassy bank as if looking for something. He is, of course, desperately looking for somewhere to pee out of sight. He looks around. There are no people about except for his two companions down on the road, and sheep, which keep their distance, but are unconcerned. There are no trees, and the biggest rock is no bigger than knee-height. The dripping crags that loom overhead feed into a small trickling stream that drains into the sea. Facing away from the road, he unzips himself and, with relief, aims in to the stream. As he does so, as if on cue, a little convoy of three cars drives along the lane. One of them honks his horn several times to draw attention to the young man as he finishes and quickly zips himself up. He turns and runs back to the campervan. By now the two females have got back into the van and have closed the sliding door. The young man approaches the van and knocking lightly on the window, says, "Let me in!" To which there is a muffled response from inside.

"You're mad!" says the young man in reply, and annoyed he walks over to the edge of the grassy bank and slithers down to the beach, hugging himself in a vain attempt to keep warm. He immediately discovers that the surface of the beach is so waterlogged that his shoes sink in up to and over his ankles, filling his shoes with a mixture of very cold water and some uncomfortably coarse grit. Pulling up one foot and the next in a kind of weird dance, he

23

curses and climbs up to the firmness of the grassy bank and complaining loudly, returns to the campervan.

He knocks again on the window, but this time more firmly.

"Let me in, it's freezing out here!" he moans. The sliding door of the van is pulled back and the two ladies emerge from within. A transformation has taken place; they are now both wearing bathing costumes. The older female is wearing a costume with brightly swirling patterns of pink, orange and white. She is wearing a white rubber bathing cap and plastic sandals, she is clutching a large blue towel round her shoulders and she is shivering. The younger female is similarly dressed, but her costume is a plain dark blue. She is not wearing a bathing cap; she just brushes her hair away from her face every so often. She is also wearing plastic sandals and she too has a blue towel, which is wrapped round her shoulders. She is also shivering. Both women are talking to the boy and occasionally giggling – or are they shrieking with laughter? The young man says something and then climbs back in the van. He quickly slides the door shut. The two women, holding on to each other and their towels, slither down the grassy bank onto the beach. They immediately sink into the sodden sand. They laugh and then hang their towels on a post, which has a faded and chipped notice board nailed to it saying, "D op no lit er!" They run together towards the sea, kicking off their sandals that by now have uncomfortably filled with grit. When they arrive at the water's edge they do a sort of dance, hopping from foot to foot and running a little way in to the water and then back again, all the while giggling and laughing. They do this two or three times. Then holding hands, they walk together on sinking tiptoes into the icey water. As the water level rises up their shins and then their thighs, they try to jump up into the air as every wave brushes past them. And they laugh again. Now the water is up to their navels and they jump and laugh and jump again. Then the older lady suddenly lets go of the younger one and, putting her head between her outstretched arms, she dives into the water and for a moment disappears beneath the waves. The younger lady says out loud to no one, for there is no one who can hear her, "Oh dear, now I must go in!" The water is well above her waist and she continues to hop up and down every time another wave passes her. Her companion has surfaced, has said something encouraging and is now to be seen doing a powerful front crawl heading straight out to sea. With her two hands joined, as if in prayer, the younger of the two women, tips herself rather than dives, and she too disappears for a moment under the water. When she almost instantly resurfaces, she stands up. Luckily she is not out of her depth. She gasps for breath and after a moment's hesitation and helped by the fact that the combination of a strong westerly wind and wet flesh make for a very cold body, she again lowers herself into the water, thinking it's warmer in than out and swims using the breaststroke in a small circle, all the while saying to herself, "I can do this, I can do this!"

Within a few minutes her older companion has thankfully returned and together they swim the few strokes back to the shallows of the shoreline and stand up. Holding hands, they run towards their now wet towels, for it is lightly raining. Not caring whose is whose, they wrap them round their shoulders and make for the campervan. The door slides open, they clamber inside and then it slams shut.

From the outside, it is difficult to see what is happening inside the van. There is a certain amount of movement and one can safely assume that the two ladies are changing out of their wet costumes and getting dressed into something warmer and more comfortable. After a while, one of the windows in the van opens a bit to allow the steam from a boiling kettle on the little stove, to escape. The occupants are making cups of tea and eating cold sausage rolls and tomatoes bought earlier that day in a nameless and already forgotten town about forty miles back. They drink the tea with great pleasure and they feel its warmth coursing down their throats. Sometime later the door slides open and the young man climbs out of the van. This time he has taken his shoes and socks off and rolled up his jeans. The door slides shut behind him and he reluctantly steps on to the beach, heading for the water's edge. He is just in time, for he has come to retrieve the plastic sandals that were discarded by the women as they ran to the sea. The tide is coming in fast now and he has picked up three sandals and is looking for the fourth when he sees it trying to float away in a couple of inches of water as a wave takes it out. He runs towards it and grabs it. The water is so cold that it makes his feet ache with pain. He returns to the van and as he does so, he is impressed at how the two ladies could have done what they did in such terrible conditions.

Not much later, the passing place is empty. There are

the traces of tyre tracks in the mud, but they are already dissolving in this light rain. There are two used teabags, now completely cold, at the bottom of the ancient and battered wire litterbin, along with a crumpled paper-bag that had held the sausage rolls. The crumbs from this bag have been scattered on the grassy bank for any passing bird or animal that sees them. There is a gap in the clouds bigger than the others; the sun shines directly through it. The rain has washed over some small black patches of oil lying in places along the road, and from a certain angle it sparkles with rainbow colours in a magical iridescence.

Dancing with Miss Edwards

(No wallflowers allowed!)

It was a Saturday, two weeks before Christmas. Malcolm was sitting in the crowded downstairs part of the old bus, which smelt of diesel fumes and damp bodies. The other passengers consisted mostly of weary shoppers clutching bulging carrier bags on their laps or leaving them cluttered round their feet. Some were trying to restrain their tired, fractious children who grizzled and grumbled. Some just ignored everything as they stared blankly into nothingness.

He was wearing a new jacket and tie, long grey trousers and black polished shoes and he felt very self-conscious. It was draughty and he was chilled and uncomfortable. It felt as if everyone was aware of him, even if they weren't actually staring at him. He was not the usual passenger and he was travelling alone. He sensed that his clothes and manner subtly set him apart from the other care-worn travellers. His recently cut hair, a short back and sides, was combed flat on top with a side parting, as was the custom for boys of his age in those days. He had had a hot bath when getting ready at home and he had helped himself to his father's hair oil and cologne; he had probably overdone it. He looked forward to the party more out of curiosity than anything else, but he had absolutely no idea what to expect. This was his first time on his own going to anything like this and he was conscious that this was a bit of a milestone for him. He lived with his family in the country and coming in to town on his own was a big adventure. His sister, who should have been with him, was at home in bed with a heavy bout of 'flu.

He was a thin, some would say skinny, twelve year old. Tall, but with a slight figure, his clothes hung loosely on his frame. As he had tied his tie – a dark purple one – in front of the steamed-up bathroom mirror and combed his hair, he had looked for any signs of facial hair or spots, signs of growing up like some of his friends at school were showing. But there were none. He thought that he looked even younger than his age; his face was pink and splotchy from the heat of the bath. He had stared at his reflection and for a while he had wondered who it was he was looking at. Yes, he knew *who* it was, he was himself after all, and he was familiar with what he looked like. As he stared at the mirror image of himself, he tried to look right into his eyes, as if to gain an understanding of his being, to get inside his head, but all he saw were two brown eyes staring back at him. Then he noticed that, although on this side of the mirror – in the so-called real world – he was holding his comb with his right hand, his reflection was holding his comb with his left hand. Where was the reality in that?

He didn't want to miss the stop so he had sat by a window towards the front of the bus, anxiously keeping an eye on the route. He was on his way to the Christmas party at the place where he and his sister were taught ballroom dancing. There would be no more lessons after this until next year. It was 1961. During the school holidays, he and his older sister had weekly dance lessons. They usually caught the bus or were sometimes taken by car to where the lessons were held; a large airy meeting hall in a Victorian redbrick building in a suburb of the local town.

They were taught the classic ballroom favourites: the waltz, the foxtrot, the quickstep and the cha-cha-cha. Even at his young age these dances seemed to have a somewhat faded air of sophistication and glamour and hinted at another world of times gone by. They would soon be old enough to go to parties on their own and they were being coached in behaviours and customs which included ballroom dancing so that they too could take their part in this adult, middle class society. They also learnt other dances, traditional folk dances: the Gay Gordons, Strip the Willow and the Dashing White Sergeant.

Their dance teacher, a tired-looking, yet surprisingly energetic middle-aged spinster called Miss Edwards, was well known in the area and well thought of. Her accompanist, who sat at an upright piano, was another middle-aged spinster, about whom he knew nothing, but then why would he? She was a straight-backed lady, petite and trim, who always wore black and never smiled or spoke and only occasionally glanced at the children dancing. She simply played the piano and followed the instructions of what to play and when to stop, like an automaton with no sign of any involvement with anybody else. Miss Edwards never referred to her by her name, she merely gave instructions.

Recognising that the bus was nearing its destination, he stood up from his seat, pressed the button and clambered towards the exit. Making apologies to the blank-faced passengers, he tried not to tread on the bags and parcels which littered his path, and deftly avoided a toddler sitting in the middle of the aisle playing with a toy car. With relief he got off and as the bus drove away with a spluttering burst of diesel fumes, he was immediately aware of the cold damp air and he wished that he had brought a coat. It was getting dark and his thin jacket and shirt gave little protection against the cold air, which wrapped itself like tentacles round his whole body, making him feel exactly as if he was wearing nothing at all on his skinny frame.

After a short, hurried, shivering walk up the hill, he climbed the steps into the dimly lit and draughty entrance hall. He was greeted by two broadly smiling ladies in ball gowns and white gloves, sitting at a trestle table. He proffered his crumpled ticket towards them. Other young people were arriving, either singly or in small groups. Some parents who had brought their children were lingering as they encouraged their more hesitant offspring to go on in alone. All were given the same announcement, which one or other of the welcoming ladies repeated every so often, trying to sound jolly and cheerful at the same time. He didn't recognise anybody that he knew in the crowd.

"You can all go straight through. Boys' toilets on the left, girls' on the right, if you need them. The party lasts

31

two hours and refreshments will be served after the first hour. Please could parents not be late in picking up their offspring at 7.30 sharp? We do hope that all the youngsters have a lovely time!"

Realising that he needed to go, he went into the boys' toilets. At the far end of the row of urinals there was a small group of three or four older boys, self-consciously smoking and sharing a cigarette. They looked up nervously as he came in, but they immediately relaxed when they realised that he was no threat to their bravado.

As he peed he couldn't help listening to their conversation, which he was probably meant to hear anyway.

"My brother says he has snogged Jane Parfitt," said one of the older-looking boys.

"Noooo!" said another. "That is disgusting, she is at least sixteen, and your brother is only fourteen." The other boys nodded in agreement.

"Well it's true, and she let him feel her bra and she felt his..."

At this point, the door opened and a man came in – someone's father perhaps – and the smokers immediately broke apart, one of them dropping their shared cigarette and immediately stamping on it. They lined up at the urinals, all innocence personified. No one spoke and Malcolm finished, washed his hands and left.

In the large draughty hall, all the boys stood in a loose huddle along one side of the room and all the girls stood on the other. The girls were, on the whole, standing quietly in groups with their hands clasped together in front of them, looking around nervously and very conscious of their new and possibly uncomfortable party frocks. The boys, on the other side of the hall, were also looking anxiously about, some standing with their hands in their pockets, some striking poses of a feigned nonchalance. He went and stood next to a couple of boys that he knew and with the minimum of acknowledgements, they greeted each other.

"Hello, Malcolm. We've just heard that the girls have got to choose a partner for the first dance," said a boy with spiky ginger hair, buck-teeth and a face full of freckles.

"Oh!" said Malcolm and he stared at the girls wondering which one would choose him.

"Well, no one's going to choose either of you," said their weasel-faced friend with a smile.

Malcolm and Ginger stared at him blankly and then, almost in unison, said, "Oh, shut up!"

And they didn't really know what to say after that and nervously waited for the dancing to begin. Elsewhere, some of the other younger boys were giggling and joking in an attempt to cover their embarrassment. One or two were just staring across at the girls in a kind of bemused bewilderment. At the back, the older boys with greased-down hair, some uncomfortably in their fathers' dinner jackets and with their hands in their pockets were trying to look relaxed. They were whispering back and forth to each other and occasionally bursting into raucous and somewhat exaggerated laughter. This caused heads to turn and drew a look of disapproval from Miss Edwards, who was now standing alone in the big gap between the two large groups of children milling about on either side of the dance floor.

The hall seemed to have been half-heartedly decorated with coloured streamers and balloons stuck along the walls and there was a small Christmas tree decorated with a few multicoloured lights on a table covered in green crepe paper in a corner at the back. All the large overhead lights were fully on, and this filled the space with a harsh, utilitarian light, which seemed to give everyone a pale yellow complexion.

Miss Edwards was wearing a homemade dress of shiny gold material. Round her neck hung a necklace of gold-coloured glass beads and she was wearing gold shoes that had seen better days. She suddenly coughed and then clapped her hands for attention. She was wearing white evening gloves, which gave her clapping a dull, padding sort of noise. The room fell silent.

"Good evening everyone, girls and boys!" she said and smiled her Joyce Grenfell smile. There was a rippled yet unintelligible response of murmuring from the crowd. "It is lovely to see so many of you here tonight and I hope that you all have a lovely time. Tonight we have Madame on the piano, whom you all know, and for an extra treat we also have her friend, Maestro, on his piano accordion!"

There was a round of muted applause.

"Now, for an ice-breaker, we are going to start with Strip-the-willow! Could you all get organised? Come along now, you all know what to do, line up in groups. Come on now! Everyone join in! No wallflowers allowed! Form lines, now, come along!"

And so after a brief pause, when everything seemed to stand still, they formed groups just as they had been taught, with Miss Edwards marshalling her troops and earnestly cajoling all the boys and girls to join in. Malcolm took his place between two large girls, each of whom took his hand firmly. They both in turn smiled weakly at him and then ignored him. Miss Edwards briefly reminded everyone what to do and then everyone waited. Miss Edwards then looked towards the accompanist and nodded. The piano struck up and the accordion wheezed into life. The music was surprisingly catchy. This so-called ice-breaker of a dance entailed everyone dancing with everyone else in turn. It involved a simple arrangement of moves spinning round and round, moving along the lines of hopping and jigging people, linking arms and skipping back again. There was no time to feel self-conscious or embarrassed, as everyone had to concentrate so hard on what they had to do next. Every child, whether large or small, boy or girl, all swung back and forth, and galloped down the rows and they soon began to forget their individual anxieties. When the dance came to an end, the boys and girls almost fell into each other, laughing and pushing while breathless. They all clapped their hands and awaited the next announcement.

"And now the waltz. We are going to start with a 'ladies-excuse-me.' Girls, you will choose your partners. Everyone on the floor. No shirkers or hanging back. No wallflowers allowed! Come along now, girls, you *must* choose a partner!"

The boys stood there like ducks in a shooting gallery, and they were picked off one by one by the girls. Most of the older girls gravitated towards the older boys and some hung back hesitantly. Malcolm was approached by one of the more confident girls. She was at least a foot taller than him. She was wearing an orange dress, with flouncy sleeves and cuffs, she also had a matching orange band in her hair and she smelt vaguely of eucalyptus oil.

"Hullo," she said. "My name is Alison Smedley. What's yours?"

She put her hand out. He gingerly took it and they shook hands and then immediately let go.

"My name is Malcolm."

For some reason, he didn't give his surname.

He was quite aware of the difference in age and height. He thought he recognised her as the older sister of one of his school friends. She had long blonde hair, a fresh pale complexion with pink cheeks and a bright yet nervous smile. She made the first move to get ready for the dance.

"Here, hold my hand," she said and she proffered her left hand and he tentatively took hold of it with his right. Her hand was a surprisingly hot and damp thing and she stretched his arm out, in the ballroom pose as they had been taught to do in the dancing lessons.

"And put your other hand here." She took hold of his left hand and placed it firmly on her side, and then moved it further round her waist; he could feel that, below the flimsy orange silk, she was wearing a more solid garment. What on earth was it? *Was it a corset*, he wondered, *or a Liberty bodice?* At this point they were standing so close together that he could feel her toothpaste-breath on his forehead. His eyes were level with her throat. He wondered if she could smell his hair oil and cologne. He turned his head to the left and the right. If he looked straight ahead he had a perfect view of a bobbly plastic necklace and when she opened her mouth he noticed that she was wearing braces on her teeth. Neither of them spoke much and as they waited for the music to strike up, they both realised how close they were to each other; he could feel her body heat and, either intentionally or not, the full length of her body brushed against his and he stepped back, just a tiny bit, and he willed the music to begin.

It soon all went horribly wrong. He tried to lead, but so did she. This resulted in them stumbling into each other a few times. They started again. This time she let him lead, but he was not too sure of his steps and they made a sorry sight as they manoeuvered round the dance floor; him treading on her orange shoes, and apologising, and then doing it again. At one point his now unwilling partner muttered something under her breath, he couldn't catch it, but he knew that it wasn't anything complimentary. All this stumbling about attracted the attention of Miss Edwards, who came over to them.

"Come along now, you two."

She spoke above the noise of the music and like some demonic puppet master, she waved her hands in the air over them as if they were on strings and chanted the instructions.

"One-two-together, one-two-together, left foot, right foot. That's better, now concentrate, that's better, you know you can do it. "

Doing it over and over again gradually they got the hang of it and she let go of the strings and moved on to another couple who had actually fallen over, and the girl was crying. Malcolm and his partner in orange struggled on with the dance and were both very grateful when the music came to an end. They willingly let go of each other. As instructed by Miss Edwards at the end of every dance, they thanked each other, they clapped the pianist and her accordionist friend and they gratefully drifted apart.

During all this he couldn't help but notice that some of the older boys and girls had mastered the dance and were moving about the dance floor with a superior sense of confidence.

The next dance was a quickstep; this time the boys had to pick their dancing partners and he went to choose one from the gaggle of girls who were standing around in the middle of the hall under the glare of the overhead lighting. He chose a girl he recognised from his dance class. He didn't yet know her name, but she looked nice and was about his height.

He went straight up to her and said, "Please may I have this dance with you?"

And as he did so, and without really waiting for her reply, more out of nerves than anything else, he leant forward and taking her hand she allowed herself to be taken to the middle of the dance floor. They stood together, he with his left hand on her waist and their arms extended with her hand in his and waited for the music to begin. This time he could smell lemons and a sweet, soapy scent on his partner. As in the previous dance, they were standing very close to each other and he tried to engage her in conversation to distract himself from the way in which his young body was responding to her warmth and proximity.

"My name's Malcolm, what's yours?"

"Jennifer," she replied, looking straight at him and continued, "I have a younger sister and we live in Henley Road."

She was a bit shorter than him, with a pretty face and she wore her hair in a bob with a small pearl slide. She was wearing a pale blue dress and matching pale blue buckled party shoes.

At this point the music started and they began to dance. Neither of them was very proficient, but they managed and stumbled self-consciously about the dance floor without any major disaster. Jennifer winced and apologised when Malcolm trod inadvertently on her foot. They stayed together for the next dance too – another waltz.

As they danced, they tried to exchange brief information about what schools they went to, what their favourite subjects were and how old they were.

And the next piece of dance music came; it was a cha-cha-cha, a Latin American dance. A dance they both felt reasonably confident about. They had been taught a simple set of steps which they just repeated over and over again. Holding hands was optional and he found that hers were warm and soft. They just had to step forwards a couple of paces and backwards a couple of paces to the rhythm of the music and as they got the hang of it, they could add other steps or flourishes as they were called. They danced confidently and when it ended, he was a bit disappointed. There was an announcement for refreshments so they thanked each other and Jennifer disappeared into the crowd. He went back to his friends who were hanging about the food table, talking about how much they were going to eat. The rest of the talk seemed to consist of commenting on various people's dancing abilities or lack of them.

The refreshments, which consisted of orange squash, well diluted and served in glass tumblers and a selection of sandwiches, sausage rolls and fairy cakes were all laid out on a long trestle table.

Malcolm had noticed that some of the older children seemed to enjoy dancing, giving themselves to the rhythm of the dance while their partners seemed always to be half a beat behind them as they tried to impress. If he was honest he enjoyed some of it too, when he was reasonably confident in the steps and when he knew what he was doing.

After the refreshments, Malcolm looked around to see if he could see Jennifer to have another dance with her, but she was already taken. She was dancing with an older boy who seemed to dance quite well and they were chatting and she was smiling and, rather than look for someone else to dance with, he was happy just to stand and watch as the two dancers swirled around the dance floor. After this there were a few more group dances where everyone had to join in, including the Gay Gordons and the Eightsome Reel. During these dances he caught glimpses of Jennifer and at one point, in the Paul Jones, they were together and then apart again and then it was all over.

Traditionally the party ended with the National Anthem being played and everyone had to stand to attention where they stood. Some of the younger boys giggled and Miss Edwards frowned at them.

Malcolm said goodbye to his friends and went out of the hall to find his mother, who was coming to pick him up. He found her chatting to another mother in the entrance hall. She saw him and waved and he went up to her and said he would go and wait in the car. Outside it was dark and raining and even colder. He was hot from the dancing but he soon cooled down. He found the car easily in a line of vehicles parked haphazardly both on and off the pavement. Icy drops fell on his head and he was grateful to get into the relative warmth of the car. He slid onto the cold leather passenger seat and waited. He watched as the rain drops trickled down the windscreen of the car and how they sparkled lit by the dim street lamps overhead. Through the murk he saw people leaving and in vain, he willed his mother to stop her chattering and take him home. At one point a big black car pulled up outside the hall and then he saw a girl in a pale blue dress emerge from the main door. She was holding a dark coat over her head with one hand as she held her shoe bag in the other, she ran down the steps and let herself into the car. As she did so she had to let her coat slip off her head and onto her shoulders and he caught a glimpse of her face. It was Jennifer.

Death of a foal

It was quite early in the morning and it was his turn to go down to the meadow to check on the bay mare that he shared with his sister. He hadn't been there since the day before yesterday. The mare was in foal and she was due to deliver in the next few days and she had to be visited regularly to make sure she was alright. The meadow was a quiet place at the bottom of a small valley, sandwiched between two very large arable fields. It was secluded and peaceful with no public roads or paths nearby. If you didn't know about it you wouldn't necessarily stumble across it. It was a scrubby patch of ground with some reasonable grazing here and there and it was not required at the moment by anyone else. It was ideal by being away from everything and it had a small stream of fresh water running through part of it. The farmer who owned it didn't even want any rent for it. He was just glad for it to be used and the grass to be kept down.

To get there, he walked up the yew path and past the grass tennis court, which he noticed needed cutting again. Its saggy net was draped like an old threadbare skirt across its middle and he continued on to the woods. On this particular morning it was fresh and sunny and the cow parsley was out, a glorious sight that always pleased him. The tall fragile stems crowned with myriad sprays of delicate white flowers moved gently as he passed by them, seemingly acknowledging his presence. From the woods, taking a shortcut, he had to slide down a grassy bank on to the quiet country road that after a few yards led to the beginning of the track down to the meadow. Once off the road, he entered the narrow path with its wildly overgrown bushes brushing against him on either side. He took care to avoid the occasional outcrop of blackthorn or nettles. It was also darker and cooler here with the thick foliage overhead blocking out much of the light. In the scattered gaps where it did shine through, it had the intensity of clusters of spotlights dappling the ground where he walked. The path, not straight but with a curve to the left, led him down a gentle incline to the meadow below. Soon he was standing at the old gate, which had started its life as a metal bedstead and was now held up by some rusty wire and binder twine. As he carefully lent on it, he scanned the field for the bay mare. At first he couldn't see her, but that was not surprising for the meadow was long and narrow, with patches of scrub growing in scattered clumps along its length. The sun was low in the sky and there were deep shadows everywhere. Along the field's boundaries the hawthorn hedges had become very overgrown and they were covered in a profusion of blossom in banks of overhanging branches. They looked just like giant waves in a Japanese print. Under this billowing foam, in relative darkness, livestock could shelter to escape the heat of the midday sun or the heavy rain in a downpour. And then he saw her way down the meadow moving about behind some scrub. She was a beautiful chestnut brown creature, with black mane and tail and a white flash on her face. He clicked his tongue in the familiar way as he always did to reassure her and he called her name. She raised her head, looking at him and whinnied. Now he could only see her head and shoulders; the rest of her was hidden by a large bush. He carefully clambered over the gate, but as he moved towards her, he knew instantly that something was not quite right. She wasn't moving towards him as she would normally do. Instead she was turning round and round, like a dog trying to catch its tail. She was obviously distressed. As he got nearer and she turned again, he could see what was worrying her – the membranous birth sac was hanging out of her back end and he couldn't help but think that it looked exactly like a really dirty grey bed sheet, bundled up and splashed with pink slime, hanging from a washing machine. She was in the process of giving birth. Through the gelatinous membrane of the amniotic sac he recognised the shape of a foal's head protruding from the body of the mare and what looked like its two front legs. He stood there transfixed. The mare walked a bit, not knowing what to do for the best; this was her first foal, after all. She looked like some weird two-headed creature, almost comical in a push-me-pull-you sort of way. She tried to lie down and then thought better of it for fear of hurting her baby. Gradually, inexorably, the foal eased out. The restless mare understood what was happening and this time she lay down gently on her side and the foal finally slid silently out of its mother and onto the soft grass of the meadow. For a while it didn't move, the poor little thing looked quite forlorn. He went towards it, the mare turned her head and stood up again, she snickered as if to ask if everything was alright. She stood over her newborn foal and sniffed it, then nuzzled it; she was trying to encourage it to move. It was such a touching sight. So he just sat down on the grass, keeping his distance and with prickling eyes, watched as the foal lay there covered in the birth sac – boy, mare and foal all waiting. But it didn't move and it lay there quite still. He knew that a newborn foal should be up and walking within five or ten minutes, or even less. It was obvious to him that something was not quite right. He looked round for some long grass and grabbing a handful he went slowly up to the foal and started to try and rub the remains of the birth sac off the foal's little body. The mare stood and watched him working with some interest, occasionally helping by brushing the newborn foal with her nose or her tongue. Eventually the entire sac was cleared away but it just lay there, its big dark eyes half open, seemingly completely disinterested and motionless. Some mares can be very aggressive to humans who intervene between them and their offspring, but this one was not. She knew him well and trusted him. She must have sensed instinctively that something was wrong and that she needed help. She had a gentle nature and was very relaxed with him being there. First of all, he tried to help it stand up by grabbing it under its shoulders and trying to encourage it to use its legs. It felt a bit like putting up a tripod for a camera, but with one extra leg. Even when he had succeeded in getting it to stand after what seemed like an age, it didn't try to walk, but stood there immobile, its head hanging down limply, and then it collapsed again. It was imperative that it got to its mother's teats and started drinking. It needed the colostrum for nutrition, to give it immunity and to help the digestive track to clear itself. Again he tried to take it to its mother to feed. The mare stood still and let him try but the filly was weak and after making a few half hearted attempts its head flopped and it lost interest. Dispiritingly, as it stood there, being held up by the boy, he could only watch helplessly as the colostrum, which it should have drunk, dripped out of the mother and was lost in the grass.

He lay the young filly down and decided to go for help.

He ran home and told everyone about the foal. His sister and another brother went straight up to the field and they took a wheelbarrow. They said that they would use it to bring the foal down with its mother, to put them in the loose box in the big barn, if it still hadn't stood up. For it was going to need constant supervision and further attempts to feed it were more and more important with every passing minute. His mother rang the vet who then asked to speak to him so that he could describe the symptoms. The vet didn't sound too hopeful, but said that he would come over as soon as he could. The boy and his mother then went up to the meadow together.

As they got to the field they could see that the foal had been put into the wheelbarrow on a bed of hay. It was still as lifeless as before. It was too big to fit in the barrow so its head and legs hung grotesquely over the sides. It looked as if it was dead. The mare was calm as she was being led by his sister, while his brother wheeled the wheelbarrow carefully across the meadow, seeking out the flattest path and avoiding the clumps of thistles.

They took it to the loosebox in the old barn. It was at the end of the central corridor, opposite the tack room. It was a cool and dimly lit place, it was ideal and well away from any distractions from the other horses. They laid the foal on to a thick layer of straw and its mother stood beside it. She occasionally nuzzled it, but she didn't seem to know what she had to do. Two of them stayed in the loose box and continued to try to lift the foal up so that it could feed itself, but it was no use, it only wore the foal out using up what little energy it had. It all began to seem futile. Then someone thought that it would be a good idea to take milk from the mare, but this proved too difficult. For the mare did not let it happen, for every time anyone tried, she kicked out dangerously. So, in desperation, someone went to get some ordinary cow's milk to feed to the foal. Using an old plastic baby's bottle with a teat, it seemed at first as if the foal was drinking, and it was, but when they stopped to give it a rest, the milk just slowly dribbled out of its mouth into the straw.

A while later the vet arrived, he felt the foal's stomach and lower abdomen gently prodding and poking with his scrubbed and stubby fingers. He took its temperature and felt for a pulse and he gave it a couple of injections. Afterwards the boy couldn't hear what the adults were saying but it didn't sound good, and then the vet left.

He asked his mother what was going to happen and all she said was, 'We'll have to wait and see.'

That night he sat up with the others until he fell asleep and then he was woken and went to bed, where he gratefully collapsed fully-clothed and did not stir till early morning. When he woke up early, he ran downstairs to find everyone in the kitchen, some standing, some sitting at the table. The vet was there again, along with his sister and two other friends of his mother, both of whom had a lifetime's experience with horses and ponies. All of them were nursing a cup of tea. The vet was smoking his pipe, which filled the kitchen with dense sweet-smelling smoke that flew out of the open kitchen window. Some were talking quietly and some just staring blankly at the floor. The atmosphere was very sombre, and when he saw his sister quietly weeping into a sodden handkerchief, it was obvious that the news was not going to be good. From listening to them talk he understood that the little foal had gradually faded away and had died just as dawn was breaking. It had not really had a chance. "There was obviously something seriously wrong with it," said someone and then someone else said that " It's nature's way." Anyway, his parents could never have afforded any serious medical intervention. The adults, who were all well experienced with horses and ponies, said that sometimes things like this happened. But thankfully it was not very common. The other mare that the family had, a Welsh mountain pony, had given birth to a succession of foals over the years. There had never been a single problem with any one of them. But now this had happened with this mare's first foal, which made it all the more upsetting. The mare was a well-bred horse with a strong pedigree and there was no obvious reason why she should not be a good mother. Someone else said that that was the problem; she was too well-bred and that there may have been some in-breeding in her bloodline. Anyway, there had to be a reason why the foal had died and it was generally agreed that it was just bad luck, a one off, something genetic possibly and that was that. The vet offered to do a post mortem but the expense of such a thing made it out of the question and, although at first his mother was reluctant to the idea, both the vet and her two friends said that they should try again next year and put the mare with a different stallion and that it was bound to be successful.

He felt guilty that he hadn't stayed up all night or at least part of the night to do a shift looking out for the foal, so he asked if there was anything he could do to help. The foal needed to be buried, it would be cheaper than asking the vet to take it away and so he volunteered to do the job. He would go and choose a spot and dig the grave and it would be done by the end of the day.

Outside the loose box, he found the foal. It had been put back in the wheelbarrow and was lying on its bed of hay. It looked at first glance as if it might have been just gently dozing, but its pose was ungainly and it looked uncomfortable and there was obviously no possibility of it being alive. He took a spade from the toolshed and laid it across the barrow, resting it on the foal's shoulder, against its chin, to prevent it from falling off. He wheeled it up the yew path to the woods and, leaving the barrow and its gentle burden, he wandered around looking for a suitable place. Over the years various pets had been buried in this area of the garden. The graves were not marked by a stone or anything, but everyone knew or thought they knew, what was buried and where.

He wanted to find a place where it wouldn't be walked on, somewhere tucked away. After a while he found the

49

perfect spot. There was a large clump of bushes that divided the tennis court from where the fruit cages stood. From the tennis court it looked like an impenetrable hedge of bay shrubbery, with some yew and some old man's beard growing amongst it, but on the other side, directly at the base of a large fir tree there was a small gap in the hedge and if you crouched down and crawled in, it opened up like the interior of a large leafy hut as the branches overhead were so dense. He and his siblings had often played there when they were younger, but none of them had been there for some years and so it had an unused air about it and he decided that it would be the ideal place to bury the foal.

At that moment his other brother turned up and said he wanted to help. He showed him the spot he had chosen and they agreed to bury it in the middle of the space, in order to get away from having to dig through the inevitable tangle of roots that they would find nearer to any of the bushes. The top surface was just layer upon layer of leaf mould and twigs. As they dug through this leafy detritus of years, they came across a couple of battered and damaged Dinky toys; one was a black Rover, like his father had had many years ago, and only just recognisable as such and the other was a red London bus, which had lost its wheels and was host to some dead woodlice.

It took them a long while to dig the hole, it was very hard going. After digging through the soft top layer of leaf mould, the hard, dry ground consisted of a complete tangle of roots and he had to go back down to the shed to look for some loppers to cut his way through them.

When he got back, his brother had gone. Eventually, after at least an hour, possibly longer, he thought that the hole would be deep enough. Picking the foal up, he was surprised at how heavy it was. Rigor mortis had begun to set in and when he had lowered it into the hole he realised that it was not going to fit. Getting it back out was equally difficult. He then continued digging and got very hot and so he took off his shirt which helped a bit. As the grave got deeper, it got easier; he was past the worst of the root layer and had hit a seam of very dark, rich loamy earth. Picking the carcase up a second time, it was strange to feel the soft fur of the animal against his skin; but it felt cold and lifeless and he shivered. This time the foal fitted more snugly into the grave. Before he started to fill in the earth, he stood and stared at it, imagining what might have been, what kind of life it might have had. But that was all now snuffed out. Its fate was to be returned to the earth. He then hurried as he filled the grave in. He did not like to see the dark earth lying directly on the clean, fresh, feathery coat of the foal. There seemed something so final, so defined about it, that it made him feel uncomfortable. He began to relax as more earth covered the animal and it finally disappeared from view. All that is, except for one small hoof poking through, which stood higher than the rest. He had to push it back into the earth and weigh it down with a large stone, plucked from a nearby rockery. He knew that he had to press the earth down hard to get the air out and when he had done that, he went and got some more old planks of wood to cover the grave, to deter foxes or other animals from robbing it. Finally he covered the planks with another layer of earth and leaf-mould and as he did so, he placed the battered old Rover car and the London bus – now devoid of its woodlice inhabitants – in the middle, and covered them over. For now it seemed a truly fitting place to leave these remnants of a lost childhood.

Walking back down the yew path, pushing the empty barrow that still held the flattened hay, with the spade and loppers laid across it, loosely rattling and threatening to fall off, he realised that in all the drama of its birth and the fight for its life, the newborn foal had never been given a name.

The persistence of pigeons

One summer's afternoon in June, 1963.

Carrying his brown leather music case, James Montacute major walked slowly down the long, echoing stone corridor with an increasing sense of dread and foreboding. No one else was about; he felt quite alone in the building. He imagined that this is what it felt like to be a condemned prisoner going to his execution. As he passed the empty classrooms, or cells as he imagined them to be on either side, he could just make out the voices of boys out on the athletics field enjoying the sunshine and fresh air of a warm and sunny Friday afternoon in June. The contrast of the bright world outside and the cool, dim, echoing stone corridor inside was not lost on him. As he looked up, he caught a glimpse through a classroom window of some boys running a race round the track. Others, out of sight, were cheering, some were laughing. As he continued on through the shadowy corridor, the old familiar sick feeling in his stomach made him feel as if he was going to actually be sick and he knew that there was nothing he could do about it except to try and ignore it. Halfway down the long corridor, he turned left and started to slowly climb up the stone staircase that led to the music room on the next floor. As he moved heavily upwards, he shut his eyes and imagined that he was climbing up the steps to the guillotine and he could hear the baying crowd laughing and jeering, wanting blood.

"'Tis a far, far better thing I do…" he whispered to himself.

"Good morning Montacute major!" said a voice, which echoed round the quiet of the stairwell in a wave of sound. "Are you all right? You look very pale. Have you been overdoing it on the athletics field?"

"Er, no, no sir. I'm fine."

James immediately opened his eyes and saw his piano teacher, Mr Nelson, holding the door to the music room open and smiling, and this reminded him of his dentist, for he stood at the door of his surgery just like that, smiling and welcoming him in before inflicting excruciating pain on him.

Mr. Nelson was known to the boys as Horatio, Mr "Horatio" Nelson. As in all public schools, all the masters had to have a nickname and with a surname like Nelson it was inevitable, if somewhat predictable and unimaginative, that the master would be called "Horatio" by the boys. He was a dapper and immaculately dressed music master, not a big man, but with a compact physique, rather reminiscent of a young Hercule Poirot. He was completely unlike so many of the other masters, who tended to wear old, patched sports jackets and shirts with frayed collars and smelt of tobacco smoke. Mr "Horatio" Nelson in contrast wore a neatly-pressed, light grey suit with a grey silk handkerchief in the top pocket, a white shirt with gold cufflinks and a dark blue silk tie.

His black Oxford shoes were highly polished. His slightly wavy hair was neatly brushed straight back with no parting, and there was a definite hint of eau-de-cologne floating about him. None of the boys knew what his real Christian name was; most masters tended to keep their Christian names a secret. Those that did tell pupils were usually treated with some suspicion by the boys. As was the norm in public schools of the time, everyone stuck to using only surnames, even among friends.

" Well, do come in and sit down, Montacute."

James entered the large airy space and moved across the parquet floor towards the grand piano which crouched, black and menacing, in the middle of the room. Each of the three exterior walls of the music room were dominated by huge metal-framed windows reaching up to the high ceiling.

"I'm sorry to drag you away from the sports outside, but needs must. At the end of this lesson I will give you a chit for the games master, so that you won't get into any trouble," said Horatio, pointing expressively to the piano stool in front of the keyboard. "I think it's the Mozart, isn't it? The minuet in C major, if I remember correctly. I am hoping that you have practised this week. Frankly, Montacute, last week was not good. Not good at all. I'm hoping for a great improvement." And he couldn't help pursing his lips as a sign of his irritation.

He may well purse his lips, just wait and see what I have got planned for you, thought James as he sat down and opened his music case for the sheet music. As he peered into the dark of the bag for a second he was a captured member of the French resistance, who was about to be unmasked by this Nazi officer, complete with monocle and gold tooth, walking towards him in the interrogation chamber and he fumbled desperately in the case for his pistol. *Merde*, he thought, for it wasn't there.

Not good last week? It was a disaster, a complete, unmitigated disaster of the first water, as his Uncle Ivo would have said had he been there to witness it. James had been having piano lessons for some time now, but he did not get on with it very well and had wanted to give up for ages. When he told his parents about his wish to abandon the piano they said that as they had already paid for the rest of the term, he would just have to get on with it. As for being dragged away from athletics, that was the least of his problems. A list had gone up at lunchtime and with the rest of his group he had been put down for the fifteen hundred yards, possibly the worst event in the entire pantheon of athletic activities. However, when his housemaster had given him the message from Horatio that the music lesson had had to be rescheduled for this afternoon he could not believe his luck.

All of Horatio's lessons followed the same pattern. First of all some scale work and being told all about the scales and chords for that week. Then Horatio would demonstrate the piece that James was currently learning, showing off and playing it through perfectly without a mistake, and then the worst bit, James would have to perform and show how far he had got on with it.

During the last lesson he had sat and watched, mesmerised as Horatio had demonstrated how he wanted the Mozart piece to be played. His perfectly manicured fingers had danced across the keyboard like butterflies fluttering over apple blossom. Every so often he stopped and said things like, "I'm looking at the value of the notes, I'm watching the timing," or "Watch the fingering here, use your thumb to keep a smooth transition," or " Don't forget. It's an elegant dance. It should be light and bright and gay." In those days the word "gay" had an ambiguity, as it was not then so universally known to mean homosexual or queer as it was later to become. James was aware of the unintended – or was it *intended* – double entendre. James blushed.

What annoyed and amazed James in equal measure even more, was the fact that, as Horatio played, he did not even have to look at the keyboard. His eyes were either fixed firmly on the sheet music, reading every note just as if he was reading a book, or to show that he really in fact knew the piece well, he would turn to James, or look up to the ceiling or even just shut his eyes, moving his head from side to side, lost in the music. His upper torso swayed with the rhythms of the piece as if he was giving a virtuoso performance in the Festival Hall, in front of hundreds of admirers and not just to one miserable school boy in a drab echoing music room. He was good, he was very good, and he knew it.

When it had come to James's turn he had stumbled haphazardly through the piece. He only pretended to read the music. There was no way he could read the music as quickly as it was necessary to do so in order to play it at a reasonable tempo. He used the general visual pattern of the printed notes to remind him where he approximately was. Learning a piece of music was, for him, a tedious process. It was a matter of going through it note by note, over and over again until he had learnt it by rote, by which time any thought of enjoying playing had long since vanished. It had become just a mechanical process. He would love to be able to sit down and play anything he chose, but he couldn't and that was that.

What had made it worse that day were the two pigeons he had seen through the window behind Horatio. He had stopped him halfway through the piece and was telling him about the importance of practising, regularly practising. How it was important to write down a plan and stick to it. While he was talking, David's attention was taken up by two pigeons on the ridge of a roof of a classroom just outside the window. The darker and larger of the two birds, obviously the male, was trying to mount and mate with the female. She was smaller and light grey in colour. Every time the male approached her back end, she hopped forward to avoid him. Or, if he managed to get aboard, she shook him off. His feathers were all puffed up and he was very persistent. Horatio then started to talk about persevering, and not giving in and the importance of seeing things through.

"If you persist, you will achieve your goals. Are you listening to me, young man? Rome wasn't built in a day. Perseverance brings lasting results. Getting good results is surely far more satisfying? Look at me when I am talking to you."

The two birds were still hopping back and forth. The male trying to get on the female's back and the female hopping just out of reach. Suddenly, it happened. The female stopped moving away and resigned to her fate, crouched down and seemed to stare straight ahead into the distance, the male jumped on her back, wings flapping, claws scrabbling. There was some tricky manoeuvring of tail feathers, a bit of shuddering by the male, and it was all over.

"Are you alright, Montacute major? You seem a bit distracted. I really am worried about you. I think I will have to have a word with your housemaster."

The male bird hopped off and strutted away from the female, with his head held high and his beak in the air like a prize fighter who had just won a bout.

"I think we will have to arrange extra lessons."

The female on the other hand, stood up, shook herself, and pretended to look for something to eat amongst a bunch of weeds growing in a gulley nearby. All this while Horatio had been talking; David had tried to listen and concentrate on what was being said, but for a fifteen-year-old boy it had been impossible. He had completely lost track. He was sent away from that lesson with the words of one of Horatio's mantras ringing in his ears, "Perseverance and persistence produce perfection in piano playing!"

James had really meant to practise during the week. He had gone to one of the practice rooms at the back of the music school, but his heart wasn't in it. He struggled to read the music; it just didn't come naturally to him. He was in awe of people who could do it. Just pick up a sheet of music and play it, without any practice. Humphrey-Jones could do it. How did he do it? It just wasn't fair. It's a gift they have. It has to be. And he realised that he just didn't have it at all.

Horatio obviously loved to play. He loved to display his talents. He could read music perfectly.

Where his plan had come from he had no idea. It had just arrived in his head. It was perfect! Fool proof! That evening he had gone down to the empty art room and he had "borrowed" a couple of black felt pens. Returning to the deserted practice rooms he had picked out the piece in the book of music he was learning from, the wretched Minuet in C major, and had got to work. Extremely carefully and trying not to go outside the lines of the notes, he had randomly filled in a selection of all the white notes in the piece, and then a few more, taking great care just to fill in the middles and not to go over the lines. And then, it was so easy, he had done the lot, every single note in the piece. It didn't take long. But he had done it. Now there was no going back. The plan had been set, if not in concrete, then in little black blobs of ink.

***

Now the lesson began, going over the scales. First with the right hand, then the left and then both together. C major, C minor, D major, D minor and so on, revealing precisely what James could do, and inevitably the ones he couldn't. When he could, Horatio would say something like, "Ah, well done!" and when James couldn't, then Horatio just tut-tutted and sighed, put his hand to his forehead, and shook his head sadly. Then it was time for Horatio to demonstrate the piece.

"I shall play the piece for you and then you will show me what you have achieved this week. Oh, by the way, I had a word with your housemaster. He suggested we draw up a plan for extra practices!" James heard, but did not react to this piece of information. He had other plans.

James took the book of music out of his case and couldn't take his eyes off it as he passed it across to Horatio. There was no going back now.

"It's the Minuet in C major on page fourteen, is it not, James?"

Horatio opened the book at the correct page and set it on the little ledge on the inside of the piano lid and adjusted the two little brass catches to hold the pages open. Putting both hands up to his temples, he needlessly adjusted his glasses.

Slightly leaning forward he peered at the music and began to play.

The first couple of notes sounded right and then it happened, it all sounded wrong, a bit like a car hitting a large snowdrift, James thought. Horatio stopped trying to play and peered closely at the open page. And didn't move. He just stared at it for quite a long time.

James held his breath and tried to relax. He felt coldly clammy and began to sweat.

Horatio's head turned slowly to face James. There was no visible emotion on his face. Just a slight pink flush on his cheeks hinted at what might be going through his mind.

"I think that will be all for today. I don't think we shall do this anymore, do you? You should go now. Montacute."

Without saying a word and grabbing his music case, leaving the music book on the piano, he quickly stood up, crossed the room and left. He half-walked and half-ran down the stairs and back along the corridor. His plan had worked, he was free, and felt elated, and yet immediately ashamed at what he had done. Part of him felt sorry for Horatio; as he had momentarily looked back, he had seemed forlorn and quite hurt. Confused and shocked at his own behaviour, he ran down the empty corridor in order to distance himself from the place of his crime. What had Horatio ever done to him, other than try to teach him to play the piano?

As he came out of the heavy double doors of the classroom block, he blinked in the brightness of the afternoon sunshine and was temporarily blinded by the light of the sun, low in the sky. He could hear voices and recognised those of the boys in his class. They had obviously finished their athletics session and were returning to the changing rooms. "Hey, Montacute, where were you?" said a friendly voice. But he didn't answer.

"Ah, Montacute major, just the young man I wanted to see!" barked another less-friendly voice. It was Mr Atkins, an ex-RSM, known as the 'Arge and Master-in-charge of PE. He was well known for being a bit overenthusiastic as far as disciplining the boys was concerned and for having an imaginative array of physically painful punishments in his repertoire, but he was highly regarded by all.

James stood still, trying to focus on the 'Arge who was standing just a couple of yards away, with the late afternoon sun directly behind him, so that all James could make out was a silhouette ringed in bright sunshine.

"Why did you not come to the training session? You knew it was compulsory."

As he spoke the group of boys continued moving away and he could hear one or two of the group of boys call out over their shoulders, "Skiver, skiver!"

"I had to go to a piano lesson with Mr Nelson, sir, I was only told at lunchtime today."

"You should have let me know, Montacute. We can't have boys skiving off at the drop of a hat and letting their house teams down. You'll bring me a chit from Mr Nelson, confirming you had the lesson. Bring it to me in the gym at six, that's when I lock up. Anyway, you will have to do the run tomorrow to make up for your absence." And he turned and walked away into the bright sunlight.

James stood there shocked; he was going to have to do the run after all!

The 'Arge then suddenly stopped, turned round and said, "If you don't bring me the note, I'll double it, to three thousand yards!" and marched off after the group of boys who had disappeared in the direction of the changing rooms and the tepid showers.

James turned to go back to his house, wondering what on earth he was going to do. He would have to get Horatio to sign a chit. That was going to be awkward, nevertheless, it had to be done; forging a note was out of the question, they were quite likely to talk about it in the common room. *Damn it!* He would just have to go and ask Horatio.

As it so happened Horatio, was coming out of the classroom block as he turned. Hesitantly, he went across to him.

Horatio stopped, probably expecting an apology or something. He stood waiting for James to speak.

"Um, er, please, sir, I have to give Mr Atkins a chit from you saying that I have had an extra piano lesson. I forgot to collect it at the end of today's lesson."

"My dear boy, I couldn't possibly give you any sort of a chit. You will just have to face the consequences. That was certainly no lesson."

And he triumphantly turned on his heels in the direction of the masters' common room already anticipating the thought of a refreshing cup of Earl Grey tea and a large slice of Battenberg cake.

On retreat

The school chaplain had sent a brief note to all the confirmation candidates announcing that there would be an initial meeting that Saturday afternoon, starting promptly at 2.30pm. I had little or no idea what confirmation was. It was just something that was expected of us. It was 1963 and I was just 14. I knew that my parents had put my name down for it and I knew that my older sister had been confirmed a couple of years before. I also knew that it meant that I would be given a prayer book by a godparent and some kind of present or money from other godparents and that it was a sign of being a 'grown up'. It was a rite of passage for every committed Christian and so if you were Jewish or Muslim then it wasn't for you. Other than that it was all a bit of a mystery.

The school chaplain trying to sound hearty welcomed the straggling groups of hesitant schoolboys into the meeting room with a wide smile and what was intended, I'm sure, to be a sincere and cheerful greeting.

"Well done, boys! Take a seat and then we can begin."

There were about twenty of us in total, all mostly from the fourth form in our second year at the school. We nervously sat in silence in the comfortable and warm first floor drawing room in the old farmhouse, which was now used by the school for clubs, meetings and a range of extra-curricular activities. The rooms here contrasted greatly with the spartan and barren rooms of the main school houses that the boys were used to and they privately appreciated the difference without openly admitting it; for to admit it, they instinctively knew, would probably sound a bit "wet".

"Well" said the chaplain, "Are we all here?" which was an odd question because none of the boys would have known who should have been there or not. He was a cheerful man, not very tall, slightly rotund with a round face and a few wisps of hair combed over his head in a vain attempt to conceal his baldness.

He began the meeting with the Lord's Prayer, during which I dutifully bowed my head, like the others were doing. As I did so, I looked at the floor and stared at the worn carpet and worried about what was going to happen next.

The chaplain explained that confirmation was the process by which each person would become a full member of the Church of England. He explained that the 'journey' had been started at our christening or baptism as he preferred to call it, when we had been welcomed into the church and now, with confirmation, we would have full membership.

He handed out some printed notes and explained that next week we would all be going on something called a "retreat" for three days. Retreating? What was that? Didn't that mean running away? He explained that a retreat was a time for quiet contemplation, an opportunity for "self examination", to open oneself to Jesus and to have an opportunity to get away from the hurly burly of everyday life at school. Frankly it all sounded a bit terrifying.

During this retreat the candidates would learn about the catechism or teachings of the Church of England. Importantly they would discuss a range of relevant topics and they could ask any questions, about absolutely anything along the way and their faith would be tested. What did he mean by self examination? I was at that age when I quite frequently "examined myself", but I didn't want to have to talk to other people about that! I didn't even know if I believed in God. I had been brought up in the Church of England as a matter of course. During the school holidays, we went to church every Sunday, partly because my siblings and I were all in the village choir. My father was a sidesman and went every week and my mother not quite so often. My parents had never discussed religion with me or my siblings. It had just been assumed, one's Christianity. I had been brought up that it was not very polite to talk in any detail about someone's religion. It was a private matter. So it all seemed rather over the top to actually have to talk about religion and to have to be "tested" on it. The confirmation itself would take place in a couple of months time when the bishop would come to the school chapel and there would be a ' laying-on-of-hands' . All the parents, god-parents and families would be invited to watch and to attend the reception to be held in a large marquee on the main school lawn afterwards.

On the appointed day of departure for the retreat, we all waited on the school drive, wondering what lay in store for us. It was a cold windy day in early January and as we stood there, small wisps of snow were blowing about in the wind and we sheltered behind a wall. When the coach eventually arrived and after handing over our suitcases to the assistant driver, we were all directed to get on board. The journey took us across several miles of bleak, flat Essex countryside under a grey, leaden sky. I couldn't see much through the smeary windows and couldn't really follow where we were going, but it felt as if we were being taken to somewhere very remote indeed. The dull wintry day seemed to suit the bleak flat countryside, which mostly consisted of sodden ploughed fields because of the continuous drizzle of rain and sleet. Finally we arrived. The retreat centre was an imposing, late Victorian redbrick house; it looked like it had once been the proud home for a prosperous merchant and his family, now all long dead. It seemed tired and faded and the flaking car park sign and the broken white lines painted on the crumbling and weed-strewn tarmac drive ironically confirmed its current status as an institution. In places, its redbrick walls were covered in swathes of dark green, rambling ivy, interspersed with lighter green smears of moss. The paint on the window frames was flaking and in urgent need of repair. In the centre of the front lawn stood a stone statue of a mother and child, which leant slightly at an angle. Once upon a time it had been painted in blue and gold and now only flakes of the paint were barely visible revealing the grey cement underneath. Scattered around it amongst the tussocky grass, was a constellation of molehills, like dark stars on the sodden grass. As the coach drew to a halt, the chaplain pointed out that the statue was the Virgin Mary and Child that she was one of the patron saints of the centre.

Inside the building it was just as bleak and cold: all bare wooden floors and bare walls. The walls had the colour and surfaces of milk that had gone off, the wooden doors and banisters looked as if they had been painted with black treacle and where the plain plank floors had been covered it was with institutionally ubiquitous brown linoleum. We were shown to our rooms by a couple of whey-faced curates who, we were told, were here to help us. Probably because my surname begins with a letter near to the end of the alphabet and therefore near to the bottom of the list, I knew that I would be one of the last to be called. And so it was, my room was high up in the building under the eaves, in what in former times had probably been part of the servants' quarters. The small room had steeply sloping ceilings and all the walls, I noticed, were panelled in heavily varnished wood. Once we had unpacked we were to assemble downstairs in the meeting room where the chaplain was going to talk to us in ten minutes time.

The meeting was led by the chaplain and the two pale curates who first stood and then sat impassively to one side. After a series of introductions the meeting started and my attention immediately began to wander. I watched the curates. Young men, obviously, but old before their time. They looked as if they were weighed down with the cares of the world. Both were tall and thin and wearing dark suits and clerical collars. One had a round face and large ears and seemed quite young; the other slightly older one had thick dark greasy hair and sallow skin and looked as if he was unwell. I wondered what they were thinking as they stared blankly at us as we sat politely listening to the chaplain droning on. My attention then wandered to staring out of the window and gazing across the gloomy gardens. It was only the middle of the afternoon, but it was already beginning to get dark. The wind had dropped and the watery sun was setting and the pale yellow streaks in the sky contrasting sharply with the dark black silhouettes of the tangled bare branches of the trees that bordered the large lawn. Just outside the window a few old gnarled and leafless apple trees stood in straggling lines, freshly trimmed and some flowerbeds were being cleared of the dead and overblown plants. The lone, elderly gardener, who was trying unsuccessfully to make a bonfire of the trimmings and plant debris, was stuffing newspaper into the pile and setting light to it. A wisp of smoke rose into the sky and the flames of the burning newspaper made a brief orange flash and slowly died down again. He stood back and then he turned round and, straightening himself up, he looked directly at the house. For a brief moment he seemed to be looking directly at me; we made eye contact. There was something very uncomfortable about his stare. In a funny sort of way I felt trapped and I forced myself to look away. The chaplain was talking about sin and forgiveness and so I tried to focus on what he was saying. I looked back out of the window. The old man was no longer there. Clouds of dense grey smoke rose upwards from the bonfire. Briefly

70

they parted and the man seemed to be standing in the middle of the fire holding his pitchfork beside him, still staring back at me. Was he really doing that, surrounded by the flames that were now appearing? It reminded me of a mediaeval painting I had seen somewhere of the devil in the fires of hell or was it of a single ordinary poor sinner roasting in Hell? I couldn't take my eyes away from the scene. I watched as the smoke enveloped him again and he disappeared completely from view with the flames lapping all around. I suddenly realised that I hadn't been listening to anything of what the chaplain had been talking about up to this point. I made myself look away from the garden and tried once again to focus on the lecture.

"Think of the catechism as a set of rules or guidelines, to be followed by all those who want to be full members of the church of Christ. You will have to learn them and be very familiar with them, and there will be a test, in fact lots of them."

This brought on yet more worries. "A test! Lots of them! When? How?"

One boy put his hand up and timidly asked, "W-w-will there be a real test, sir?"

"Not exactly, not in the sense that you are thinking of," replied the chaplain patronisingly, with an unctuous smile. He continued, "Rather the test is, in a manner of speaking, your life. You will be continually tested throughout your life. You will find yourself in situations where you will need guidance and that is when God's teaching helps and guides us. Life is about choices and we want you to be able to make the right choices. Now, shall we begin?"

There was a pause and he cleared his throat.

"The heart of the Catechism is the Ten Commandments. God's commandments brought down from the mountain by Moses. Do any of you know any of them?" There was an embarrassed silence and shuffling of feet. One boy put up his hand and said, "Thou shalt not kill, sir?"

"Yes, that's one. We all know that one," said the vicar rather unenthusiastically. "Any more?"

"Thou shalt not steal, sir," said another.

`No one else offered any more.

"Well. We shall start at the beginning. You should all make yourself familiar with the Ten Commandments. Look it up, Exodus, chapter twenty, the first seventeen verses. *'Thou shall have none other gods but me.'* This is the first commandment. This is where God is establishing his authority. All Christians believe that there is only one god. All the other gods are false gods. What does anyone think about that?"

A boy sitting at the front said, "But what about the Buddhists and the Muslims, sir? Are they all wrong, sir?"

Another boy said, "What about the Hindus? Sir, they have hundreds of gods. I know, sir, because my ayah in India was a Hindu and she said they have lots and lots of gods. Was she lying, sir?"

"Um, er... not exactly. You see we are all searching for the truth. We are all looking for answers. For example, why are we here? What is the purpose of life? And so on. Over time different peoples of the world from different cultures have followed different paths and created different routes in their search to find the reason for our existence. The moderate people of the major religions of the world are coming to accept that we must all work together and tolerate each other, rather than fight each other. We must accept each others' differences."

"But will people go to Hell if they don't accept Christianity?" piped up the youngest member of the group called Perkins minor.

"We used to think so," replied the chaplain, "and we used to burn non-believers at the stake, but we take a more tolerant view, nowadays." He chuckled nervously. "Anyway, I want to move on now to the next commandment, *"Thou shalt not make to thyself any graven image, nor the likeness of anything that is in heaven above, or in the earth beneath, or in the water under the earth. Thou shalt not bow down to them, nor worship them; for I the Lord thy God am a jealous God, and visit the sins of the fathers upon the children unto the third and fourth generation of them that hate me, and shew mercy unto thousands in them that love me, and keep my commandments."'*

"You, boy! What do you think that means?" And with horror I turned to see that the chaplain was pointing directly at me.

I was jolted by the shock of being asked a question. I had been watching again as the flames took hold of the bonfire. It was getting darker outside and there were occasional glimpses of the old man moving about poking at the fire with his fork. His face was momentarily lit up by the flames. It was the last time I saw him and as I looked I think he waved. I was embarrassed. I didn't know what to say, for in truth I hadn't really heard the question.

Knowing full well that I had not been paying attention, the chaplain repeated the question, helpfully putting it into some kind of context. "What does God mean when he says that thou shalt not make any graven image, nor worship them?"

"Well, sir," I began hesitantly. "God means that you shouldn't worship idols. You should only worship him and he is invisible." I felt relieved with my answer.

"Absolutely right. Well done. But it does go on to say 'nor the likeness of anything that is in heaven above or in the earth beneath, or in the water under the earth', what do you think that means?"

"You shouldn't make or worship statues of a God or anything, sir."

"Absolutely!"

"But what about the statue of the Virgin Mary and Child in the front garden, sir?"

The chaplain stared at me and then said, "That's not the same!"

Trying to ignore me he then addressed the whole group and continued, "Before we next meet, I want you to write out the commandments and make sure that you are completely familiar with all of them. And now we come to the business of trespass or sin. We are all sinners and we need to ask God to forgive us our sins. God knows the innermost secrets of our hearts and we have to confess our sins. In order to confess our sins we must face up to what we have done and then be completely and utterly repentant. Later on this evening, after supper, and tomorrow morning after breakfast, I will be in the small chapel here and I want you all, or as many of you

74

who are truly penitent, to come and confess your sins to me and I will, through God's Grace be able to grant God's forgiveness to you." He paused and looked across the group of boys as if looking for someone to ask a question. His beady eyes swept across the 'sinners' as if like searchlights, as he decided whom to question next. All of the boys sat there, feeling guilty of some sin or crime, and stared with embarrassment at the ground not wishing to give him any eye contact. A sort of collective guilt pervaded the small group. They were all thinking of how many so called sins they had committed. Then he continued;

"You have all heard of the Seven Deadly Sins? Can anyone tell me what they are?"

Only two boys put their hands up. One, Perkins minor, was a small, quiet boy with a round face, national health glasses and a scholarly and earnest disposition. The other was a larger, confident and more surly looking boy with pallid spotty skin and a downy moustache on his upper lip and who played rugby for the junior colts. The chaplain pointed to the smaller boy and said, "Well, go on, tell us, Perkins."

In a small, thin, unbroken voice the boy trilled, "Pride, envy um, er, anger... um—" He stopped, his face was turning rapidly pink and he had to think for a while. The boy sitting next to him whispered something in his ear, he then continued, "And laziness and I can't think of any more, sir."

"Well done, that's four, a good start." And pointing to the other, older boy with his hand up he said, "Can you tell me the last three, Morton major?"

"Yes, sir! I think so, sir." He said, rather too enthusiastically. "They are greed, gluttony and *lust*, sir!" and he had answered with relish in the cracking voice of a confident and self assured adolescent, stressing the word 'lust'.

"Well done, Morton major. Now are we all sure we know what all these words mean?" Morton major saw his opportunity and put up his hand.

"Yes, Morton major. Do you have a question?" Little did the chaplain know it but he was about to be drawn into a trap.

"Yes, sir. Lust, sir. I only know the word, but I'm not sure what it means. I'm only asking because sometimes people call it forkin er, forkination, sir, and I don't really know what they mean by that either, sir! Could you explain, sir, *exactly* what they mean, sir?" This time he had stressed the word 'exactly'.

There was a long pause as his question hung in the air. One or two of the boys at the back of the group, suppressed an embarrassed giggle. Morton major stared wide-eyed and unblinking, straight at the chaplain, he was like a cat playing with its prey. Coldly he waited for his answer and watched the poor man realise that he had no escape. I looked at the two curates, the round-faced one was trying to suppress a smirk and the older, dark-haired one was ashen white and his lips had disappeared into a straight line. The chaplain meanwhile was giving a good impression of a fish caught on a line and being hauled up out of the water. He was opening and shutting his mouth, his eyes were swivelling from side to side and he was moving nervously from foot to foot. The group of boys was getting restless. After a while he took out a handkerchief and mopped his forehead. The rest of the boys were waiting in silence, some were watching in wonder, some were whispering encouragements to Morton major, some started to talk just loud enough to be heard, asking each other such things as, "Are they talking about shagging?" and, " Is forkination the same as screwing?" and, "And what's self-abuse sir?" The meeting was beginning to become chaotic. Morton major menacingly played with his quarry by just watching and waiting with a feigned air of innocence and patience. The chaplain tried to gather his thoughts and then choosing his words carefully, he said,

"Quiet please, everybody, quiet. Settle down now. The word is 'fornication', Morton major." There were more titters from the group, which he ignored. He mopped his brow again and continued. "Well, I mean it's like this, um… er… it's difficult, er… let me see. L-L-Lust is having wicked thoughts of the flesh, and you must not give in to… to… temptation. You must fight it! Do you see, Morton major?" There was an almost pleading tone in his voice, he did not want to have to spell it out, but Morton was going to make him.

"Er, flesh sir? Is that like wishing you had a roast for supper or a bacon sandwich, sir, and then having to have beans on toast instead, sir?"

"Er, no not exactly, um, sins of the flesh refers to bodily functions, er to do with, to do with, er, um… procreation or—" he hesitated, sighed and then said one single word, "sex, Morton major, sex!"

"Like having dirty thoughts, sir?"

"Er, yes, Morton major. You have to put those impure thoughts out of your mind."

"What impure thoughts, sir? Does everyone, do you, sir, have dirty thoughts , sir?"

"Er, no um yes, no of course not… Well now, I think that that is quite enough questions for now."

"But what about forkination, sir?" persisted Morton major.

"The word is fornication, boy, fornication, and it means two people – a man and a woman – having sex together."

"You mean when men and women 'do it', sir, making babies, sir, that it's a sin, sir?"

"For pity's sake, Morton, no. It's not like that at all. Really, I have had enough of this."

In a futile gesture, the chaplain turned to the two curates for some kind of help and guidance. They both sat there inert and immobile, about as much use in this situation as a pair of large Chinese vases which they now, in an uncanny way, seemed to resemble.

The chaplain had no choice but to bring the meeting to a speedy conclusion and we were hastily dismissed and told to go to our rooms and wait for the bell for supper which would be rung in fifteen minutes.

Walking back up to my room, I felt a bit bewildered for it seemed to me that we had not really learnt anything and that so many questions had not been addressed let alone answered. Everything was so contradictory. In fact, there were more questions than answers. I was climbing up the stairs following some of the boys and I could hear Morton major bragging to a small group around him about how he had stitched up the chaplain.

"That showed him. It's all bollocks really. I don't believe a word of it anyway. I'm just getting confirmed because my godfather has told me if I do he is going to give me a hundred quid! And a new racing bike!"

Later, after an almost inedible supper of overcooked and rapidly cooling cauliflower cheese and congealing lumps of bacon, eaten off cold plates in silence in the draughty dining hall, we were told by the two curates, in a bizarre sort of double act, to return to our rooms in silence and to study our bibles, with particular reference to the commandments and sin. A bell would be sounded when we were to get into our pyjamas and go and get washed in silence in the communal washrooms, after which we must return to our rooms. After another bell, we must put our lights out, and we were not to forget to say our prayers and to ask God to forgive us our sins. However, anyone who wished to go to confession to confess their sins should do so now.

I went to bed in a bit of a turmoil. All the contradictory ideas swirled around in my head. I wanted black and white answers and it seemed that there were only ever going to be shades of grey. Nobody's perfect; nobody could ever be perfect. It seemed to me that if people are going to be human then they will inevitably "sin". Therefore sinning is kind of natural, and if it is natural how can it be a sin? People were born in "sin". How silly is that? Why were people created sinners? I tried and failed to imagine my parents "doing it". Although I knew that they must have, I couldn't or rather didn't want to imagine it. I went to the communal washrooms and washed in cold water. There were one or two other boys in there washing but nobody spoke as one of the curates was standing in a corner making sure of that. He stared blankly at the boys as they washed and did their teeth. The boys ignored him. I returned to my room and quickly changed into my pyjamas. I knelt down by my bed and thought that I ought to try and pray, but I didn't know what to do or how to speak to God and, when I tried, it felt silly and ridiculous. Why should I kneel down? Why should I grovel before a god? Surely no true god would expect me to kneel down. So feeling both foolish and annoyed simultaneously I got up and crawled into bed.

A whole string of random thoughts were swirling around in my head and I eventually fell into a fitful sleep. I felt so exhausted by it all. Man is made in the image of God. All men and women are created equal. I was not a sinner; I was a normal human being. I was a teenage boy and whatever my body did was quite natural. I had nothing to confess. Nothing. Then I was searching for something. I was in a maze, on my hands and knees. I was crawling along a tunnel. There were all sorts of obstacles in my way. I was in a darkened room and there were lots of doorways of different sizes and I needed to get out. Every time I tried a door it came away in my hands, it had no hinges. Then there were piles of unidentifiable clutter lying in my path. I crawled and stumbled over or through everything. I felt that I must get out of this place if I wasn't to suffocate – it was stifling. The nightmare of stumbling over stuff and crawling went on forever. After what seemed like an eternity, I found another door, a small door, with a shelf in front of it. I felt for the handle and turned it and was immediately aware of a cold rush of air, I clambered onto the shelf and started to climb through the door, but everything was dark, and there was nothing there. My arms waved about in a void... Was I at the entrance to a vast tunnel? I looked up and saw lots of little white lights. Strangely and inexplicably, I could just make out a series of trees against a skyline in the distance. I could smell woodsmoke. There was nothing to put my feet on. Suddenly I felt sheer panic. My hands clutched at the doorframe. In a flash I realised instinctively that I was high up. The door was a window and I was in the crazy process of climbing out of it. I felt a shock as if I had been electrocuted, and pulling myself backwards, I slammed the window shut. In the same movement, I fell back onto the wooden floor, hitting something as I fell. Whatever it was fell over and there was a crunching sound. Breathless with fear, I groaned softly to myself. I waved my arms about and I half-walked and half-crawled in any direction, hoping to find the bed and blindly groping for it, in the process, knocking a bedside table and lamp over. At last I felt the coarseness of the blanket on the side of the bed and dragged myself on to it. The sheets and blankets were completely churned up and knotted in a lump, but I managed to cover myself. Instinctively I curled up into a foetal ball, my breathing calmed and my fear subsided and I fell into a deep and dreamless sleep.

I was awoken by a loudly clanging bell, being rung by someone who was calling out, "Chapel in fifteen minutes! Chapel in fifteen minutes!" As I opened my eyes, I looked round the room. It looked as if the room had been ransacked. I noticed that the wood panelling was scattered all round the room. They were in fact a series of loose hatches. By removing them I had revealed all kinds of stored clutter: chairs, enamel buckets, jugs, bowls, and piles of cardboard boxes full of toilet paper. It all looked a complete mess. I struggled out of bed and quickly tried my best to put everything back as I assumed it should be. I picked up the bedside table and put the lamp back on it. Miraculously the lightbulb still worked. I looked round and the window was closed. I realised that I had been sleep walking and had been on the brink of falling out of the window. It was the rush of cold air at the window that had woken me up and it had probably saved my life.

The rest of my time on retreat was spent in a kind of blur. I listened to all that I was told and tried but failed to make any real sense of anything.

Confirmation day arrived and a huge white marquee had been erected on the lawn beside the school chapel for the reception which would follow the service.

At the climax of the service in the school chapel all the confirmation candidates had lined up and one by one they had knelt in front of the bishop who laid both his hands on each person's head and muttered a blessing. As I walked up to him for the blessing, I realised that he looked a bit familiar. I knelt before him and looked up at him briefly, he smiled and I quickly looked down again. As he leant forward and put his hands on my head I got a distinct whiff of a pungent smell, it reminded me of… wood smoke.! Of course! He was the gardener, all those weeks ago, the man in the bonfire at the retreat house!

"Have you been a good boy?" he asked rather creepily.

"Yes, sir." I replied.

I realised that there was the possibility that I was being blessed by Satan himself as he said:

"Confirm, O Lord, your servant with your Holy Spirit!"

Sailing

He kept his dinghy at the sailing club and yesterday he phoned me up to ask if I wanted to go sailing with him. I knew he had a boat, but I had not been out sailing with him before and I was really excited at the prospect.

This was the summer of '68 and we had been sort of 'going out' for a few months now. We had first met when he joined the art school at the local college where I was doing my foundation course in art and design. He had joined the course halfway through the year; something about wanting to keep his hand in before going to university where he already had a place, so he wasn't quite like the rest of us. We still had to do all the business of interviews and preparing portfolios and things like that and he didn't. I always remember that first day of college in the new year. It was a liberal studies class and when my friend Kay and I went into the classroom, there was this boy who we hadn't seen before, sitting on a desk and I didn't know who he was. He said hello and smiled at us. He looked quite young. He was wearing a jacket and jeans and he looked a bit uncertain and sort of vulnerable, yet oddly confident at the same time. Amazingly, Kay recognised him and whispered to me that she knew him, something about ponies and horses. Kay knew his sister as well; they had all belonged to the Pony Club when they were younger and she went over to talk to him. I don't know if he even noticed me. I found out from Kay what his name was and he seemed OK, actually. He told us that he was joining the art school and he asked if he was in the right room. Kay assured him he was. Whenever we are together, Kay seems to dominate the conversation and she seems to do all the talking; I'm not one to butt in. Soon other people in our group started to arrive noisily: Eddy, Paul, Theo, Maggie, Jan, Verena and some others, and we all began finding seats and settling down. Most of them acknowledged him and were friendly towards him, but you could see some of them sizing him up and wondering what he was doing there. Once the lesson began, I found myself sitting across the class from him and I couldn't help watching him. I couldn't keep my eyes from wandering in his direction. Not staring exactly, but I kept finding that I was looking at him a lot. He must have been eighteen or nineteen. I don't think he had even started shaving. One or two of the boys in the group had stubbly chins and one or two had quite long hair, but his hair was quite short.

Kay turned to me and whispered, "What do you think of him? Do you fancy him?" I blushed; he did look quite nice, but I didn't think I fancied him. During the lesson he was one of the few who were concentrating on what the teacher was saying. He was chewing a pencil and making notes in his sketchbook from time to time. The lesson was about the French Impressionists, Monet and people like that. I love Monet's work, but if I am honest, the teacher was not making it very interesting. The new boy seemed to know a bit about the Impressionists, while in contrast the other students didn't seem to be taking much interest at all. As I looked in his direction, he turned towards me and looking very intently at me he smiled shyly and then he blushed and quickly turned away again.

**

"Ouch! Careful!" I said. The fingers on my left hand had been squashed in his grip as the bike wobbled and he struggled to keep it upright. I had been hanging on to the handlebars and his hand had been on mine as we freewheeled down the hill, getting faster and faster. He was holding on to the handlebars, which seemed to lurch from side to side of their own free will, and he gripped ever tighter as he squeezed the brake and slowly brought the bike to a standstill. We had hoped to get a lift from one of his parents, but when I got to his house neither of them were there. And then he had the bright idea of going to the river on his bike! The sail bag and bits of wood called battens were tied on to the rack behind the saddle, along with the lifejackets on top. I sat sort of side saddle on the crossbar and he had to do all the pedalling. He had to stand up on the pedals to keep us going and he had begun to get hot and I could smell his sweat and feel his hot breath on the side of my neck, every time he sat back on the saddle. It wasn't an unpleasant experience, I realised that I loved this, but it was just a little uncomfortable. But I didn't care; we were together. As he held the handlebars, I was surrounded by him; his head just inches from mine, his hands gripping the handlebars, my hands just touching and occasionally being overlapped by his. I think he enjoyed it as well. It gave him an excuse to have his arms around me! His hand on mine felt warm and a bit bony, but reassuring. If I turned my head, our faces almost touched; his eyes looked into mine, my eyes looked into his and we smiled at each other and briefly kissed. It was a light, fleeting butterfly of a kiss.

I definitely remember the very first time we kissed. We had been sitting side by side on a small, red wooden box – a sort of stool – in the middle of a very crowded room, at the tiddley winks competition at the college. I think that we had both randomly contrived to accidentally-on-purpose find ourselves next to each other. I could feel his body against mine – our legs touched, our elbows touched and we must both have been very aware of each other. We had not really spoken much before this. It was the final of the competition and the room was very crowded and everyone was squashed in together. Lots of people were calling out to their friends and cheering on the players and yet all I was really thinking about was this boy and very much aware of his proximity. It was almost as if we were in a bubble of silence, just us, and I could feel the electricity between us. I didn't know what was going to happen, and I know he was thinking about me, because he turned towards me several times and sometimes smiling again at me, and then, embarrassed, he turned away again. He moved his hand and held mine, and we sat very still. Then it happened. He suddenly turned to me, bent his head forward and kissed me full on the lips and his arm came round my shoulders, quite roughly, and pulled me towards him, without having said anything, and then, just as quickly, he turned away. It was all over in a second. He just stared ahead, and I noticed that he was breathing rather fast. It had all happened very quickly; he seemed as surprised as I was. After a while he turned to me again and we kissed a bit more. He still didn't really say much. This time he was more relaxed I felt really happy because I knew that in his own way he was trying to show me his feelings towards me that he obviously found difficult to put into words. The tiddley winks competition was soon over and then he just got up and said he had to go home. Just like that! He said goodbye and everything, but I remember thinking that it would have been nice to stay together for a bit longer.

The day was getting hotter all the time and after a while we decided to stop for a rest. We were in the middle of nowhere, on a country lane deep in the Suffolk countryside in high summer, and we had found a small pull-in. I clambered off the bike and he leant it against a tree. We went through a gap in the straggly hedge and sat on a grassy bank with our backs to the hedge, looking across a field of beans that were in flower. The bank was thick with tall grasses, wild flowers and the heady, sweet smell of the bean blossom, the dappled shade from the old oak tree above us made for a magical place. We both lay back on the ground and I lay beside him, our bodies touching. The long grass tickled my legs, and it wasn't very comfortable. I turned my head towards him and he smiled and I smiled and I took his hand and kissed it. I lay back and looked up to the canopy of trees above us. I love that; it's one of my special things. It's quite an inspiring feeling, staring up at the network of leaves and branches. I noticed a pair of long-tailed tits flitting from branch to branch, looking for insects, and then I saw some more and pointed them out to him. He looked for them, then he saw them too and we just lay there in silence, watching them. We didn't speak for some minutes. We counted nine or ten of them in all; they must have been one large family. They methodically moved across the tree, hunting for little insects, and then they were gone. They vanished as quickly as they had arrived. I turned to him; his eyes were shut, and he was breathing gently. I watched his Adam's apple bob up and down as he swallowed, and studied his profile. He had a boyish face and a fair complexion. And his hair was a mop of light brown, which he had let grow a bit.

"Did you see that? Weren't they amazing? I have never seen so many at once."

"Yes," he said, his eyes blinking. He slowly rolled on his side to face me and I rolled on my side to face him and our faces were just inches from each other. Our noses almost touched and we just looked into each other's eyes and smiled and then kissed. We just lay there. A great feeling of happiness washed over me. We were holding each other; his arms around me, my arms around him.

Then he suddenly said, "We ought to get on, we're supposed to be going sailing." He got up quickly and turned away from me and walked towards the bike.

" Come on , all aboard the Jolly Roger! " he said.

We found his dinghy in the dinghy park. He told me it was a Firefly. It was made of beautifully moulded varnished wood, unpainted. I watched and tried to help

89

as he rigged the boat and then we dragged it down the slipway on its trolley and pushed it into the water. He told me to stand with my back to the wind and keep the boat pointing into it and so I hung on to it as he took the trolley away and dumped it at the top of the slip. I was standing in freezing cold water up to my knees with my jeans rolled up. He came back and told me to get in the boat and I clambered in, as he hung on. Suddenly he pushed the boat into the river. As he did so, he told me to move to the front, crouch down, and watch out for the boom, but he didn't tell me what a boom was. Suddenly the wind filled the sails, the boat picked up speed and we headed up the river against the current. He seemed to know what he was doing, he was steering the boat and controlling the big sail. After the speedy and frantic launch when everything had happened very quickly, we were now sailing along quite steadily. He had begun to relax and I turned to him. His face was flushed and his eyes were squinting into the sun as he steered the dinghy out into the river, past the moored boats with their taut bowlines as they pulled against the outgoing tide.

"What do I do now?" I asked.

"Hang on to the jib sheet and keep your head down. Only haul it in if you feel it slacking off, the trick is to keep it filling with wind," he said, without looking at me. He was concentrating on looking ahead.

"What's a jib sheet?"

"Oh, sorry. There, it's that thick rope there. There's one on either side and depending on which side the wind is coming from— hang on, we're going about! Keep your head down!" And with this, the boat heeled over and seemed to turn a corner through nearly a hundred and eighty degrees. As it did this, the sail whipped across the boat and the bit of wood along its bottom edge just missed my head by inches. Luckily, I ducked my head quickly and I was left on the bottom of the boat, uncomfortably half-lying half-crouching in a pool of cold water that was sloshing about among the tangle of ropes, paddles and the remains of our sandwiches.

Later on, when the boat was back in the dinghy park and the sails and other bits and pieces were tied back onto the bike, we began the long trek home. It was getting dark, I was cold, my clothes were wet, I had a couple of bruises on my legs and I had scraped my elbow. He was pushing the bike through the sand, I was walking beside him. He turned to me and said,

"Well, what do you think of sailing now?"

"I love it," I lied.

Ropehawn

Getting down to the house was not easy or straight forward. They first had to leave the cars parked in a small sheltered place known locally as the 'ledra', which led off from the steep sided lane that wound endlessly through the Cornish countryside. Unpacking the car, they carried with them as much as they could, knowing that they would have to make several return journeys later to get it all down. They didn't mind. Having been cooped up in a car with only one break, for the six hours that it had taken to drive down from East Anglia, the fresh air and physical activity were very welcome. The anticipation and a sense of freedom made them impatient to get to the house. Leading off into the trees the winding path which in former times had been a donkey track down to the old pilchard house had been worn into the sloping sides of the cliff by generations of hooves, feet and varieties of iron-rimmed wheels. A tunnel had been formed by the ancient and twisted trees arching low overhead and they could feel the cooling breeze on their faces and smell the faint tang of the sea. On dry sunny days like this the well-trodden surface was easy enough to negotiate for it was strewn with layers of crackling and desiccated leaves with a soft damp mulch underneath. In wet weather it was an entirely different proposition, for it presented the unwary visitor with a slippery and unforgiving surface. When wet, the ubiquitous dark loam turned to a slimy sludge underfoot and that combined with the sloping angle of the path made it almost impossible to walk on without serious risk of falling over. Every so often low outcrops of rock from the underlying strata of strong Cornish granite broke through the surface and crossed the path at angles like rows of rotten teeth, both molars and canines. There were also roots, some hard and wooden, which had risen above ground, snaking across the path and ready to trip up the unwary walker. These obstacles had caused many a pony-trap or dog cart in days gone by to break an axle or a wooden wheel and to tip its terrified passengers out onto the earth, with many shrieks and cries. For in those times the visitors were gentle folk, usually Victorian ladies in black bombazine, who wished to visit the pilchard house and to purchase some fish to take back to St Austell, and they did not expect to be so mired and stained by the dark mud on which they rolled. Their accompanying gentlemen, who were walking some distance behind, could only watch helplessly from afar, and then rush to the scene of the accident, breathlessly muttering endearments to their beloved, furrowing their bushy eyebrows, and stroking their mutton chop whiskers impotently.

Relishing the fresh air and the gentle cooling breeze as they walked, our visitors were aware of the sunlight breaking randomly through the leafy canopy casting bright shafts of light in which dust motes and insects busied themselves before disappearing into darker shadows. If they looked carefully through the leaves and branches of this natural leafy corridor they would catch glimpses of sparkling waters, way below them. This sight would instantly lift their spirits and distract them from the work of carrying their heavy burdens so that they would momentarily forget the dead weights of suitcases, rucksacks and food boxes. Light, bright images would come to mind, of carefree summer days, splashing water, laughter and happiness from times gone by and the anticipation of times yet to come now, on this their summer holiday.

They were never very sure how long the descent down the track took but after a while of carefully negotiating the ancient path and being anxious not to trip on the rocks and roots which tried to surprise them, the tunnel of trees and bushes suddenly gave way to allow an unhindered and refreshing view of the open sea and its rocky coastline.

Around the next corner they had to stop at an old five-bar gate, which was closed and tied with a piece of wire and on which they now leant breathing in the sea air with relish. Nobody said a word. They had gladly put down the luggage and boxes so that they could stare in satisfied silence for a few moments at the place where they would be spending the next two weeks.

From the gate, looking down the clipped grassy slope, they saw the house in profile. It sat comfortably on a high piece of ground at the base of the steeply sloping bank behind it. This bank was covered in a thick mass of trees struggling to grow vertically above a dense undergrowth of ferns, trailing creepers of old man's beard and ground elder. The house had been built at the turn of the century on the firm stone foundations of an eighteenth century pilchard house. Little of that building now remained, except for the cellar with its eighteen inch thick stone foundations on which the current house now stood. From the outside of the building most of these foundations were hidden from view by overgrowing ivy, grasses and mosses. The plaster walls of the house had been painted white and there was a geometric pattern of black painted timbers which gave the house that typical Victorian look. The back of the house stood only a foot or so from the cliff against which it had been built. This created a magic place behind but it was too close to the bank for anyone to walk into, because of its narrowness and the mass of climbing plants and vegetation. It was said that the house was built on rocks which would in several generations time bring everything down to the sea, but they were not worrying about that now.

They fumbled with the wire loop that held the gate shut and freeing it they pushed it open and leaving everything where it lay, they ran down the path towards the house. Some flung open the front door and went happily inside, while others went straight past, down to the little slipway, just happy to be there. At the top of the slip they stood some with hands on hips and silently stared out over the flat calm sea. Across the bay they could make out the familiar shapes of the Carlyon Bay Hotel and Charlestown and everything was in the clear bright morning light. The sea was like a mill pond they said, for it was high tide and the water was crystal clear. As they peered from the slipway, down into the depths they could clearly see the miniature forests of kelp swaying back and forth with the surging waters and the many darkened colours of the stones; ochres, bull's blood and slate grey, which lay scattered on the sea floor. Once the tide had peaked, and the waters had receded, they would explore these same grounds with nets and buckets to search in the pools for shrimps and prawns to have for their supper that evening which they would eat in front of a smouldering log fire in the sitting room. On impulse someone said, "Let's swim. It'll be great!" Someone else said, "What about our things?" Yet another one said, "Oh don't worry, no one is here to see. Let's go in, in our pants!" Someone else said, "But we haven't got towels!" "Who cares?" said yet another.

And with that, most of those who were there, after throwing off their clothes and shoes and in varying states of modesty and undress with minimal cover, ran down the slipway and noisily entered the water, splashing and laughing. The sensible ones, who didn't want to swim, stayed at the top and sat on an old upturned boat and watched, some came down from the house to see what all the noise was about. They enjoyed the shrieks and gasps of the bathers as they entered the water, hobbling over the stones and splashing each other, which was evidence enough that the water was very cold indeed. For this was early summer and the sea would not yet warm up to an agreeable temperature for several weeks. They didn't stay in long and beginning to shiver, they returned to the slipway and clambered out, folding their goosefleshed arms across their chests. They walked up towards the others who couldn't help but notice that the few underclothes, now sodden, that they were wearing had been rendered virtually transparent as they clung to the swimmers bodies, clearly revealing outlines and darker shapes which left precious little to the imagination. This embarrassed some, intrigued a few and yet mesmerised others, but no one said anything about it at all.

Much later, after the rest of the luggage had been collected and when it had been decided who would have which rooms and who would have the prize of sleeping in the summer house and everything had been unpacked and put in its place, a simple picnic lunch was taken outside.

In front of the house there was a patch of lawn surrounded by high stone walls with a little door set into the seaward wall, looking straight across the bay. This favoured place was the spot which they often chose for their picnics and they agreed that it was a bit of a sun trap. The walls provided shelter and added to the sense of privacy and seclusion. Some deckchairs were retrieved from the summer house, a couple of rugs were thrown on the ground and they all sat down to eat the pasties and to drink the wine and cider which they had brought with them. Someone had also prepared a salad and a simple cheese board with biscuits, but with just one cheese, the all-important family favourite, Stilton.

With the midday sun now high in the sky, after the meal a contented silence settled on the group. One sought out a quiet shady corner to read a book by a favourite author, another relaxed on a rickety deckchair to do the cryptic crossword in the paper, yet another went into the house for an afternoon nap on one of the beds, leaving the windows open so that the curtains billowed lazily in the breeze. Two more retired into a quiet whispered conversation on the high grassy bank, exchanging news and the latest information and idle gossip about mutual friends and family, for they had not seen each other in a while and needed to catch up. Another went to sort out the fishing equipment; for it was planned to make an expedition first thing tomorrow morning to catch some mackerel for breakfast. With the tide falling, the afternoon fishing would not be very good. The most they might do would be to go shrimping and anyway, most were too tired from the long journey and wanted to relax this afternoon just getting themselves settled in.

All the paraphernalia for fishing was kept in the small cellar. This could be accessed by either the steps down from the kitchen or by a little door from the outside. It was a small room, with thick stone walls which inside had been painted white some time ago and which were now crumbling and flaking with age. The room was part of the older original pilchard house, which probably dated from the eighteenth century or earlier. As Malcolm entered the room he couldn't help but notice the stink of rotting fish. The source of this stink was immediately obvious. There were two buckets filled to the brim with mackerel and the flies had already got to them. Lying on the little table was a note on which someone had written in a scrawl of green crayon, *'Thought you might like these, we caught too many for ourselves!'* and there was an illegible signature. God, it made him angry when people did this. They had got carried away in the excitement of it all and now he had to chuck out the fish they hadn't eaten. It was such a waste. Picking up the bucket he went out into the garden and walked down to the water's edge. At least the resident local seal, which everyone called the 'Lord Privy Seal' , might enjoy them, he thought as he hurled them angrily into the water. As he rinsed out the bucket he thought he could make out a crab or two lurking nearby in the shadows under the waves. As he was returning to the cellar, a voice called out, "Daddy, Daddy! Come here quick look at this!" He looked up to see his son on the high grass bank at the edge of the property, he was pointing to the ground near to where he stood. He soon clambered up the bank and walked over to where his son was pointing. There on the ground lay at least another twenty or thirty mackerel. Obviously from the rest of the catch, which he had just thrown into the sea. They were buzzing with flies and their drying scales had lost any shine and their eyes were cloudy and blank.

"Daddy, why do people do that? It's so cruel, it's not fair! They've just killed them for nothing!" He looked up imploringly at his father with an anguished expression on his face; he really didn't understand.

"They are just stupid people who are careless and thoughtless. Nobody should ever catch more fish than they need in any one day. You must always remember that. Come on we had better put them in the sea with the other lot. At least they will be eaten by something. Would you like to come fishing with me tomorrow morning?" The boy didn't answer immediately and then said, "Yes, OK," but without much conviction.

Later father and son returned to the cellar and selected the fishing gear that they would need for the morning trip and checked it through. They had a choice of spinners and feathers but thought that they would take both. Whatever they used depended on the weather. The lines of twine were wound round roughly fashioned frames of wood and the boy was warned by his father not to catch his fingers on the hooks and spinners as if they got too deeply embedded in to their flesh they would have to take him to hospital to have it cut out. The boy stared aghast at his father and quickly put the set of feathers that he was holding back onto the shelf with all the others.

The interior of the house seemed to truly welcome the visitors. They had been coming for several years and loved the place. It belonged to a distant relative who was too old to visit it anymore and was just pleased that it was being used. In the old kitchen, supper was prepared on the scrubbed pine table and cooked on an ancient gas cooker in two huge enamel saucepans, one for spaghetti and one for the Bolognaise sauce. The salad was washed in the stone butler's sink and the plates and tureens, that they would need, were taken down from the dresser shelves and quickly dusted. Eventually the table was cleared to lay the cutlery and the others were called from the sitting room where they had been playing a noisy game of racing demon on the old Persian rug which lay on the bare wooden floor, while two of the older members of the party sat on the window seat and had watched and smiled.

During a lively supper while excited plans were made for the following day, the meal of spaghetti Bolognaise and accompanying garlic bread and a good Chianti was enjoyed and consumed to the very last suck of spaghetti. Then apples and cheese were followed by cups of coffee and pieces of chocolate.

Two bars of chocolate were produced, one plain and one milk chocolate. This was a bit of a ritual after every evening meal. The guardian of the chocolate, an aunt, always presided. The chocolate bars were broken up and pieces were offered round the table as "pearl" or "plain".

They gradually drifted back to the sitting room, with some staying in the kitchen to wash up and clear away the remnants of the meal. There was only one standard lamp lighting the room and the curtains had been left open. There were a few old faded photographs of the house and the surrounding cliffs hanging randomly on the walls. These must have been taken in the late nineteenth century, for there were photographs of a small donkey cart posing stiffly with its driver. The cart was loaded with faggots of wood. The cliffs in the background were devoid of trees and only covered with small bushes and scrub. All available wood would have been cut down for firewood. This was in complete contrast with today as the need for firewood was now not so great and so the cliffs were now covered in dense woodland and scrub.

The fire had gone out and there were one or two half-hearted attempts to relight it. Someone lit a couple of candles on the mantelpiece and drinks were poured. They settled down to talk about the old days. Did they know that one year some people brought dinner jackets and evening dresses and invited friends and relatives to lavish candle lit dinner parties in the garden, and the time when they got to the house and almost caught some burglars red handed trying to load furniture into a boat? When the burglars had seen them they had jettisoned the furniture on to the beach and roared off into the dusk, with their outboard motor spluttering like an angry mosquito.

Eventually they went off to their beds. One lucky couple had been designated to sleep in the summer house, others to the various rooms upstairs. All the bedrooms were simply furnished with the bare essentials of beds, cupboards and a few chairs. They were comfortable and clean with old rugs on bare floorboards, simple light coloured curtains that gently moved in the breeze when the windows were opened. There would be a bookshelf with a few well thumbed novels or comic annuals and here and there would be hung old faded photographs of people on holiday from long ago now with frozen and faded smiles behind dusty glass . At the top of the house there was a "boys' dormitory" and a "girls' dormitory" and this was where the various younger members of the group slept. These were more sparsely furnished than the other rooms and so there was not too much tidying for the rooms' occupants to have to do.

Eventually after saying goodnight to the others left in the sitting room, the young couple that had been given the summer house to sleep in slipped out of the front door into the black night. As they hurried together down the dew-covered grass path, shivering and holding hands they gazed up at the sky and marvelled at the myriad stars and tried to identify the familiar constellations. They wondered at the vastness of space and time of which they knew that they were only the tiniest speck. The tide was coming in again and they could hear the waves crashing on the slipway below in the dark. A stiff breeze was getting up and it was coming straight off the sea. All day the sea had been calm and tranquil yet now it was promising to be quite a stormy night. There was no key and the young man had to push on the wooden door to open it. The dampness in the air had swelled the wood and it had stuck in the door frame but was soon cleared. The summer house was quite a substantial Edwardian timber building constructed of pitch pine with a slate roof and was built at the same time as the main house was being converted from a pilchard factory. The interior consisted of one large room with a faint but distinct smell of creosote. It was filled with the paraphernalia of a beach house which had been used as a holiday home for several generations. There were oars and spars leaning up in one corner. At the back some old cotton sails hung from one of the beams that stretched across the room. Some old deckchairs and wicker ones with their seats blown out were stacked to one side and there were cricket bats, stumps and a badminton net in another corner. Up in the rafters hung myriad cobwebs made visible by layers of dust. On a small rickety table someone had started to repair the rigging of a model boat and it now lay on its side forgotten and incomplete. The main feature of the room was the large lattice windows which looked across the dark sea. The only light in the room came from the moon and it cast a gentle grey shadow over everything. There was a large mattress which had been put in the middle of the room and had loosely been made up with pillows, sheets and blankets. As the young lovers looked out of the window they could just make out the white horses skittering and dancing across the dark waves. Rain was now splattering loudly against the windows, revealing small unseen leaks so that water trickled down both sides of the glass at once and pooled on the sills and under the cushions on the window seat. Quickly and quietly they undressed and as they did so they admired glimpses of each other's nakedness in the moonlight. Hurriedly they slipped gratefully under the bedclothes and reaching for each other they clung together, giggling as their cold hands and feet warmed as they explored the new familiarity of each others' young body. Sometime later, as they fell into a deep sleep, the storm abated and a gentle rain fell on the slate roof and soft water dripped onto the small model boat, which would never be repaired, lying on the table.

Up at the house the rest of the inhabitants were settling down for the night. There were only two bathrooms so turns had to be taken and people had to be patient, especially with the older occupants. People in dressing gowns and with slippered feet would bump into each other as they walked along corridors to find a vacant bathroom. Much earlier most had left their windows open to air the rooms. When they returned later they quickly shut them again to keep out the wind and the rain which had blown itself in, in their absence. As they drifted off to sleep they could hear the noise of rain against the window panes and the crashing of the waves on the rocks below and they dreamed of shipwrecks and dramatic rescues as people were hauled to safety in a bosun's chair or they desperately clung to wreckage and in some cases, with eternal gratitude, to each other. The lovers in the summer house were by now asleep in a tangle of blankets and bed-sheets, with their bodies entwined and their faces bathed in moonlight while the storm had raged outside and then had eventually blown itself out.

The young boy and his father got up earlier than the rest to go fishing. They crept downstairs and had slipped unnoticed out of the front door and into the fresh, crisp brightness of a summer's morning. The wind and rain of the night before had long since died away and it had given everything a shiny, fresh and recently washed appearance. They decided not to take the outboard motor, the noise would wake everybody up, this meant that they would row and fish with feathers. The boy, holding a couple of the fishing lines, wound onto the frames, held them carefully so as to not catch his finger on a hook. He felt both excited and apprehensive at the same time. His father started to drag the clinker built rowing boat down the slipway. The boy put the lines onto the back seat and helped his father by pushing at the transom. Reaching the water, which lapped at the bottom of the slipway and before pushing the boat into the water, they quickly took off their shoes and socks. When the boat was half in the water, the father told his son to jump in and to go and sit at the front. The water was icy cold and he hopped from foot to foot as the boy clambered in. Pushing the boat a bit further he felt it float clear of the slipway and so he quickly swung his leg over and jumped aboard.

The little rowing boat was one that was always used by visitors to the house. It was a solid and well made craft and he quickly settled into the rhythm of rowing as it glided out into the bay. As he rowed he gazed back at the house and tried to imagine what everyone else staying there would be doing at this moment. Some, the older folk would be getting up, the younger ones would lie in longer and eventually would surface when they smelt bacon being fried or coffee being brewed. Breakfast was always a very relaxed affair, with everybody getting up at different times. They helped themselves to cereals or tea and coffee, or made toast, some made boiled eggs or fried bacon. They sat at the kitchen table, some looking dazed yet thoughtful as they sipped tea and chewed on toast and marmalade. Others chattered about the weather, the state of the tide and their hopes and plans for the day.

The oars cut through the clear water with a comforting splash, and as they came up, they left a trail of bright sparkling droplets looking just like glass beads that quickly fell back into the water. The sun was out, in a cloudless sky, but it was too bright too early. This usually meant that during the day the clouds would build up and then later there would be rain. But now it was clear, the air was cool and pleasant, the sea was flat calm and it all looked like the perfect conditions for fishing for mackerel. The man pointed out to his son that the fish were jumping and that this was a good sign. The boy, who had moved to the stern of the boat, was leaning over staring thoughtfully into the water and trailing his hands, creating a little wake behind him.

"Be careful that doesn't attract a shark!" said the boy's father.

The boy quickly pulled his hand out of the water and squinted into the bright light as he looked up at his father with a frown.

"There aren't any sharks here, Dad!" he said.

"Then why did you pull your hand out of the water?"

The boy smiled and put his hand back in to the water as if to show that he knew he was right.

They continued in silence as the boat went further out into the bay until his father was in the "best" place for mackerel, which was traditionally when facing the house you could line up the hotel in Carlyon bay on your starboard side with the tip of the headland out on the port side. He therefore shipped the oars leaving them in the rowlocks. There was little or no current so they were not going to drift too far.

"Now," said his father, "let's catch breakfast." He reached down to the bilges of the boat and picked up the two sets of lines which they had brought with them, and handed one to his son, who seemed to be suddenly nervous and was looking rather serious.

"It'll be fine, you'll see, now lower your line into the water from that side of the boat, I'll lower mine from this side, like this."

He paused as the line snaked through his fingers into the darkness below and then continued, "and then let it down till you feel it hit the bottom, or until your line runs out. There it is." The line went slack.

"When you get to the sea bottom, haul it back up about six or eight feet, just wind it up like this, to make sure that you are free of any rocks or weed, mackerel like a clear bit of sea to run in and to hunt for food."

Each line had been wound round a small rectangular wooden frame. On to each line had been attached a line of hooks, each with a brightly coloured feather tightly bound to it. His son then tentatively lowered his line over the opposite side of the boat.

"Now," continued his father, "when the line is at the

depth you want, you just lift it up and lower it like this." And holding the line in his hand, he raised his arm up and then down and he repeated this several times. "And that's all there is to it. You just keep going until either you catch a fish or you get bored and stop. The fish think that the feathers are live bait and they just go for them. Don't raise it up and down too fast, do it like this and he moved his arm up and down in a gentle rhythm."

By now the boy's line had hit bottom and he started to wind it up. When he had wound it up far enough he started to wave the line up and down.

They both continued to haul the lines up and down in silence. The boy looked at his father; there was an air of worry in his expression. His father did not notice and said, "Hopefully we will catch a shoal soon, this is the best time to come fishing for mackerel. Come on you fish!"

Suddenly the boy's line juddered.

"Dad, I think I've got something! Something is pulling on my line!" For a fleeting moment he felt exhilarated and happy, but at the same time a little overwhelmed by the situation. The immediate realisation of what was about to happen. He had seen people catch fish, but this was the first time that he had ever caught one himself...

"OK, then, haul it in, take your time, just let the line down onto the floor of the boat but don't tangle it with your feet!"

The boy seemed to be smiling and he was breathless with elation, but he was not too sure what he would find on the end of his line. As he hauled it in, coiling it at his feet, he peered over the side of the boat into the dark blue-green depths below, at first he could just see iridescent streaks of sun light but then as he watched he could see small silver flashes and they seemed to be darting to and fro, and as he continued to haul in the line and they came nearer and nearer, he realised that he had actually caught some fish.

"Dad, Dad, I've got some. I've got some fish!" He was grinning excitedly, but then as suddenly as a cloud casts a shadow over a sunny day, his mood went from complete atavistic elation to a terrible feeling of dread and even shame at what he was realising he had done. He stopped hauling on the line and stared down into the water where he could see three fish darting back and forth, and again back and forth, trying to escape.

His father quickly tied his own line round the rowlock on his side of the boat and then moved over to the other side and it tilted heavily, half-standing and half-kneeling on the thwarts. He grabbed the line out of his son's hand and with one large sweeping action hauled all three fish into the boat, where they landed in a flapping tangling mess of silvery blue fish, multicoloured feathers, line and hooks. He didn't notice that his son was staring, immobile, in horror at the fish as they flapped and impotently tried to escape their inevitable doom. His father grabbed the first one and then, picking up a small piece of wood with his free hand, he hit the fish firmly on the back of its head. In quick succession he meted out the same treatment to the other two fish and then briskly wiping his hands on an old rag, he looked up at his son and said, "Well done, your first…" He halted mid-sentence as he noticed the tears streaming down his son's face, and he said, "What's the matter?"

"Why did you have to do that?" said the boy, as he wiped his tears away with his sleeve. "It's so cruel!"

"I had to, it's the kindest thing to do, and you wouldn't want them to have a long, lingering death by suffocating out of the water."

There was a pause and then the boy said, "Anyway, why *do* we have to kill fish to eat?"

His father thought for a moment and then said in what he thought was a succinct and simple reply, "Because they're there. It's nature's bounty, food for us. I would never kill anything that I would not eat. You mustn't worry so, they have no feeling in their mouths and if we didn't catch them and eat them, then someone else or more likely something else would. They are going to make a tasty breakfast. Come on let's go back to the house."

And with that they packed away the fishing lines and the father began to row back to the house. The boat hadn't drifted far out and as he rowed he looked at his son, who was now sitting quietly at the stern of the boat blankly staring past his father at nothing in particular.

With the falling tide it was not necessary to drag the boat up the slip, so they just tied it to a convenient metal ring on the harbour wall. His father threaded the fish together through their gills and offered them to his son to carry proudly up to the house.

At first he hesitated, but his father said, "You must take them; it's your first catch." The boy's instinct was to refuse but, not wanting to let his father down, he took them from him and walked up the path feeling very uncomfortable.

Later, in the kitchen after they had been cleaned and

fried in butter, his father offered him a fillet from one of the fish. "Come on, remember what I said, if you catch it you must eat it."

The boy looked at the pallid white strip of fish meat on his plate with a mixture of revulsion and disgust. This now felt like a nightmare in which he was trapped.

"Come on, it won't bite you!" encouraged his father.

Slowly he picked up his knife and fork and detached a piece of the flesh. It was grey and greasy, but he put it into his mouth and chewed. The taste was of salt, fish and fried butter, but there was also a stronger background taste: the taste of the sea. As he chewed he remembered the terrified fishes being brought to the surface, unable to get away from the line and being hauled up into the light and his father smashing them into unconsciousness. He chewed and swallowed the lump with some difficulty.

"Isn't it delicious," his father said. "You can't beat it, can you? You can't get fresher than that. To think that a little while ago it was swimming out there. Amazing! Don't you just love it?"

"Yes," he lied. He looked intently past his father, through the open kitchen window, out to the huge expanse of water. He imagined all the other fish that hadn't been caught, swimming free in the shimmering waters of the bay and he felt like a monster as he took yet another bite of the mackerel. It didn't seem so bad this time, a strong and fishy taste. Perhaps he would like it when he was older, when he was grown up and then, silently to himself, unnoticed by anyone else, he mouthed the words "Thankyou!".

Seat of kings

It was noticeable in the morning that the continual and incessant wind coming from the North West was much colder than it had been on any of the previous days of their stay so far. Winter was about to arrive. They had got there just a week before and were staying in an isolated, stone-built farm cottage beside a track only suitable for tractors and 4x4 vehicles. They were cat-sitting-cum-house-sitting for two weeks while their retired friends, the owners, were away for a holiday. The cottage had been built some two or three hundred years earlier and had served as a home for generations of farm labourers and their animals until the present owners had moved in. It was situated on the side of a hill with views right down the river valley and beyond to the high moors on the range of hills in the far distance which were usually shrouded in mist. Today the mist had gone and the views were crystal clear. The cottage had a steeply sloping garden with outbuildings that housed an existing earth privy, now no longer in use, but complete with a polished pine seat and lid. Just a few paces along the lane was a field house, typical of those in the area; a rectangular building, the design of which harked back many centuries to the settling of the Norse invaders, and which had originally been built for livestock, storing the harvest and as accommodation for jobbing labourers and itinerants. The cottage was of a more compact design. Downstairs there was a small parlour, a kitchen complete with an Aga, a larder and an adjoining couple of utility rooms; one had originally housed the pony and the other was a store room for logs, hay and vegetables. Upstairs there were three bedrooms, a bathroom and a large sitting room, sometimes used as a workroom. There was also a study as one of the owners was an academic and the other a theatre designer. The cottage was sympathetically furnished in keeping with its history. The current owners used traditional old oak furniture, antique watercolours, prints in gilt frames, comfortable chairs, thickly lined curtains, warm carpets, and dim lamps to give it a truly homely feel. In the kitchen, the original flagstone floor had been discovered under layers of compacted earth and was well preserved; it was probably as old as the house itself. The larder, with its whitewashed stone walls, was built on the north-facing wall of the house and kept a very cool temperature; it was stacked with every conceivable food stuff stored in jars and bottles, packets and tins in row upon row on the stone shelves. There were Kilner jars of bottled rhubarb, apples, quinces, redcurrants, gooseberries and plums. There were chutneys, curry pastes, jams, jellies, sauces and condiments of every kind. There were jars of pulses, pastas, seeds and grains, wholemeal flours, plain flour and strong flour. All the ingredients for bread-making, cake-baking and pie-making were there sealed in plastic boxes. Tins of baked beans, corned beef, sardines, tuna and pilchards stood along the shelves in great number. Every spice or dried herb which you could think of was neatly stored in alphabetical order on a long, narrow shelf along the length of the larder. Whole racks of wines and spirits, beers and cordials filled another space. There was also a well-stocked freezer in the storeroom and a very full fridge with all the usual essentials. In short, within the cottage one could find all the food necessary to survive being snowed in for weeks, and possibly months or a even a whole year.

The cottage was surrounded on all sides by green fields sloping steeply down to the river, which snaked though the countryside and which was shrouded with overhanging trees. The fields were divided from each other by dry stone walls. In some places these had collapsed and seemed to be ignored by the scattered sheep which inhabited these pastures, wandering from field to field at will. These walls seemed ageless. There is no way of being certain, but some of them are undoubtedly centuries old. If they had been built say, two or three hundred years ago and had not fallen or been pushed over, then they would have stood the test of time. Some seemed to be built with more care than others and to be tighter and neater in their construction and it could be assumed, possibly wrongly, that the better the construction the older the wall. In some there were lines of stones protruding as what, decoration? The steep incline of the hills added to our admiration of all those unnamed builders. Were some still alive, and living down the road? Or were they taking their well-earned rest in the churchyard where they had lain peacefully for hundreds of years or more? How they must have sweated and toiled to create such endless monuments to man's ingenuity. Just looking at the walls and imagining all the hard work that was necessary for their construction was in itself a humbling experience. Some of the stones, especially the end-stones for gateposts or corners would have needed at least two, three or even four men to lift them and put them in place. But first they had had to be hacked out from a nameless quarry, chipped into shape, loaded onto carts or wagons, hauled along uneven tracks, carted across fields, most of which were sloping at unbelievable angles, and then sorted into piles on the ground. Once construction started, each wall-stone was chosen for its shape and placed next to its companion in a continuous living arrangement for ever. The walls were built to describe boundaries between neighbours, either feuding or friendly, to prevent any argument and to keep the peace. Each landowner guarded his property jealously and would not want there to be any misunderstanding about who owned and therefore controlled each plot. The walls also had to keep livestock in or separate them to prevent fighting, or were used to encourage tupping and to make sure that the right ram was with the right ewes or for a host of reasons now long forgotten.

The track up to the moor clung to the sloping hillside for the first part of their walk. On their left it was bordered by a high stone wall, which in a couple of places housed colonies of mice. On one occasion they had seen the little black house cat sit by this colony and patiently wait for a careless mouse to emerge. Beyond the wall was a large field, empty but for a few rabbits. As they passed the rabbits would stare indignantly at them. Sitting up, they would pause their endless crunching mid-chew and then, their courage deserting them, they would scamper off into a burrow or a convenient crevice in a nearby wall and disappear. On the right of the track the field rolled far down to the river hidden by trees in the gully below, and there was another wonderful view of the full length of the valley.

After a while the path turned upwards to avoid the boggy ground ahead. There were fewer walls on this part. Here on this higher ground, there was a noticeable change in atmosphere. This place had no shelter and the wind came fast and cold down the valley. As they struggled breathlessly up the steep hill, they heard the 'craak-craak' of the grouse as they were startled in the scrubby brushwood around them and scuttled into the heather on higher ground, muttering that 'gutt-gutt-gutt' sound to each other just as if they were complaining about being disturbed.

A fine mist had begun to blow across their faces and they wound their scarves more tightly round their necks. If they had looked back they would have seen the complete semi-circle of a rainbow arcing across the valley. The garage, for visitors' cars, stood isolated and alone at the end of the track by the road. It was a basic structure of timber and corrugated iron. It served its purpose well, having been blown down at least once in the winter storms, and quickly reconstructed by a local farmer so that no interfering planning officer could deny its existence in such a remote and isolated place. The doors were never locked, they didn't have to be, but they hung there on their rusting hinges so that the garage was always generously available to anyone who needed it. As they rested, panting at their exertion, they looked back and saw the glory of the rainbow, and they forgot their aches and pains.

Now, taking the small, single-track road, they walked up amongst heather and rock; this was another steep climb and the wind continued to blow against them, so they bowed their heads and plodded resolutely upwards, only stopping now and again to straighten up, take a few deep breaths and remark on the amazing scenery. At last they made it to the place where the road levelled out and they were sheltered from the worst of the wind by a high stone wall, which, although giving welcome respite from the wind, blocked any view of the valley below. However the sight of the undulating moors to their left, with its patches of heather and sunken boggy pools rising to higher hills in the distance, took their full attention. Here there were a few birds too. A mere twenty paces away, they noticed a couple of grouse standing stock still, in the shadow of a clump of heather. They stood as still as each other and stared; neither human nor grouse moved. The grouse thought that they were well camouflaged, which they were, and the humans wanted to have a long look at the birds and admire their plumage, especially their white feathered stockings, red wattles and permanently startled eyes. However after a few moments the birds flew off with a 'craak-craak' and disappeared from view.

The narrow road wound on, the hills receded and soon they could see further across the moor. It put them in mind of the blasted heath of the Scottish play. A line of butts was clearly visible, a dozen or more at fifty yard intervals along the lower banks. For this is where the landowner comes with his well-connected friends or wealthy paying customers to indulge in the noble sport of shooting game. The gamekeepers have spent the year looking after the stocks of grouse by burning the heather to encourage new growth and other tricks and strategies to encourage them to stay, so that his Lordship and a chosen few have something to shoot at when the beaters shriek and clamour, waving flags to drive the birds into the air and into the line of fire. It is no wonder that the grouse are always looking startled and complaining to each other and anyone else who'll listen!

Now here in a small gulley off the moor, and not six paces from the road, lays a millstone on some rocks. An ancient round table perhaps, it is in the middle of a small pool, like an island and the waters divide past it on either side before joining up again and flowing away down the hill. It is said that this is the very spot where His Royal Highness, the heir to the throne has taken his lunch on the few occasions that he has graced the local landscape with his presence for a day or two of shooting. The security would be discreet and tight. Two black top-of-the-range land rovers would be parked a few yards away each with three royal protection officers pretending to look like members of the royal shooting party, but the loaded guns which they carried hidden were not for shooting game. They would sit in their vehicles or stand around nonchalantly but at all times they would be scanning the horizon or checking the lane in both directions without relaxing their state of alertness for a single second. When the shooting party breaks for lunch, one can imagine HRH enjoying the occasion, smiling and chatting with those he can trust. Always correctly dressed, for that is the sign of a gentleman of his elevated rank. He would be wearing a matching tweed shooting jacket and plus fours, thick woollen stockings and sturdy hand-made brogues. He would perch himself upon the millstone, perhaps with a cushion for the royal seat or a folded tartan rug to prevent the cold in the stone seeping through. He would be joined by a close chosen friend or two, and they would dangle their well-shod feet just above the shallow flowing water, while other guests and friends stand about or sit on shooting-sticks or nearby rocks. What would they eat? Perhaps they would start with a good strong whisky, a single malt, sourced and decanted from a barrel as big as a car. This had been laid down at HRH's birth at a well chosen distillery in the far north of Scotland, it's location a closely guarded secret. It would be served in cut glass crystal tumblers, and be quickly followed with slices of game pie, sautéed potatoes and asparagus spooned out on to crested plates with solid silver cutlery and white linen monogrammed napkins. The pie would have been made the night before in his Lordship's castle kitchen by his old faithful cook, who has worked for the family for, who knows how many years. There might be mugs of thick, warming broth served from a crested leather-bound vacuum flask and drunk from hefty Wedgewood china mugs. To follow the pie there would be a memorable lemon syllabub in pretty china pots with lids and eaten with silver spoons. To finish there would be that king of cheeses, the Stilton, with the finest water biscuits and small sips of piping-hot best Colombian coffee from elegant little bone china coffee cans on saucers. All this would be served from the back of a pair of large, dark green Landrovers by two young ladies of breeding. They are his Lordship's daughters, no less, who having been sworn to secrecy had accepted the job of serving lunch to his Royal Highness and friends, with amused yet nervous alacrity. His Lordship, the host on whose land this shooting party is taking place, surveys the scene with satisafction but will be mightily relieved when everyone has gone home.

It is strange to wonder how the millstone got there. It must have been brought up the hill for the very purpose for which it is now being used. There never was a mill up here; it must have been hauled up from a disused mill from somwhere else in the dales. The stone mason would have fashioned it all those years ago from local stone, itself some several million years old. The wheel had been used to make the flour for the bread for generations of Dales folk, including those very men that may have built the walls nearby and herded the sheep. Neither he nor they could ever have guessed, as they ate their humble portions of home-baked bread made with flour from his mill, that this royal rump, this princely posterior, would have sat upon it eating good food and discussing the morning's bag.

Leaving the royal seat behind, the road begins to climb again and once more they are trudging, head to wind, up a steep incline. They are surrounded on all sides by heather and the occasional startled grouse. Looking up into the watery sun they can see the silhouettes of several birds sitting on a rocky outcrop on the brow of the hill, looking down at them.

"Strange to think that those birds are completely unaware of the date and time of their imminent and inevitable demise." He said.

"Well, not so strange, for us it may not be so imminent" she said, "but neither are we, of ours!"

The flint wall

"Shit!" said Gary out loud to himself. He was standing looking out of the open window, enjoying the sensation of the cool fresh air on his body after having had a long hot shower. He had been shaving; carefully crafting his dark black sideburns to make sure that they were absolutely symmetrical. Tipping his head from side to side, he thought how they framed his face perfectly. He had been thinking about last night and trying to remember what exactly had happened, but it was all a bit of a blank. Never mind, whatever it was his mates would tell him later. He stood there in front of the mirror. He was wearing just a pair of bright red boxer shorts as he leant over the sink. The bottom half of his face was slathered with streaks of shaving foam partially scraped away. Then from the window he had been reminded of what had recently happened in his back garden.

The night before last, the central part of the old flint and brick wall that had divided the two cottage gardens for more than a century had finally collapsed after a heavy downpour. The soft ancient mortar had been so waterlogged that it could no longer hold the flints together and it had become fatally weakened. Unseen at some point in the night, a major section of the wall had silently and slowly, subsided like a large melting ice cream into a pile of sand, flints and bricks. The old dark crimson climbing roses that had clambered up on his side of the wall for so many years were left without their prop. Unsupported, they lurched rhythmically in the breeze. Like weeping mourners these surviving sodden blooms wobbled and worried over the remains of the only support that they had ever known. They had scattered their dark red petals across the whole soggy mess which looked like a macabre confetti of congealing blood.

Gary finished shaving, rinsed his face, drew his breath and winced as he slapped his cheeks with a liberal splash of his favourite minty-fresh aftershave. He then loaded toothpaste on to his electric toothbrush and polished his teeth for the regulation two minutes each side. After rinsing his mouth out with some bright green mouth wash and flossing vigorously he bared his teeth and admired their perfection. He sprayed his armpits with his mountain-fresh deodorant and when he had done so he stepped back and admired his lean, toned body in the long mirror. He stared critically; his arms hung straight down by his sides, fists clenched ready to strike, chest muscles tensed, concentrating on his reflection, scanning intently for any defect. He was not excessively tall, five foot eight, but he had a well-proportioned, compact physique of which he was very proud. His lack of height had always niggled him, but he felt that this slight imperfection was more than compensated for by the fact that he had what he considered a fantastic body, which he kept fit and trim in his job as a plasterer and jobbing builder. He had a dark almost Mediterranean complexion and the tan to go with it. His shaved head, his brown eyes, a small aquiline nose and a narrow, some would uncharitably say, mean mouth made up the features of the face which stared back at him. His square shoulders, well-defined chest and stomach muscles and narrow slim hips were smooth and tanned. Showing just above the waistband of his shorts, his tan ended in a line where the contrasting white skin of his flat stomach began. There was a vertical line of body hair from his navel that disappeared into his shorts. He slipped the waistband an inch or so further down, to admire the contrast between his tanned stomach and the pale skin further down, and with a small sigh of satisfaction considered himself to be nothing short of… well, perfection.

Gary currently lived alone; his girlfriend had moved out two weeks ago, following endless rows about his 'wandering eyes'. As he freely admitted at the time, he couldn't always help himself if a pretty girl walked by. It had been a Saturday and they had been sitting on a bench eating fish and chips when he had seen her walk past. Gary had been instantly transfixed and had stared at her. Time for him had stood still and it seemed that all was silence in his little bubble of existence. His mouth, half open and full of fish and chips, had stopped churning. Was it a dream? She looked about seventeen and wore a red summer dress and not much else. As she walked away from them he had continued to stare after her, open mouthed. He watched as her body moved freely under the taut fabric of her dress and he was completely mesmerised. His girlfriend hadn't failed to notice him staring, slack-jawed, a chip hanging half-chewed from his lips, with a smear of ketchup on his chin and that's when the rows had started. They had rowed on and off for the next couple of days. Eventually she had stormed out, dragging two bulging suitcases of clothes with her and taking her CD collection and a dried flower arrangement and screaming at him that he was a '*selfish, randy, fucking little shit.*'

Truth to tell, their relationship had started to go wrong some weeks before. Gary had begun to get fed up with her constantly trying to organise his life and to check up on him all the time. He had bought this cottage, his own first home, just under a year ago. It had been in need of modernising and he had planned to do it up and make some money. He had just about finished the renovations when they had met at the fair. They had had an immediate magnetic and animal attraction for each other and she had moved in that very night. At first he loved the way she took control of him, bossed him about even, cleared up after him and planned his day for him.

From the start, their relationship was a very physical one and they had greedily coupled at every opportunity; in the car, on the floor in the sitting room, under cover of dark on the grass in the public gardens, up against the wall in the side alley outside the cottages, and in fact in every room in the little cottage itself, including on the stairs and on the dusty floor of the attic box room which he was planning to make into a guest room. In the main bedroom Gary had built a four-poster bed from a kit and the noises of boisterous and unbridled coitus that they made at all times of day and night had regularly disturbed their neighbours, who were just too polite to complain. Suddenly after six months it was all over. Seemingly and inexplicably, their passion for each other vanished as quickly as it had arrived. Even they didn't really know why. Once their hungry lust was satiated they didn't seem to have anything else left. Life had settled into a dull domesticated routine; he went to work, she went to work, they both came home tired in the evenings. He then went to the pub and enjoyed flirting with other girls; she stayed at home, watched telly, and went to bed. They certainly didn't want children; and the topic had never really arisen. They were young and unencumbered and wanted to keep it that way. They only ever seemed to eat take-aways as her cooking skills were negligible. She did once try to cook a roast, but it was a disaster; she got all the timings wrong. The chicken was raw in the middle, the sprouts turned to mush and the gravy was lumpy and it destroyed any shred of confidence she had ever had. It had begun to dawn on them that they had very little to say to each other and nothing much in common. Their physical attraction for each other slowly faded away, and whenever they did try to rekindle it, usually helped by a little alcohol or weed, it too, like her cooking, was totally unsatisfactory as they just went through the motions and it was all over rather quickly. It also began to emerge that they were each getting more and more annoyed by the other. His vanity and concern about his appearance, which had once amused her, now grated. His constant tidying up and messing with the decor of the cottage irritated her too. Her fussing over him and domination of him, which once had aroused him, now in turn annoyed him. She wanted to know where he was going, what time he was getting back and what he would be doing. She reminded him of his domineering mother when he had been a teenager. When he got back late from the pub last Friday night having had just a few beers with his mates and fallen asleep, dribbling slobber onto the new leather couch, she went wild. Then the next day, he had stared at the girl in the red dress and he had that ketchup on his chin.

The doorbell rang. He quickly pulled on his old pair of work jeans but he had to hold them up with one hand as the buttons had all gone and he had not had time to find a belt.

He wasn't expecting anyone. It was probably one of those annoying "unemployed" foreign migrants selling overpriced kitchen tat. He snatched the door open with his free hand ready to give them a piece of his mind. Instead he just stared with his mouth open, suddenly conscious of the fact that he was standing there, bare chested and with his mouth just gaping, unable to say anything. It was the same girl who had been wearing the red dress. She smiled at him and hesitated. Now, he couldn't help but notice that she was wearing a tight-fitting ripped white t-shirt stretched over her firm youthful breasts and her jeans were frayed at the knees and he felt that old familiar feeling wash over him.

"Er, hi, er, hello?" he said. He was excited by her presence but didn't want to appear to be mumbling, and he couldn't think why she was there.

"Hi. It's Gary, isn't it?"

"Er, yes. It is."

"My Dad said that you were looking for someone to help you build a wall. You told him at the pub last night. Will I do?" As he stared back at the girl, it all came back to him. He had been bragging about how he was going to sell the house he was just completing for loads of money. He also had his eyes on a barn just outside the town that belonged to a mate of his dad's and he was going to do it up with him and share the proceeds, but that he needed someone to help him. Someone who wouldn't muck him about, as you had to be careful. The collapsed garden wall was going to delay these plans. He now needed to fix it as soon as possible. You can't sell a house with a garden that looked like the proverbial bomb site.

Maisie stared back at Gary. Her eyes couldn't help but flicker up and down his body and she liked what she saw; his lean firm muscles, his snake hips. She couldn't help noticing too the red flash of his boxers where the broken zip of his jeans gaped with nothing holding them together. She also noticed that he had to hold his jeans up with one hand, as he didn't have a belt.

They both stood there speechless for a while, quietly appraising each other as they tried to think of what to say next.

Gary broke the ice. "Er, yeah, er, you'd better come in."

***

The summer's heat was intense. It was the last day of the first week of working together. They had sorted the piles of stones and bricks into neat heaps on Gary's small lawn. Old reds stacked in a neat pile, beside large flints, medium flints and small flints in three heaps carefully laid on an old canvas paint cloth. Gary's work was always meticulous. He was well known for it. That's what made it stand out from the others. The preparations for building the new wall were well ahead. He had discussed it with his neighbours who were quite happy with the thought of a new flint wall to replace the old crumbly one. All the loose mortar and rubbish had been bagged up and taken to the dump. Gary had dug the trench for the new wall and together he and Maisie had carted the heavy clay soil away in wheelbarrows to a spoil heap nearby, in the neighbours' drive, to get it out of the way. Maisie had worked the mixer, making load after load of concrete for the foundations and Gary was finishing the task of smoothing down the last load with a shovel as it began to harden off. Every so often he stopped to check the smooth surface of the concrete against a spirit level held up to the pegs and string which marked out the lines of the planned wall. He took these opportunities to look up at Maisie as she worked the mixer, measuring out the cement, sand, ballast and hard core. Her sweaty brow furrowed in concentration as she counted out the measurements and occasionally the tip of her tongue poked out between her lips and licked her top lip as the sweat trickled down her face. Patterns of sweat spread down her front and back and darkened the fabric of the t-shirt which she had borrowed from him. She worked as well, if not better, than any bloke he knew. Bizarrely he was reminded of his mum when she was making a cake; rhythmically mixing the rich thick mixture of flour and eggs, dried fruit and brown sugar with a wooden spoon and then smoothing it all down in the baking tin. Afterwards and against his mother's better judgement and as a result of his ability to pester her for it, he had always been given the bowl to lick and scrape clean and he could still remember the guilty pleasure of the sickly sweet smell of it all and the way it got onto his chin and the tip of his nose. The heat was speeding the setting process up and small lumps of concrete were sticking to the sides of his shovel. As he pushed it back and forth he could feel the sweat trickle down his back and chest. The sensation wasn't unpleasant. He wore a red and white bandanna on his head which went some way to keeping the sweat off his face. As usual he was bare-chested and wore his old jeans using a piece of rope as a belt and a large safety pin to fix the zip. He had worn them all week and he made a mental note to chuck them in the wash tomorrow.

Maisie was enjoying the work and was pleased how things had worked out. She could not help but stare at Gary's body with a sense of curiosity and if she was honest, admiration and wonder. Her eyes were always drawn to the gaping fly now held together with that safety pin. Was he doing this on purpose, wearing red boxers (red is the colour of danger, after all) or was he completely guileless and unaware of the fact that she found it all both provocative and exciting? She was familiar with the male body. She had seen her brothers in the bathroom on many occasions showering and changing on the beach as they were growing up. But this was quite different and she instinctively knew that her fascination was potentially highly dangerous. His latest plastering job at the building site had finished and that had given him this opportunity to build the wall. Any possible work on his barn project was way in the future. He had offered Maisie the job of helping him rebuild the wall, what was the harm in that? She knew what to do, her dad and brothers were builders, and as a child playing amongst them she had watched enough times as an extension or whole house was built. In that way she did have a basic understanding of the building process. The rest was just hard bloody graft and sweat. She had immediately accepted the offer of work without a moment's thought. She was planning to go to college in the autumn to do an office management course with the ultimate aim of working in her brothers' construction company and now she needed the money. And anyway she enjoyed all the physical work. It would keep her fit and toned. She was proud of her body and went regularly to the gym and the local tanning salon.

Gary had offered to pay her the going rate for the work and that was it. But there was more to it than that. Gary really fancied her, but did not want to make a move too quickly. After all he knew Maisies's Dad and his reputation and if he… the thought of what he would do to Gary if he took advantage of the situation wasn't worth thinking about. But Gary was by nature an optimist and a chancer and he was well aware of what could happen if he didn't rush things. It had been a while now since his girlfriend had left and there was something exciting about the inherent danger in his plan, but that only added to the thrill of it.

Maisie was only seventeen and naturally her family, particularly her father, Ron, was very protective of her. Some would even say over-protective. Gary's fears were confirmed when Ron had come round to see how the work was getting on. While he and Gary were having a beer in the kitchen and Maisie was out of the room, Ron had made it quite plain that he was happy for Maisie to work for Gary. But there had been a warning.

"Yeah, it's good for her. Workin' in the fresh air an' that. Better 'an workin' in an office an' it looks like she's doing a good job. Mind you, Gazza, don't you go tryin' anyfin' on, mate. I know what you're like. Coz I'm warning you. The last bloke that got a bit fresh with her well… let's just say I will have your balls on a plate and make a purse out of your scrotum. Get my drift? Oh look my can's empty." He smiled benevolently, *or was that malevolently*, thought Gary.

As Maisie stood waiting for Gary to fill the barrow, she secretly stared at him as he worked. He obviously took care of his body and she liked that. She also noticed as the muscles on his back and arms tensed as he bent over the trench, moving his cement encrusted shovel back and forth across the wet surface. Slowly he stood up and found himself looking directly at Maisie. He put his hand to his forehead to shield the bright sunlight and squinted as sweat trickled into his eyes and stung them, making them water. Gary stood breathless for a moment, his free hand leaning on his shovel. He smiled at Maisie. The heat was intense. There was not a breath of air and Maisie watched as a rivulet of sweat ran vertically down his chest across his stomach and finally joined others darkening the waist band of his boxers and turning the bright postbox red into the colour of dried blood.

Maisie realised that she was blushing, and trying to sound unflustered said, "Would you like a beer or something? You look *so* hot."

As soon as she had said it, she realised the unintended double meaning. This made her flustered even more and she blushed and hoped that he hadn't noticed. He had noticed but pretended not to. She carried on, "There's some in the fridge. I could bring it out for you."

"Yeah that would be great. But we'll go in. I could do with a break. You must have a beer too. The foundations are now finished, just got to wait for them to harden and set, so I think we'll call it a day."

In the relative cool of the kitchen, having kicked off his boots and socks, Gary washed his hands at the sink, and wiped his upper body down with a damp towel. Maisie went to the fridge and took out two bottles of ice cold beer. She opened them and stood them on the counter, and watched as the beer foamed out of the bottles and dribbled down the sides. She passed one to Gary who immediately put his mouth over the neck of the bottle and tipping his head back, he took a long satisfying gulp of the icy, refreshing liquid. Maisie sipped her bottle in a more restrained fashion, and sitting on a breakfast bar stool, watched Gary as he finished the bottle in what seemed like a couple of mouthfuls. When he had finished it, he put it down and moved up closer to where Maisie was sitting. Somewhat to her surprise, he gently took her bottle out of her hand and took a swig from it and put it down on the counter. As he looked at her, she smiled.

Leaning forward he kissed her gently on the lips. She gasped, smiled, gently pulled away and then she kissed him back. This time it was a more urgent kiss and her tongue flicked against his teeth and he stood up to hold her to him, kicking the stool away as he did so. She rose to meet him and their bodies pressed together. He could feel the pressure of her against his body. She could feel him against her stomach. And then it seemed like a hunger took hold of them and they were ripping at each other's clothes. She could smell his sweat mixed with the slightly sickly smell of his after-shower balm. They stood apart briefly to gasp for breath. Seductively, Maisie raised her arms in the air in the manner of a plea and he gently but firmly pulled her t-shirt up over her head and let it fall to the floor, and in the next movement he undid her bra and that too dropped to the floor. He stared as if transfixed at her generously full breasts and dark nipples and then, holding her to him by her shoulders, he kissed her neck, her face and nibbled first one ear and then the other. Maisie's fingers began hungrily pulling at the waistband on his jeans and, as she pulled ever harder, the large safety pin popped off and clattered across the floor. His jeans, with no help at all, slipped down his legs to his knees. Despite the care and protection of her father, Maisie was no virgin. Over the past couple of years her parents were completely unaware that she had had three boyfriends and had enjoyed a full-on physical relationship with all of them.

As one they slipped down onto the Indian rug on the newly laid wooden floor. Their love-making was impatient and hungry as they rolled around as if trying to eat each other. She was crying out with a pleasure that she had never known before and they simply coudn't get enough of each other. Afterwards, he cried silently into her hair with a sense of happiness and completeness but he did not want her to hear him or see his tears.

They must have both slept where they lay on the rug, for some time, side by side. Gary was on his front with his arms across Maisie's stomach and when they woke up it was still light and the phone was ringing.

Gary quickly crawled back into consciousness. He struggled to stand up and even though his trousers and shorts were round his ankles he hobbled to the phone and held it to his ear.

"What kept you, mate? Are you still on the job? It's nearly six o'clock." It was the unmistakeable voice of Ron, Maisie's Dad.

"Er, yeah, we've just come inside and we're finished for the day actually." The irony of Ron's initial question was not lost on Gary. He tried to sound calm, matter of fact, even though he was breathless from scrabbling across the room and now trying to pull up his trousers with his free hand.

"Me and the wife have just been out doin' some shoppin'. Just ordered a beautiful white leather settee at the Furniture Warehouse, just up the road from you, so we thought we'd pop by to see how you're gettin' on. I hope young Maisie has been useful to you."

"Yeah, great. She's been very good. We've finished the foundations and it's filled with hard core. It's hardening off as we speak."

"Great! See you in five. I'll bring some cans." He hung up.

"Shit. That was your Mum and Dad. They're going to be here in five minutes."

In a whirl of sheer panic and terror at the consequences of being found out, Gary and Maisie gathered up their things, dressed and put everything to rights as quickly as they could. In her panic Maisie struggled with her bra strap and only just succeeded in doing it up and getting her t-shirt on when the doorbell rang and her Dad was banging on the door.

***

Over the next few days Gary made a start on constructing the wall. It was a traditional design consisting of panels of flint work with piers of red bricks every eight feet or so to stabilise it. Although he was a plasterer by trade, Gary knew how to do this as he had seen a similar wall being built on a job he did a couple of months ago.

Things fell into an almost domestic routine. Maisie arrived each morning at about eight. They had breakfast together. Sometimes, either before or after breakfast, they made love then and there, in the sitting room, or in the bedroom. Sometimes they waited till they stopped for lunch, but Maisie complained that the kitchen floor was too hard and, anyway, they were afraid that someone from the adjoining cottages would see through the kitchen window if they came round to borrow something. Sometimes they made love in the shower at the end of the day as they washed the sweat and dust off their bodies and they would fall damp and exhausted onto the king-size bed in the 'master' bedroom and usually slip into a deep sleep.

Work on the wall progressed slowly.

Soon the first of three panels of flint work were completed along with the accompanying brick piers.

It was important to get the pattern of flint across each panel consistent and matching in terms of colours and shapes, otherwise it would look a mess. When it came to his work, Gary was always insistent on making no mistakes. On one occasion a section of wall did not look right when he took off the shuttering boards, so he tore it down and did it all again.

The second panel was soon completed. Gary couldn't help but notice how well Maisie looked. All the fresh air and sunshine throughout August had certainly done its job. They were both aware that their time together was not going to last. Maisie was going off to college in about three weeks and Gary was going to finish the cottage, sell it and then try to buy the barn.

When he was working on the third and final panel of the wall and coming to the end of the flint work, certain unforeseen events started to change Gary's plans for the future. They had just emerged from the shower after a full day's work when the phone rang.

Dripping wet and with only a towel round him Gary answered the phone.

"Is that Gary?"

It was the familiar voice of his mate, George.

"Yeah."

"Can you talk?"

"Yeah."

"There's a plastering job for you in Portugal, starting next month if you're interested. Working on an office tower block in Lisbon. Loads of work, and very good pay. Should last ooh, a couple of months or so, are you up for it?"

"Oh, that's great, sounds good."

"I've got to talk to some other guys, so I'll get back with the details later. All right?"

George hung up.

"Who was that?" asked Maisie,

"Just George. Got some work for me next month."

Gary didn't elaborate with any more details. He didn't tell Maisie that the work meant going abroad for a while.

Work progressed well on the wall during the next few days. In fact it was all but completed except for the last six inches or so on the last section of the flint stone panels. Gary was pleased with the look of it so far. It was not easy to do. And he had only had to redo that one bit. The technique required him to use scaffolding boards as shuttering held against the brick piers with wooden stakes driven into the ground to hold them in place until everything had set. Behind the shuttering he laid the flint stones individually so that they nestled comfortably together in a bed of lime mortar, and he did this for each side of the wall. The middle gap was then filled with clean hard core and more mortar. The whole thing was left to set, usually overnight. Over time the shuttering boards were moved up and now at last the wall was nearing completion. All he then had to do was to lay the cap stones on top. He had managed to retrieve most of the old ones from the rubble of the collapsed wall, and would have to source a few replacement ones from a reclaim yard to replace the ones which were broken.

The next day Maisie was late. It was already nearly ten and there was no sign of her. Gary didn't worry, however. He was enjoying the work, it was going well and it was nearly finished. The sun was on his back and Bob

Dylan was singing "*Where have all the flowers gone*?" on the tinny radio perched on the other end of the wall. His mind started to wander and he thought about his forthcoming job in Portugal and the opportunities that it would bring for further work in Europe. He liked to travel. It was good of George to remember him. He had put a lot of work his way. He looked forward to getting the work documents and booking his flight but he still hadn't told Maisie anything.

He didn't notice that Maisie had come into the garden until he heard her blow her nose. He looked round and noticed immediately that her face was streaked with mascara and that she had been crying. She was trying to blow her nose on a small damp crumpled piece of tissue.

"Hi. Are you all right?"

"Oh Gary…" and she subsided into more sobbing and blew her nose again and a few shreds of white tissue fluttered to the ground.

Gary moved towards her.

"What's up, love? What's the matter?"

"Oh Gary, Gary. I'm late."

"That's OK, love, there's not much more to do anyway."

"No, you don't understand. I'm late. My period is late. I'm worried I might be pregnant!"

Gary's heart seemed to miss a beat. These were words that he did not want to hear and he immediately felt his stomach churn.

"Are you sure? How do you know? Did you get a test?"

"No, not yet. I can't go to Boots to buy one 'cos Mrs Knight works there and she knows my mum and she would tell her straight away. Oh Gary, what are we going to do? I'm supposed to be going to college and everything. Oh this is awful…" and she collapsed into his arms, sobbing uncontrollably.

***

Some months later Gary's neighbours were choosing a spot against the new flint wall for the white rambling rose that they had been given. After months their driveway had finally been cleared of the piles of sand, earth and stones that had begun to annoy them. They were celebrating the final completion of the wall and getting rid of all the mess.

The pretty young wife turned to her husband and said, "Do you see that?"

"What?" said her husband, as he tried to dig into the earth that seemed to contain more rubble than anything else "Can you see what I am having to dig out? He's just buried all the broken bricks and lumps of mortar here. I've already dug out two buckets full just to plant one rose."

"Look. Do you see that?" she repeated and she pointed to the top right hand corner of the third panel of flints.

Her husband stood back and looked to where she was pointing.

"Do you see? It's all different. Up until this point, it's all perfect; all the flints are well laid and really evenly spaced. All across the panels. Except for this last six inches. It's just a mess. You can hardly see the stones. It looks as if it was all finished in a bit of a hurry!"

The life class

Maudie was so upset. She had just overheard Marjorie, whom she had thought of as a friend, and Marguerite talking about her in the small kitchenette in the village hall as they were putting the cakes back into a plastic storage box. They did not realise or perhaps they did, that Maudie was behind the large cupboard doors, drying up the cups and saucers and putting them away after the coffee break.

"Did you see Maudie's work?" Marjorie had said, with a note of disdain in her voice.

"I just caught a glimpse. Very weird, wasn't it?"

"Yes, I thought so too. She's always done work like that. You know, so-called modern art. I think it's a joke myself, but I haven't got the heart to tell her. She went to art college years ago in Paris, I think, that's where she gets her crazy ideas from. Frankly, I can't stand it; I just can't see what it's all about. And she knew all those types, Henry Moore and the other one, whats-er-name Hepworth, not Audrey, no, Barbara, that's it, Barbara."

"Yes, it is odd, but each to their own."

"Anyway, I thought her drawing today was a dreadful thing. I can't get on with all this semi-abstract nonsense, or whatever it's called. So pretentious. Why does Elspeth keep asking us to do something different every time? Why can't she let us just draw what we want?"

And with that, they had left the kitchen to rejoin the life class for the second half of the session.

Maudie's first instinct was to go straight home early, but then she thought that not only would that be rude to dear Elspeth, who had organised the class, but it was the last session of life drawing till September and she did so love it. Not to mention the fact that all her materials and workbox were out there in the life room. Smoothing down her pinny with her arthritic hands, and holding herself up as straight as she could, as her physio had frequently advised her, she entered the main room of the village hall where the class was settling down.

The village hall was typical of its kind, found throughout the kingdom. About sixty years old, of a wooden construction, in need of paint and varied maintenance. It was home to all sorts of groups and clubs, which told of their business on a crowded notice board in the dimly lit entrance hall. Small homemade posters jostled among each other. There was a dizzying array of forthcoming attractions such as "Flower arranging on a budget" or "Drawing for all" and even a small discreet notice for a forthcoming talk on family planning and STDs by a national organization.

The class members had an average age of about fifty-five or so. The organiser, Elspeth, a part time lecturer at the local art college, was a large and breathless lady, given to wearing brightly-coloured scarves in a manner reminiscent of throws, cast over furniture in need of reupholstering. Her short, spikey-cut hair was dyed a bright orange. Large, ceramic, brightly-glazed, lapis lazuli Moroccan earrings dangled on either side of her weather-beaten face. She often crewed for her husband, Jeff, who was a keen sailor. He enjoyed haggling for local handmade costume jewellery in souks and bazaars that they found on their travels across the length of the Mediterranean Sea and down the North West coast of Africa.

As Elspeth tried to settle everyone down, she was remembering that Jeff wanted her to go with him on his next trip to West Africa. There were so few people in the class, just seven or so. By the time she had paid the model and the rent for the village hall, there would be precious little left for her. She made a mental note to increase the fees next term.

Clapping her hands to attract everyone's attention, she announced, "Ladies, we are ready to start again, oh, and gentlemen." She suddenly remembered the young curate and his friend Brian, who had joined the class just last month and who were fussing over their easels and fixing paper to their drawing boards.

"We have an hour left and I thought it would be nice if we did one long pose. I've asked Betty if she could do us one of her reclining poses. Is that alright for everyone? She's going to lean back on the end of the sofa, with one foot touching the floor and her arms draped wherever they are most comfortable."

Maudie's resolve to keep a straight back failed her and as she moved quietly to her place, she could only look down at the floor. She sat down on the plastic chair, and busied herself setting up her drawing board on her easel. She thought that she would do some warm-up sketches for the first few minutes before starting on the final piece.

She leant forward and fished an old sketchbook out of her green canvas bag. She had been having a clear-out of her studio some weeks ago and had come across it in a long-forgotten folder of her work from her younger days in Paris. She was going to throw it away, but then she had second thoughts; after all it was unused and it would be a waste to discard it. It inevitably reminded her in a bitter-sweet way, of her days there, all those years ago. She had been so happy and then it all went horribly wrong. It had been such an exciting time. Much to her parents' horror, she had run off with her childhood sweetheart Bernard to be an artist and to see the world. The first few months had been wonderful. They had rented a tiny flat on the left bank and had painted and drawn and made love. They had tried to make a living by selling their work in the local galleries and street markets. Maudie had been very successful and began to make a name for herself. Bernard was less successful and this had led to arguments, tears and the eventual breakup of their relationship. Bernard went off with a Spanish waitress he had met and, inevitably, he disappeared from her life. Maudie was devastated. However, she hung on and she managed to keep up with the rent on the flat, having been commissioned by a gallery to produce a set number of works a year. By then she was mixing socially with several of the up-and-coming artists in the Parisian art scene. At a private viewing in a smart gallery she was introduced to an established world-famous artist, known affectionately as Monsieur, old enough to be her father, and he offered her work as an assistant in his flourishing studio. She readily accepted the job. She was completely in awe of him. It meant that she could continue with her own painting and drawing, whilst at the same time working in the studio of one of the greats of the twentieth century. She felt she got on very well with him and through him met some of the really big names in the art world at that time. She so enjoyed her new life that the loss of Bernard did not seem so terrible after all. She was paid well and showered with small gifts by her new employer. As well as a couple of simple pieces of jewellery, she was given art materials bought from his own suppliers and a couple of signed photographs.

Then, one evening, it all went horribly wrong. There had been a particularly lively party at the private view of Monsieur's latest show; he had become very drunk. She too had had one too many. After all the guests had gone, as she was struggling to clear up the last of the mess, he had pulled her onto a day-bed and had raped her. In the fight to escape his clutches, when crawling on the floor she had knocked her head badly against a heavy wooden table leg and had eventually lost consciousness. When she came round, feeling utterly wretched, she realised that she was alone. She dragged herself to a washroom and tried to clean herself up. She managed to get herself back to her flat, had a proper shower and telephoned her friend, one of the other assistants, Marie-Louise. She arrived at her flat within twenty minutes. Maudie told her what had happened and asked her what she should do. Marie Louise told her that if she told the police Monsieur would deny everything; it would be her word against his, and, frankly, her reputation would ultimately be ruined. After all they had both been drunk.

She would be labelled a gold-digger and a liar and no one would want to buy her work. He was a powerful and rich man, the chief of police was a good friend and a client, so, really, the best thing she could do was nothing. Marie-Louise knew all this because exactly the same thing had happened to her. Exasperated, Maudie asked her why she stayed working for Monsieur. She explained that she had had a child from a previous relationship and could not afford to lose her job. Where else would she get that kind of money? She just made sure that they were never alone together. Marie-Louise explained that after a few drinks, Monsieur's personality would change dramatically and he became a devil and that, afterwards, he always claimed to have absolutely no memory of his evil deeds.

Maudie was shocked and horrified. She didn't go back to work and she didn't leave her apartment for the next week. She ignored all phone calls. Once she felt well enough, she gave in her notice to her landlord. She told the gallery that she wished to terminate her contract. They reluctantly agreed, but said that they would withhold payment for the last of her paintings, which they had sold, in lieu of notice. She sold or gave away everything in her flat. She kept her few other remaining paintings, her art materials and equipment and fled back to London. Once back there, she discovered to her horror that she was pregnant. Through a friend she managed to find someone who could "take care of things" and she submitted herself to the nightmare of an abortion. Her elderly parents were too frail to be burdened with her worries, so she suffered in loneliness and silence. She found a part-time job teaching art in a private girls' school and so led a reclusive life, hoping for obscurity. She avoided getting too close to people, especially men, and only had a few carefully-chosen female friends. One of the closest, or so she thought, was Marjorie, which made the overheard conversation all the more upsetting. It only helped to confirm her general lack of trust in most people.

Wearing her partner's red, green and gold bath robe, Betty, the forty-five-year-old model, left wafts of cheap, sweet perfume trailing in her wake as she moved into the middle of the room. She undid the loosely-tied belt and with a shrug of her shoulders, the bathrobe slipped off on to the floor. Her generously-sized breasts hung pendulously as she leant forward and clambered on to the sofa. Turning round, she lay down on her back with her head propped up and settled herself as best she could into the pose, which had been suggested to her a few minutes earlier by Elspeth over a cup of lukewarm, sugarless tea and a ginger nut biscuit. She was an extremely large lady of indeterminate yet substantially voluptuous weight and yet she moved with the fluidity and gentle grace of a ballet dancer that belied her size. As she had gently lowered herself down onto the seat of the old sofa, it had seemed to sigh – or groaned – as her bulk came up against the combination of some random foam cushions and the old springs within. She took a while to get comfortable. Betty had four children under twelve by three different fathers and she was now living with a forty-two-year-old DJ called Winston. Her face was round and friendly and she looked over the class, checking to see that everyone could see her. She imperceptibly shifted her weight as she arranged a large cushion so that she could lean her head back more comfortably. There was no way she could keep up a long pose such as this without supports. Her plump, pale white skin seemed to glow unnaturally in the greenish glare coming from the few working overhead fluorescent tubes. Her ash-blonde hair was loosely, yet artfully, piled up in a cottage loaf style chignon, and was held in place by a large amber-coloured tortoiseshell clip. Her bright red lipstick, rouged cheeks and black mascara attracted attention away from her double chin. Her breasts spread themselves loosely to either side of her chest, the large, round dark nipples hinting at her fecundity. When she moved, the many folds of flesh across her stomach and at the tops of her thighs rippled gently like torpid waves, for she was finding it difficult to get comfortable. Her large thighs lay slightly apart revealing a dark patch of neatly trimmed pubic hair, which contrasted sharply with her pale white skin and the light blonde hair on her head. Her right leg, slightly bent at the knee and supported by a cushion, lay along the seat of the old sofa; her left leg hung over the side of the seat so that her left foot, with the adornment of a 'gold' ankle-chain, rested regally on an old burgundy velvet cushion balanced precariously on a small pile of books put there for that very purpose. Betty had finally settled in her pose and tried to empty her mind, which in the circumstances was difficult, given that that morning she had discovered that she was pregnant yet again, and she was wondering how Winston would take it. Would he do a runner like all the others?

To complete the pose, Elspeth draped an emerald green silk shawl over her right shoulder so that the tasselled end lay on the floor. Once all was settled, Betty benignly surveyed the class, like a monarch gazing majestically at her subjects.

"OK," said Elspeth. "Don't forget we're having a go at doing something in a semi-abstract manner, if you would like to try… Shall we begin?"

With the earnestness of the chosen few, the class began to draw. The only sound was the gentle scratching of pencil or charcoal on paper. Elspeth wandered around behind her students just looking thoughtfully at what each one was doing. If she thought someone was struggling, she would talk to them quietly with a hint or some helpful advice. Most of the time she let everyone just get on without disturbing them, which was how most of the class liked it. They knew that they could ask if they needed help, anyway. Elspeth was well aware of the few that constantly needed her advice . She knew the signs: fretful sighing, tut-tutting and lots of rubbing out. From across the room she watched Maudie. She really was amazing. She worked with total focus and concentration, completely absorbed in her work. She produced very stylistic, idiosyncratic drawings, quite unlike the rest of the class's predictable and it had to be admitted, pedestrian efforts. It was difficult to pinpoint, but the freedom and energy in her drawings reminded Elspeth of the work of artists like Picasso, Modigliani, or was it Matisse or Chagall? They were a delight to behold, and she never ceased to be amazed. Maudie, however, had made it quite plain on several occasions that she didn't like anyone drawing attention to her work, so Elspeth left her alone.

Crouched over her old sketchbook, with her tongue just peeping out between her lips, Maudie was completely engrossed. She was currently using the same sketchbook for all the life classes. Her emerging drawing captured the large free-flowing and generous shapes of Betty's corpulent body with a freedom and confidence that accentuated some parts and reduced others, playing with the light and shade. Although quite physically unnatural in a textbook sense, it uncannily was Betty, in every way.

Marjorie struggled with her work, a small, tight piece of ill-proportioned, unconfident work, and she was beginning to get a headache.

Marguerite was having fun painting with her new set of cheap bright acrylics that her son had given her for her fifty-sixth birthday. She was thoroughly enjoying her work, which resembled a tortured, unidentifiable mass of colour, in which Elspeth thought that Betty looked just like a bloated, inflatable doll.

The new curate, Jeremy, was struggling with a large mass of charcoal lines, which were getting more and more blurred and indistinct as he went over them again and again. His partner, Brian, had persuaded him to come along; however, he was regretting his decision to join in and secretly thought that he would not come again. He would rather be at home in their small neat flat having a quiet evening in, listening to La Traviata, and eating a vegetable lasagne. Brian, on the other hand, was confidently producing an accomplished, professional study of a large lady in the traditional conservative style

150

of the competent academician; after all, he had trained at the RA about ten years ago.

Nicola and her friend, Gemma, whispering now and then to encourage each other, both from the local sixth form college, took up all of the rest of Elspeth's time and attention until the end of the session.

***

Thirty years later.

Mark, the "picture expert" wasn't having a very good day. The stuff that people had been bringing in was not up to much. So far, he had been asked to value a string of uninspiring work: a couple of really bad, flood-damaged Victorian oleographs, an etching that turned out to be a photocopy, four drawings purporting to be by Walt Disney but definitely weren't, and a watercolour that the client had insisted was by Thomas Girtin, but the watermark within the paper had distinctly said 1963.

Then in came this young man with a medium-sized sketchbook in a tatty carrier bag. When he took it out of the bag, Mark's heart missed a beat. He recognised it instantly as the kind of expensive, handmade sketch-book supplied exclusively and individually to certain artists in the 1950s and his hopes flew into the stratosphere. It was a pad about two centimetres thick, containing thirty sheets of creamy white cartridge, every sheet with its distinctive watermark. The front cover of pale green paper, and a backboard of thick grey cardboard convinced Mark that here was something extremely special. The distinctive name of the Swiss company that had supplied it together with its Zurich address was printed quite clearly on the back. As he turned the book over, his blood pressure rose further, for he saw a handwritten message: *'Maudie, tout pour toi. Merci pour tout. Grands baisers!'* and it was signed *'Monsieur'.* The signature had been written across a slightly faded stamp, which clearly stated *'Ausschliesslich zu 'Monsieur'.*

Mark, who never did have a strong constitution, thought he might faint. All in a nano-second he wondered what the sketchbook contained: how many drawings, how much would it fetch and what would be his commission? Trying to stay poker-faced and calm, Mark quickly flicked through the sketchbook. It was stuffed full of Monsieur's drawings! He counted them, there were twenty-six. Twenty-six little beauties! It was as if all his Christmases had come at once.

"It was among my Aunt Maudie's things," said the young man who had brought it in. "She died about six months ago. We know that she used to work for Monsieur as his assistant in the 1950s. He must have given it to her as a leaving present, when she left. I found it among all her stuff. You should have seen her studio; it was a glorious arty muddle. She never tidied it and nothing had been touched for years. We have burnt all her stuff, complete rubbish it was. But this might be worth something. Monsieur is quite famous, isn't he?"

"You can say that again," said Mark. "He was one of the greatest artists of the twentieth century."

And, without telling the young man, he reckoned

that the sketchbook would fetch a seven or possibly an eight-figure sum and that would be on a bad day.

In the Golden Days nursing home a ninety-seven-year-old Marjorie was lying bedridden and partially paralysed in her room. She was propped up on several pillows so that she could watch the television. She had just been fed lunch and had had difficulty swallowing the tepid rice pudding, which was not a favourite. The afternoon news was rambling on; war in the middle east, economic gloom and doom, a dreadful murder, in fact the usual endless stream of misery. Through the miasma of cloudiness in both her vision and hearing that was brought on by her daily cocktail of several prescription drugs, she tried to listen to the programme. Despite her physical collapse and deterioration, her brain was still very active. There was some dreary news about football and then suddenly she saw an image on the large TV screen on which she managed to focus and which she knew that she recognised from somewhere deep in her past.

"And finally news of a new record in the art world. Today in London's Knightsbridge, at a top international auction house, a small sketchbook complete with twenty-six original figure drawings by the late, world-famous twentieth century artist, known to most, affectionately as Monsieur, was sold to a Russian oligarch. All experts who have studied it say it contains some exquisite examples of his finest work from his middle years."

On the television, Marjorie watched the clip, open-mouthed, as the auctioneer's porter was shown holding up a small sketchbook, open at a page displaying a figure drawing of a large nude model lying on a couch with a green shawl draped over her shoulder and one foot resting on a pile of books." As Marjorie struggled to listen, she heard the auctioneers hammer slam down as he triumphantly said "Sold for twenty-two million euros!" as the noisy clapping and cheering erupted from the crowded saleroom.

Marjorie, tried and failed to sit up, she took a sharp intake of breath and gasped "But it's Maud-mm... she dr-dr-drr." Alone in her room she suffered a massive and fatal heart attack.

"And now let's go over to the weather," said the newsreader brightly, as the nurse came back into the room saying,

"Oh dear, Marjorie, you've brought up all your pudding. What *are* we going to do with you?"

The river trip

A cautionary tale

It was a hot and dreamy summer's day. Time just seemed to drift by. '*Heatwave to last all week!*' had been the useful headline in last Sunday's paper. The subheading had proclaimed: '*Hosepipe ban on the way!*' During the rest of the week it had proved to be an accurate and most welcome forecast. But now, the weekend had arrived and the heat was still lingering and people needed a break. People like Bill and Daisy, who had recently bought a boat, wanted to get out on to the water and enjoy the all too rare warm and balmy weather. It was going to be so good. Their boat, named *Viking*, which was moored close by to the boatyard, lay motionless on the flat mirror-like water. She looked almost as if she knew that she was going on a trip Bill thought. She had an expectant air about her, or was he just being daft? He was rowing the dinghy with some difficulty against the tidal current, and he turned his head to look at her. His spirits had lifted as they always did when he saw her and he felt a simultaneous rush of both excitement and nervousness. Excitement because he enjoyed being out on the water and nervousness because they had not had the boat very long and they felt, well, inexperienced.

Viking was a good-looking boat, solid and reliable, and built in a very traditional way. She had a clinker-built hull, but this was only an illusion; it was in fact made of fibreglass but with a wooden superstructure. This comprised of a very compact two-berth cabin complete with cooking stove and a small, wood-burning stove whose chimney poked out of the roof. There was a small for'ard cabin with a pump-action loo in the foc'sle and there were lots of well-stocked lockers and cupboards with everything that they would ever need. A gaff-rigged mast, complete with furled sail and a bright blue cover stretched over the cockpit, completed the setup. She was about twenty feet long and had a decent-sized diesel engine mounted amidships, and both Bill and Daisy had grown to love her. She conveniently lay on a double mooring across the channel only a few yards from the boatyard's pontoon.

From a distance, the river looked deceptively calm and placid. Close up, the more observant and experienced sailor would notice the fast-flowing incoming tide. There was not a breath of wind and the rising water crept in quietly with an unseen urgency, and as Bill well knew, with a great unstoppable power. As he rowed out to her, Bill could feel the bite of the tidal current trying to push the little dinghy off course and he had to compensate for this by working the oars extra hard as he crabbed sideways across the water. Daisy sitting in the stern of the boat was surrounded by a collection of bags at her feet; they contained food and provisions and everything else that they anticipated they might need for the trip, including sketchbooks. As they drew alongside *Viking*,

Daisy grabbed one of the side rails and the little dinghy nudged against the hull of the larger boat with a familiar thump. She quickly looped the painter round the cleat and made it fast. As she did so she said, "We must get some fenders; this side of the boat is going to get so damaged."

Bill mumbled his agreement and smiled to himself; she always said this when they came alongside. Then, holding firmly to the larger boat, he indicated for Daisy to clamber aboard first. Taking care not to slip and with great caution, she stood up and undid the edge of the covers so that she could get in and then she climbed up onto the decking and into the cockpit.

Bill had reached out with his spare hand and had gone to cup Daisy's proffered behind and said, "Do you want a steadying hand?"

"No thanks, darling!" had come the reply

Bill then passed up the bags that they had brought with them for their journey. Daisy then took down the cockpit cover and unlocked the little companionway door and started to stow everything away in the cabin. Having checked that the dinghy was secured to *Viking*, Bill too then climbed up and dropped down into the security of the cockpit and then Daisy joined him. They both sat down to get their breath with a quiet sense of contentment and a slightly nervous anticipation for what they were about to do. They were feeling the heat and Bill, now sweating profusely, immediately took the opportunity to take off his shirt. He relished the air on his skin; there was invariably a pleasant cooling breeze when they were out on the water. As they sat there they looked around them; they were pleased with what they saw and smiled at each other.

"She's just so right for us. We could not have managed with a larger sailing boat, especially one without an engine. And what a fabulous day it has turned out to be." As he spoke, he looked at Daisy and watched for her reaction.

"Yes, she's perfect, just right in fact. I'll go and finish off inside the cabin. I hope that we haven't forgotten anything. Then I'll get her ready for the off."

Although they had only bought the boat a few months ago, they were still getting used to her. They had spent time in the spring doing the small amount of painting and maintenance that had needed to be done; and they had left the servicing of the engine to the men at the boatyard. They had already taken the boat out several times during the summer, but always with others, family and friends and such. Bill, from years of dinghy sailing as a boy, was reasonably confident with the use of the sails and all that that involved. He was, however, unfamiliar with the use of a diesel engine. In fact it was a totally alien thing to him and so he had been grateful for some experienced company on their first few trips. Today's trip was to be their first time out on their own and they acted calmly and relaxed with each not wanting to show the other their slight feelings of nervousness, but they each knew that too.

They had developed a well-rehearsed routine when setting off on a journey in the boat; Daisy stayed in the cabin to do her bit with the engine, opening up the sea cocks and turning on the electricity and so forth, and Bill remained in the cockpit to control the tiller, gears and throttle. They could easily reverse the roles, but somehow this was how it had stuck.

"Are we all ready in there to make a start?" Bill asked, trying not to sound too officious.

After a few moments, Daisy called up, "Sea cock open and electrics on!"

Daisy then lifted the lid off the engine to get at the decompression lever and to check the oil level in the little reservoir. She had to struggle a bit as it was heavy and unwieldy, but she was used to it. Bill checked that the gear lever was in neutral and pushed down on the throttle. He then leant forward and, grabbing the crank handle, he turned it over a couple of times. He switched the ignition on and the engine spluttered in to life. Bill immediately yelled, "Decompress!" and Daisy flicked the leaver back and the engine responded and settled into the familiar chugging sound. Both of them sighed with relief, all was well. *Viking had decided that she would behave today.*

"Let's cast off shall we?" said Bill, his voice cracking with some emotion. Although this was just a simple trip down a river, for some inexplicable reason he always felt a bit moved in this way, but kept it to himself.

Daisy climbed out of the cabin and along the deck towards the bow and loosened the for'ard mooring rope from around the stanchion, with Bill staying in the cockpit and casting off the aft mooring. Simultaneously he yelled to Daisy to cast off the forward mooring and she flicked the hawser well away from the boat. Once free, *Viking* started to drift forward and went clear of the buoy and its mooring rope and so he eased her into gear. Bill then steered the boat clear of the other mooring buoys and into the main channel of water, heading down river. He had to make sure to keep clear of the many buoys and other boats that cluttered this part of the channel. Once clear of them, he increased the speed and peered ahead looking for the first of a succession of red or green navigation buoys that would guide them safely down the main navigable channel. Before coming aft, Daisy untied the small bits of cord that held the anchor in place on the fore deck. She did this so that the anchor would be immediately ready to chuck overboard in the event of an engine failure or some other disaster. This was one of Bill's pet worries; what would they do if the engine died? He had to have a contingency plan for every eventuality. The tide was still coming in but this made little impact on the performance of *Viking's* speed when driving against it. Bill noted that her engine had settled into her comforting, if slightly noisy, rhythm.

"Well done old girl," He said quietly. Was he speaking to Daisy or the boat? Daisy couldn't hear a thing anyway. She had returned to the cabin and with the engine going flat out between them, any conversation was completely impossible. *Viking had heard him but she didn't say anything.*

They had no firm plan about where they were going to go that day other than that they were going on a journey and would see where it led them. They had packed sleeping bags and plenty of food the day before so that they were ready for anything. First stop would be at a place known locally as The Anchorage. This was a popular spot which gave good shelter from any biting easterlies. If there wasn't a really high tide there would be a sandy beach to enjoy. They had often travelled past it but had only ever anchored there once before and that was on their maiden voyage a few months ago and they had had two other experienced sailors with them, one of whom was an expert on diesel engines.

They sat in the cockpit, enjoying the trip and revelling in the fresh air. They just loved watching the ever-changing shoreline with its mud banks and inlets and the mercurial river slipping by. Each was deep in their own thoughts. With the warm summer breeze on their faces they both looked up river, their eyes half-closed against the glare of the sunlight bouncing off the water. The cooling breeze caused small tears to trickle from the corners of their eyes. They marvelled at the amount and variety of sea and river birds that they saw. Flocks of small, black-headed gulls would rise up from the water and scatter before them like autumn leaves. Oystercatchers would shriek their distinct staccato chatter as they pattered across the mud. Bill and Daisy's union was a happy one, and they had always thought of getting a boat and exploring the river and now at last it had all become a reality.

During the dark winter months and out of necessity they had both done a training course in river and coastal navigation and happily they had both passed the test at the end of the course. This had boosted their confidence no end and in making this trip they were now putting much of what they had learnt into practice.

"Tea or coffee, darling? Or would you prefer a wine or beer?" Daisy asked.

Although the thought of a refreshing cold beer was very appealing, Bill opted for a coffee. He always felt that, when on board and especially when travelling, he should refrain from alcohol and should always have all of his wits about him, just in case.

After a while Bill felt like getting out of his clothes and putting on something cooler. When Daisy returned with the drinks she had already changed and was just wearing her bathing costume and a large, loosely fitting shirt to protect her shoulders from the sun.

"Darling can you come and take the helm?" asked Bill. "I wouldn't mind going and changing into something cooler. I feel a bit overdressed."

Daisy took the tiller and Bill went below. He stripped off his trousers and rummaged in their overnight bag for something to wear.

"Darling," he called out. "My shorts aren't in the bag!"

Daisy, who could see him down in the cabin saying something, hadn't a clue as to what was being said, due to the noise of the engine. She put a hand up to cup her ear, frowned theatrically and shook her head.

Bill sighed and crawled up to the open hatch.

"I said that there are no shorts in the bag."

"Well, wear your swimming trunks."

"They're not there either."

Daisy was quiet for a bit and then she said, "Oh dear, I've just remembered. I had just folded them up, both the shorts and the trunks and was about to put them in the bag when the phone rang. Do you remember? It was my cousin in Canada – you know, dear old Barbara – and I must have put them down somewhere. Sorry."

"Well what am I supposed to do now? I've only got my pants on!"

"Just come up here in your pants. I don't mind and anyway, no one else can see. Nobody's going to mind even if they do. There's a heatwave on!"

As she spoke, she looked about her. The nearest boat was at least two or three hundred yards away. And, after all, it was probably the hottest day of the year so far and no one was going to bother about a man wearing just his pants. Anyway, they were black and non-descript and any onlooker would assume that they were swimming trunks.

Reluctantly, Bill joined her in the cockpit feeling rather vulnerable, but glad to be feeling a bit cooler.

After nearly two hours or so of chugging up the river they eventually arrived at the Anchorage. Here was a large sweeping curve in the river with a sandy beach and plenty of trees along the top of the bank fronting a small wooded area, affording plenty of shade and it looked idyllic. There were just a couple of other boats anchored but with no sign of their occupants and some people walking at the far end of the beach. It was a young woman with two boys, they looked like twins and they were throwing a stick repeatedly into the water for a large dog to fetch. They were all just enjoying the freedom of the space. She watched as they then all happily moved off out of sight into the distance.

The place was perfect, they both thought as Bill eased up on the throttle. When they were in exactly the right spot, with Daisy now at the tiller, she put the engine into neutral and turned down the throttle even more. Bill then heaved the rather heavy anchor over the side of the boat. They waited to see if the anchor had bitten and then Bill played out the anchor chain to what he calculated to be the right length and then secured it.

"Perfect," said Bill, as he returned to the cockpit. " We'll leave the engine running for a bit longer just to be sure that we are not moving. It's great here, isn't it?"

He looked at Daisy, who was busy concentrating on lining up the relative positions of a couple of trees on the bank, in order to check for drift.

"I think it's perfect, darling. And we don't seem to be drifting at all. Let's have some lunch."

After waiting for several more minutes the boat hadn't shifted so they felt it safe to switch off the engine.

"Ah! The peace and quiet is lovely," said Daisy. Bill nodded and smiled in agreement.

Oddly and from nowhere he suddenly said, "It's so strange, that a place can be so lovely and yet so dangerous, deadly even."

Daisy realised that he must be thinking of a friend of theirs who had drowned in an accident on this river some years ago.

"Yes a river can hold so many happy memories and yet it can also be a very unforgiving place," she said wistfully.

Sometime later after a simple meal of homemade bread, ham and cheese, some wine but not for Bill and coffee, Daisy picked up her book and settled down for a good read. She was reading a paperback, *How the mind works* by Stephen Pinker which had been suggested by someone in her philosophy group. Bill watched her fondly as, lost in deep concentration, she made occasional jottings with a stub of pencil into a well-used, spiral-bound notebook, crammed full of bits of paper, some letters and a train ticket or two, all of which had their own important reason for being there. Daisy had an ability for deep concentration; an ability that Bill knew that he lacked. If she was involved with reading or when working on costume or prop-making, which was something she did from time to time, it was as if she was completely focused and unaware of anything else. Bill envied her that and he loved to watch her at work.

He was beginning to feel hot and a bit sleepy, they had had an early start, and so he made his excuses and went below. He opened the little port holes to let in some air as he sprawled out on the bunk. In the privacy of the cabin he dragged off his pants and threw them in the corner and, lying naked and feeling completely relaxed and at peace with the world, he fell quickly asleep. Gentle, cooling breezes wafted through the opened port holes and cooled his hot, sweaty and slightly overweight body.

***

Bill was swimming under water and it was surprisingly warm. What was that down there? He was sure he saw something move. Yes, it was a fish, quite a big one and it would make a good meal. With some difficulty, he dived down and tried to stab it with his spear and missed it.

The fish turned to look at him and said, "Why did you do that? That's not very nice, and I'd prefer it if you'd put that thing away."

Feeling rather foolish, Bill let go of the spear and it turned into an eel and spiralled off into the murky depths.

"Now," continued the fish, "if you don't mind, I'm on my way to see a friend of mine: one of our river gods. He's a very important being who looks after this place and is in charge of everything and lays down the law. He's pretty benign, doesn't interfere too often. Sometimes he gets it all wrong, though. Like the time the river flooded and drowned all the cattle. But you can't get everything right all the time, can you? External forces with a greater power always interfere, you see. Not even a river god can overcome those. You can come with me if you like, but you've got to be on your best behaviour. He'll turn you into a mud-bank if he doesn't approve of you. He's done that to several folk already, as you can see, and he's not too fussy about how often he does it!"

As they swam along, the fish told him his life story and Bill listened intently, but instantly forgot everything that he was told.

***

The prow of the long wooden boat cut through the water surprisingly quietly, leaving hardly any wake behind in the failing light of the early evening. The carved head of the sea dragon with jet black unseeing eyes gazed down on to the dark grey waters of the river flowing past. Its snarling mouth bared open, revealing a set of white, needle-sharp teeth. The blood-red sails had been lowered at the mouth of the river and the men now rowed the longboat silently up the middle of the winding channel. A young boy in the bow lowered a weighted length of knotted twine into the water every few minutes and whispered a number to the man standing in the bows beside him. The boy's hands were cold and raw but he didn't complain. To do so would only cause the man to be angry. If he became too angry he would hit the boy and if he became really angry the boy could even be thrown overboard. He had heard what had happened to others. If he could swim back to the boat, all well and good, but if he couldn't… so be it. He would be considered a weakling and therefore a gift to appease the gods of the river.

Since leaving the fjords and rocky coastline of their homeland they had been at sea for nearly a week and they now needed food and supplies. They had stopped once on the coast just north of this river, but the foraging had not been good and they had decided not to waste time and to continue further south as they had originally planned. Some of the crew had been up this river before and they had said that the pickings had been good. Last year they had surprised the small settlement on the shores of the river and had taken food, water and a couple of slaves. Anyone foolish enough to stand up to them had been despatched before they could draw breath. They had liked the way the land laid and how the higher ground overlooked the small collection of thatched huts which made up the riverside village. The hunting was good and it was a secure and relatively sheltered anchorage. The place had possibilities and they had decided to come back to make their own settlement here, for how long they knew not. They were the first of an armada of boats that their king had sent to take the river, the surrounding lands and all it contained. The king himself would soon follow. Too bad if the locals didn't like it. Back home there was not enough arable space for all

167

of them; they wanted to stretch their wings and this seemed an ideal spot. Just like a ripe apple waiting to be picked.

***

"Oh no, you've woken up!" exclaimed Daisy. "Don't move. I'm drawing you. Put your arm back up where it was."

Bill opened his eyes and looking across the cabin saw that Daisy was sitting on the steps with an open sketchbook on her lap.

"Just stay still. Put your arm back where it was and don't move." she said.

Bill had fallen asleep on the bunk in a rather uncomfortable half-sitting position. He was leaning against the sail bag, which had doubled as a large oversized pillow. He put his arm back to where he thought it had been, but didn't really know and then he looked down at his legs.

"Oh God! I've got no clothes on. What are you doing?"

"Well, you fell asleep and I have taken advantage of the situation to get some drawings done for my latest commission. You know the one for the Riverbank Arts Centre. They want me to do a sculpture of one of the river gods. And you are a perfect specimen of such a thing!" She smiled.

"What! A river god? You must be joking! I'm hardly the best advert for a river god. I'm overweight and over fifty."

"That's alright, darling. Most of the Roman and Greek river gods were old men with beards. Some of them were even quite paunchy! You just seemed perfect lying there.

Look!" She held up a small photocopy of an ancient Greek river god. "You were sleeping in virtually the exact same pose as the river god from the Elgin Marbles, which went to Russia as part of the exchange programme! Admittedly, he has a younger body than you, but it was too good an opportunity to miss. Stay still, I just need a few more minutes."

Bill was uncomfortably aware that he had pins and needles in his left leg and he just had to move it. At this exact moment a very disorientated hornet flew into the cabin and started buzzing about. Bill hated bees and wasps and, worst of all, he had really bad memories of hornets.

"Oh no! A blooming hornet! I'm out of here!" cried Bill, flapping his arms in the air.

"Oh for goodness sake!" said Daisy. "Don't flap at it and it'll go away. It's more afraid of you than you think. You're just making it more panicky!"

Without thinking, he jumped up and stumbled up the steps to the hatch, pushing past Daisy and grazing a shin in the process. He just had to get out of the cabin as quickly as he could. Once in the cockpit he looked back to see that the hornet had followed him and was now circling his head. This was too much for him to bear and he clambered on to the narrow bit of decking along the side of the cabin to move as far away as he could and yet the hornet still hovered round him. He let go of the hand rail and turned to flap at the wretched thing and in doing so he lost his balance, because at that precise moment Daisy had come out of the cabin on to his side of the boat to try to calm him. Their combined weight just tipped the boat enough to propel him over the side and he landed with a perfectly executed belly-flop into the cooling waters of the river.

The resulting smack on his front stung every part of him quite painfully, which also immediately reminded him that he had not got a stitch on. The water was surprisingly cold and the graze on his shin began to sting. He seemed to struggle for some time to get to the surface and when he did he was gasping for air. Treading water and twisting himself round and round he couldn't see *Viking* anywhere. *Viking* with Daisy on board had completely disappeared. In fact, there were no boats at all anywhere in the river. He felt that he was going mad. He had no idea of the time but the light was fading and he began to feel a bit panicky. How long had he been underwater? It can't have been very long. He can't have drifted so far away that all the boats were out of sight. It had been a sunny day and there had been lots of people about enjoying the river.

***

The boy thought he had seen something in the water up ahead. Yes, there it was. What was it? A seal? No, it was floundering about too much! He pointed to it and said something to the man standing next to him. The man immediately gave orders for the oarsmen to slow their rhythm and for the tillerman to take care to avoid the beast or whatever it was. The boat slowly closed in on the thing. Bill, who had seen the boat appear out of the shadows had watched as it drew nearer. Although it was a welcome means of rescue there was an uncanny sense of menace about it, He realised it was being rowed by about twenty or so men, one or two of whom were turning their heads and staring at him. It was probably just a load of obsessed re-enactors. It reminded him of the Old Norse longboats. A look-out in the bow was talking in a loud guttural voice giving commands to the oarsmen but it was a language he did not recognise, let alone understand. Slowly the boat drew alongside and as it did so one of the crew threw him a rope with a loop in the end. He said something to Bill, but it just sounded like gibberish. He guessed that he was meant to put his foot in the loop like a stirrup and so he did. Then holding on to the line as it became taut, two men hauled him up and after clambering over the side of the boat, he dropped onto the deck just like a large fish. He lay there and then tried to stand up. He was cold and shivering and embarrassingly naked. Someone then threw him a roughly-woven blanket for warmth, for which he was grateful, and he covered himself as best as he could. The fact that it was extremely itchy and that it stank of human sweat,and worse wasn't going to worry him. He wanted to cover himself and he was cold. Someone motioned for him to sit in a large chair positioned in the stern of the boat and he obediently sat in it, feeling very odd. He looked around him and saw that in the middle of the boat a small group of women and children huddled against the chill air. A young boy came up to him and gave him a drink in a horn cup: a sweet and sickly liquid. He wondered if it was mead or something like that. As he sipped at the drink it dawned on him that the reason the boat reminded him of an Old Norse longship was because it really was an Old Norse longship. And the people in it were not re-enactors aiming for authenticity.

Everything was too realistic and no pretend Vikings would stink as highly as these folk did, for they reall stunk. They really were... By this time, he had drunk a few mouthfuls and he began to feel heavy; he wondered if he had been drugged and realised that he probably had been. All this time the boat continued on up the river as the daylight faded and Bill, suddenly feeling very tired and very sleepy, lay back in the comfort of the large chair and fell immediately into a deep and dreamless sleep.

The men of the ship were not too sure what they had found. Was it one of the fabled mermen? This area was famous for them. Why was he alone in the river? Was he a human out hunting and if so, why was he naked? Or was he a spirit? Was he a river god? He looked human, but he was plump and pink, he had no beard and didn't look as if he had done a day's work in his life, then he might be royal. The men's own faces were weather-beaten and unshaven; their arms, hands and feet were rough and calloused because of the way they lived. This strange creature which they had found looked so different; he looked, soft and pampered. They discussed this among themselves. Perhaps they could sell him? After a while the general consensus was that of course he could not be a lazy aristocrat or prince for there were no tattoos on him. Those kind of people were renowned for the magnificence of their tattoos. So why would he have been in the river? After some debate they unanimously came to the conclusion that he must be a spirit of the river in human form. Anyway, they needed to go ashore, to stretch their legs and to forage for food. They decided to beach the boat at the next suitable place and all of them that could do so, eagerly scanned the river banks for the ideal spot.

Bill awoke with a start. There was a massive thump from under the boat and he instinctively grabbed the arms of the chair. He could only watch in amazement as the boat which had been deliberately rammed onto the sloping beach was being skilfully handled. Any one not hanging on to something would have fallen forward. But then all the men in the front end of the boat jumped ashore and began to pull the boat up the beach, singing a loud rhythmic chant as they did so. The rest of the men then leapt out and seemed to be getting organised. Some had gone off into the woods with spears and axes, some were unpacking boxes from the boat and some had started to put up a couple of primitive looking tents on the higher ground. A group had started to stack up driftwood into a pile as if they were going to make a large fire. The most fearful thought then came to him; that they were building a pyre, a sort of funeral pyre… to make a sacrifice of him! He had read about that somewhere. As if to compound his fears a group of men came and gestured for him to leave the chair and to climb off the boat onto the beach. He felt so afraid he thought that he was going to be sick but then they pointed to their mouths as if eating. Did they mean come and join them for a meal or that they were going to eat him?

He should not have worried. He was being treated like the guest of honour. He was placed in the large chair which had been carried from the boat and set on the beach in the centre of what became a large crowd of the men, women and children. He ate and drank his fill. By the light of the fire and some burning torches he watched as some of the men formed a circle round him and started singing and dancing about, as if in some kind of trance. Others laid

173

fur hides, pots of food and weapons at his feet. Then the hunters returned and put a newly killed deer before him on the ground, with its throat cut and blood running into the sand. A couple of women came and stood around him and danced seductively. With all this going on, he was covinced that they thought he was some kind of god. He even began to enjoy it all and relaxed. He smiled at them, they smiled back. He laughed and they joined in laughing. He hadn't had so much fun for ages. Wait till he told Daisy about all this, she would never believe him.

If he could understand Old Norse he would have realised that he was very mistaken as to these people's intentions. They were celebrating the fact that the shaman has told them that Bill would make a perfect sacrifice to the gods of the sea and the rivers as a gift and they were going to return him to the water. It was the best way to guarantee success in all their endeavours. The music and singing was getting louder and louder and the dancers were getting more and more frenetic. It was just as well for Bill that, as the cacophony of sounds was at it loudest, he did not turn to look behind him. The shaman was walking slowly towards him with a huge war club raised in the air and, when he was within reach and as some of the dancers seemed to start swooning in ecstasy, he brought the club down onto Bill's skull with such force, that he was instantly and painlessly sent spiralling into the infinitely black void of total oblivion.

***

Bill twisted his aching body round and round looking for *Viking* and there she was! He called out to Daisy who was shrieking with laughter, or was it panic? God, his whole body hurt, like it was on fire, and he had the godfather of all headaches. Daisy was waving her arms about like an opera singer. He had drifted some way from the boat and he decided to swim towards it, but, he was not very fit and he quickly tired, he could make little or no way swimming against the tide, he was getting out of breath and a sense of panic began to grow within him, which only made things worse.

"Ev-ev-everything hurts, I'm not making much h-h-eadway so I shall make for the beach. Can you row over in the d-d-dinghy and come and get me? And b-b-bring some clothes!"

From where he was, he could see Daisy start to haul in the dinghy and he turned towards the shore saying to himself that he must calm down. He was still drifting and he was also gradually getting nearer to the shore, even though he was moving diagonally and it was exhausting. Luckily there were not many people about and those that he could see in the distance in their boats were not really paying him any attention. As he got nearer to the beach and the water got shallower the strength of the current lessened and he made better progress. He was relieved to see that there was no one else on the beach. After all, the tide was now going out, they had dropped anchor at its highest point and anyone wanting to swim from the beach would soon have to wade through mud to get to the water. He could feel the cool mud beneath him and then he was crawling and slithering towards the safety of the firmer beach where there was less mud and more sand and gravel. With a sense of relief and childish enjoyment he rolled around in the mud and completely slathered himself from top to toe. Some people pay a fortune for a mud bath like this! He had also thought that, if he was going to lie here waiting, he might as well make himself at least blend in with his surroundings, something he remembered from his old army cadet days. But he had never ever thought that he might have to do it naked. The swim had really tired him and he was aware that the intense heat from the sun was warming him up. He lay on his back staring up at the sky and he just tried to relax and to wait for Daisy. It was just as well that he did not see that Daisy, having managed to get into the dinghy and to cast off from *Viking*, was finding that rowing against the current was not easy and she was getting further and further away from the beach.

After what seemed to her like an age, but in fact was ten or fifteen minutes, Daisy finally managed to get the boat to land at a little inlet further down the river. She quickly tied it to an old metal gatepost nearby. Then after struggling through the mud and reeds she made it to the path and once on firmer ground and taking her sandals off she ran along the shore to where she hoped that she would find Bill. When she got to the beach she quickly scanned the wide expanse of sand, shingle and mud but could see no sign of anyone. She felt sick and started to panic. She couldn't think straight. What if he had never made it to the shore and drowned? She ran down the grassy bank onto the beach and looked up and down the shore line more carefully. And then she noticed what looked like a grey seal at the water's edge, lying inert in a mass of churned up mud. She slowly moved towards it. As she got nearer she realised that it was not a grey seal, but a human being. It was Bill! He was quite immobile.

"Oh Heavens, no!" she cried out, "No, no, Bill, Bill." as she ran towards him.

He was completely covered in mud, which had started to dry on him giving him the appearance of having been made of stone or clay. Bits of weed and stones stuck to him in various random and somewhat startling places.

She dropped to her knees and grabbed his head and sort of shook him, all the while calling out his name.

"Bill! Bill! Are you ok? Come back, come back. I'm here, don't do this to me!"

Bill's eyes opened wide and then instantly closed because of the glare. With one eye half open, he said, "Oh, my head it feels like someone has hit me with a sledgehammer." He paused and was quiet then he said in a strange whisper, "I had an amazing dream. But I have already forgottten it."

"You've been lying in the sun for too long, you've probably got a bit of sunstroke", said Daisy, trying to make light of it. "I'm glad I woke you when I did. Any longer and you would have been well and truly cooked."

"Er um... I must have drifted off; sorry that's a rather unfortunate pun. I haven't got any clothes on. Did you bring any?"

"Oh no I haven't, sorry. I left them in the boat in my hurry." Daisy suddenly turned away and saw some people moving through the trees at the far end of the beach.

Then they both heard their voices as they got a bit nearer . The young woman and two boys, who they had seen earlier, were coming down the path. One of the boys turned round and called back up the path.

"Ted, Ted, come on, good boy!" A young and bouncy golden retriever came bounding down the path and with its tongue flopping out of its mouth, and a smile on its face, made straight for Bill and Daisy.

"Oh crumbs!" sighed Daisy quietly. She quickly began picking up bits of the disintegrating wreck of a boat which lay nearby and started covering Bill with them. She also threw on a bundle of old rope to cover his modesty.

"Ow," gasped Bill, "mind where you put that stuff. I am human."

"Sssh! be quiet!" hissed Daisy.

When the dog was about thirty yards away, its owner yelled, "Ted! Ted! No! Sit!" Miraculously the dog stopped in its tracks and sat down, its nostrils twitching as it tried to smell the air in front of it.

Looking directly at the young woman who had started to walk towards her dog, Daisy called to her, "I think this is a dead seal! Probably died from the virus that is killing off so many of them round here. I wouldn't let your dog get too close; you never know it might be catching. I'll cover it up and then call the coastguard to ask what they want us to do about it!"

The two boys who had heard this conversation ran up to their mother and one of them said, "Mum, can we go and have a look? We've never seen a grey seal close up!"

Daisy carried on furiously flinging anything that she could find on to the dead seal.

Luckily the young woman called out more urgently for her dog to return to her. "No, no! Ted! Ted! Come here, good boy!" and turning to her two boys she added, "Boys, it might have a virus. And anyway we really must get back, we've been out for ages. We have to pick up Dad from the station. Come on, Ted. "

The family and their dog moved off the beach and up the path to the woods.

During all this time Bill just lay there inert with his eyes shut. He had only opened them briefly when Daisy had referred to him as a dead seal. Daisy was now trying to work out how they were going to get out of this mess.

Once the woman, her boys and dog had disappeared into the woods, she told Bill that they had gone, saying, "The coast is clear, but stay there."

"What are you going to do?" asked Bill.

"Just a couple of snaps!" and after moving some of the things that were covering him and rearrranging others, she started clicking furiously.

"Oh no!" said Bill and started to try to get up.

"I wouldn't get up, if I were you. You're being watched from the wood. The two boys are standing among the trees and one of those boys has got a pair of binoculars trained on you as we speak."

As she said this she moved her body to block the boy's view of the dead seal and she could hear the woman calling to the boys and they reluctantly turned to go after her. She couldn't hear but would have been relieved to know that one of them said to his twin brother that it wasn't fair because he hadn't even had time to get his binoculars focused.

She then persuaded Bill to let her take a few more photographs. He said that all he wanted was to get the mud off, but Daisy persuaded him that it would waste time and anyway, from a distance it looked as if he was wearing clothes, albeit ragged ones. He looked around for something with which to cover himself. There was an old tarpaulin draped over a dinghy nearby and with some difficulty he wrapped it round his waist and they set off in the direction of their dinghy, hoping not to bump into any more people. Luckily nobody else was about. At several points along the way Daisy asked Bill to strike various poses so that she could take more photographs. One had him sitting on a log deep in thought, one was of him leaning nonchalantly against a gnarled old tree with his arms folded, looking rather pleased with himself, another was of him pointing to the east as if he had seen something and yet another was of him sitting on an upturned boat looking like a shipwrecked sailor. The best of all, however, was of him emerging from the reeds just like the phoenix rising from the flames with both arms raised to the heavens and his face set in a determined grimace, which Daisy thought quietly to herself looked more like an advert for a man with really bad indigestion but with a bit of work it had definite possibilities.

They eventually waded through the mud and reeds to get to the dinghy and clambered in. Bill threw the tarpaulin back beside the path for its surprised owner to find some weeks later. They managed to get back to *Viking* without any further incident, with Daisy rowing and Bill crouching in the stern of the boat. Passing boats paid them little or no attention; the light was fading fast and the various skippers out and about were more intent on getting back to their moorings before dark than staring at distant rowing boats and waving at them.

Once aboard they both had a complete overall wash with each in turn standing over a bucket of fresh water. As Daisy washed his hair for him, Bill flinched, as having seen the livid purple scar on the side of his skull, she had tried to touch it through his thinning hair.

"What on earth… you look like you've had a real bash on your the head. You've got a massive great bruise the size of my hand just here."

And she gently put her hand on his head just above his right ear. Bill flinched again and yelped.

"We ought to get that looked at… There is a bag of ice in the freezer box."

"No, no," said Bill, the thought of cold ice on his head made him feel quite nauseous, "it's nothing that a stiff whisky won't cure." Daisy poured out a couple of whiskies and they clinked them and then drank a toast.

"To the river!" said Bill.

"To the river!" they both then said in unison, and each took a large mouthful. Daisy then heated up some lasagne, which they enjoyed with a bottle of red wine and then feeling completely exhausted they snuggled together under the large duvet and switched out the lights.

***

Some months later at dawn, for that had been at the special request of the artist, the unveiling of Daisy's commissioned artwork at the opening of the River Bank Art Centre took place. A large cloth was draped over the sculpture concealing a monolithic shape about twenty or thirty feet tall. There was a long and worthy speech by the chief executive of HARPIES aka Heritage and Art for River People In Educational Studies, followed by suitable applause. He humbly accepted the invitation to pull a piece of old rope and the cloth, a recycled boatcover slithered to the ground. Immediately there was a sharp intake of collective breath and a stunned silence. There followed a pause as people took it all in. Then to the relief of Daisy there erupted a long and sustained round of rapturous clapping and cheering that just went on and on. The large, mixed-media sculpture was made up from an assembly of dried and fired river mud, stones, fossils, reeds, twigs and branches, wood of all kinds including drift-wood, salvaged bits of old boats, oars, propellers, anchors, old sails and fenders. There were bits of wire and rope and everything which at one time or another had been in, on or under the river; all of which had served a specific purpose or not. A very imposing and uncannily life-like figure of a river god was revealed in all its natural and awe-inspiring glory and yet it seemed to be just a random collection of riverside detritus. The longer one looked at it the more one saw. Every detail of a strikingly well formed but slightly overweight, human male figure, was there and yet at the same time it wasn't; it was as if some kind of magic was taking place. Were the spectators seeing what they wanted to see rather than what was there? It was surely some kind of clever trick of the eye? People didn't know whether or not to look away it was all so anatomically accurate and embarrassingly exposed.

Yet it was quite ethereal, indistinct and vague, just a collection of well… junk. It was dreamlike and yet it was made up of very real solid things. People whispered to each other, how can this be? There were things natural and manmade, some things exquisitely beautiful and yet also broken beyond recognition. Things that had been expensive and things that had been cheap. It was completely and utterly extraordinary, breathtaking and shocking all at once. The figure stood majestically on a plinth made of fired river-mud studded with myriads of sharks teeth and shells and it was placed in the centre of the vast entrance foyer of the new brutally modernist building which had been built on a spit of land at the river mouth. Gazing out to sea, the god's left arm was extended as if holding something and his right arm was raised and pointing due east, where across a sea of golden, blinding light, exactly on cue, the sun was just emerging from below the horizon.

As Bill stood there, somewhat aloof, empty coffee cup in hand, he gazed up in wonder at the river god's face. The eyes were the most striking feature, being made from hundreds of bits of amber and so naturally translucent. Bill was half-listening through the noise of the applause, which was beginning to subside, to the reporter nearby talking to Daisy. He was saying what a fantastic creation it was. He was asking her where she had got her inspiration from. She turned to him and with some emotion tinged with an element of sadness in her voice said,

"Why, it's a combination of both my late husband and the river, of course. They are as one! "

At that precise moment, Bill, still staring up at the mesmerising face, had just noticed that it did have an uncanny resemblance to him. He was then amazed as the river god seemed to look down and wink at him.

Keeping fit

Fifteen stone exactly. That's the same as yesterday and the day before, and I did thirty lengths yesterday and every other day for weeks now. Shall I bother to go again today? Look at you. Head and shoulders, no spare fat there, in fact, you look quite healthy, but then there's your stomach. All that spare fat hanging about, and your skinny legs, what a contrast. You look OK from the front, but from the side… you look like a tortoise standing on its hind legs. No clothes on, not even my watch; I can't blame the weight on anything extra. These scales lie. They do. If I use Stephen and Kelly's, it puts me at fourteen and a half stone, which is marginally better, I suppose, but still too much. The doctor says I should only weigh twelve and a half stone. What does he know? I would be stick thin. It's so difficult. The only way to lose weight is to do more exercise and to eat less, we all know that. But that's easier said than done. If I cut out bread, potatoes and sweets that would help. Why is it that some of my favourite foods are the ones that I should leave out? I am trying to think of an excuse not to go to the sports centre. I can't think of one so there is nothing for it; I've just got to do it. I ought to go and do yet another thirty lengths. What day is it today? Since I've retired, it sometimes takes me a while to work out the day of the week. The old joke that once you've retired every day is Saturday has worn a bit thin. In fact, I can see the look of annoyance and irritation, on some peoples' faces when I say it. Especially those who haven't retired. Why are they so uncharitable? Let's see, where is that timetable? It goes up to the end of Feb, it's now April and they still haven't printed a new one. Although there is no need really as not much has changed. Wednesday. Public swimming: 12 noon to 1.30pm. God, it was awful the other day. Half term – kids shrieking and shouting. Anyway, where's my towel and trunks? On the radiator, I think. What a strange name: trunks. Where does that word come from?

Lovely sunny day, walking up the lane past all the garages. Why do so many people chuck litter? And the dog mess. God. I would shoot the lot of them. Past old Jim's garden on the corner, he's a real old fashioned gardener. Neatly mown lawn, primroses and daffodils, and then a perfectly laid out vegetable patch. Broad beans, spinach, carrots, potatoes all labelled and marked out. And the washing! Absolutely everything on display: socks, y-fronts, big knickers even, for all to see, billowing in the breeze and without a care in the world. Along the road, I turn left. I notice that a garden that used to be old-fashioned and traditional has changed. New people have moved in and ripped all the old traditional stuff out – the roses and the pansies – and laid out raised rectangular beds made with railway sleepers and planted with tall grasses. And they've put in a play area, with car tyres and a barbecue and brick-paving everywhere. Past the school, the local comprehensive. Why are so many state schools so god-damn ugly? Hideous sixties buildings. Some kids are hanging around in the sports centre car park, doing some sort of traffic survey with a harassed, overweight volunteer with frizzy hair. Behind the bus shelter, two kids are smoking with an air of guilty bravado.

At the reception desk there is a small queue. I wonder who is on reception today. It varies. There is a nice, friendly mumsie one for whom nothing is any trouble. There is an officious one who always gets confused by her own efficiency and has to go into the back office and ask for help and there is the grumpy-and-downright-rude one. I peer round the group of people in front of me. Oh, it's the grumpy-and-downright-rude one on duty. She is having to cope with a family who want to buy two pairs of goggles and pay the entrance price all at once. The mother can't find her purse with her bank card in it and the grumpy-and-downright-rude receptionist has the kind of face that says, "*Why are you messing me about like this?*" The queue grows behind me, and one or two people mutter, including me. Eventually it's my turn. "Swimming, please." I say. "Do you have your card?" "No.I'm afraid I might have lost it" "Where is it?" "I don't know!" "Well next time you come in, you will have to ask for a temporary one." I explain that I am a fully paid up gym member and anyway, swimming is free for the over-sixties. "I know that," she says between pursed lips. As I walk away, I wonder why I have to wait till next time. Why can't I ask for a new card now? I begin to turn back, then I think better of it. That's one thing this government has got right: free swimming for the over-sixties. When I say 'free' it means that I don't have to pay at the point of entry, but you can be certain that I have been paying for it for some time, in increased council tax, VAT on fuel, or elsewhere in one of the myriad stealth-taxes somewhere along the line. There is no such thing as a free lunch or, in this case, swim!

Now there is a new notice at the entrance to the changing rooms. *No outdoor footwear to be worn beyond this point.* Everyone has to sit down at the entrance and remove their shoes; it doesn't say socks, but I take mine off anyway as I don't like the idea of walking in my socks on these wet floors. It makes me think of visiting a mosque, everybody taking their shoes off, and, after all, it's for the same reason: cleanliness. But the mat under my feet is the same filthy doormat that has always been there, so it rather defeats the object. Have I remembered the pound for the locker? Yes. Go into a changing cubicle, start to strip off and carefully put my clothes on the bench; don't want them to fall on the floor. I can see traces of someone's powder. Talcum powder or worse, athletes foot powder or something for eczema? Put on my trunks. Ready to go. Don't forget your watch. Put it in my trouser pocket. Gather everything up, unlock the cubicle and look for an unoccupied locker. Why do I walk on tip-toe at this point? The first locker I open is full of somebody's clothes, but they haven't locked it because they didn't have the pound. Next one I try is the same – God, this is annoying. Finally I find an empty one, put the clothes in and then the towel in on top, then put the pound in the slot, shut the door and turn the key. I hear the satisfying clunk as it connects and the pound drops into the mechanism awaiting my shivery return. It's number forty-two. I put the numbered, bright yellow plastic key-cum-bracelet on my wrist.

Need to pee. Walk to the men's loo. Luckily no one has peed on the floor by the urinal, this sometimes has happened and it is a question of which urinal is clearest of someone else's pee or is there a cubicle available. Rinse my hands; is that strictly necessary as I am about to have a shower? Still walking on tip-toe. Then out towards the pool and a quick hot shower, which starts off cold. I look across to the pool and weigh up which section of the pool to swim in. Both of the two lanes are very busy. The 'slow' lane is full of ladies, of a certain size and age, swimming along as slowly as it is as humanly possible to do: some are chattering side by side, some of the more thoughtful are not. There is one older gentleman, swimming in a rather weird style, which actually looks as if he is walking along the bottom of the pool. The ladies that aren't swimming are standing in the shallow end gossiping, elbow on the pool edge. The 'fast' lane contains three impossibly fast swimmers in swim hats and goggles doing the front crawl. That just leaves the public area with the noisy kids playing. There are also some dazed parents trying to entertain their two crying children, encouraging them to at least try to swim. There are a couple of besotted teenagers who want to snog each other, but can't do so under the stares of the lifeguard.

I decide that the public area is the best bet in the circumstances. I reckon that if I swim up and down, right against the dividing rope then maybe I can get a length of clear water. Or that is the theory, anyway. Climb down the ladder. Keep going down, let go, go under. Slightly chilled, but this will pass. Move over to where I am going to push off from, trying to ignore the mayhem of the kids. I usually aim to do thirty lengths, but the problem is remembering which number I have got to. I read somewhere recently that lots of people who go swimming for exercise are wasting their time because they don't do it correctly. I prefer to swim the breaststroke because I have never really mastered the breathing in the crawl. Anyway, I am taking extra care in swimming properly, making sure that I use both my arms and legs fully. It does make a difference. I am easily bored when swimming. When I am in a crowded pool, all my attention is taken up by avoiding the kids who are larking about and who appear to be completely unaware of my presence. The lifeguards sit at each end of the pool on their high chairs, staring blankly at the people swimming. At the deep end is a sign that says, *No jumping,* and I watch as two girls jump into the water repeatedly, and shrieking as they do so and the lifeguard just ignores them. There is also the besotted couple of canoodling teenagers. The boy is doing his best to either drown the girl or snog her and she half-heartedly tries to get away from him, again shrieking, but then stays around for more. He splashes her, holds her under and all the while the lifeguard watches blankly. He doesn't know whether to intervene or not. He opts not to. The couple disappear beneath the waves their only chance to thoroughly enjoy the closeness of their bodies to each other. The girl comes up, gasping, saying something to the effect that he shouldn't try to do that in a public place. Is this my third or fourth length? I glance over to the other lanes. There is now only one person in the 'fast' lane and he doesn't look that fast. I decide to move and go to that lane. I have already been bumped into and splashed by the kids. I settle down to do my lengths. Seven, eight or was that nine, ten? I think about it for a bit and decide that it is seven; eight, then I do two more and stop in the shallow end for a breather. I set off again, eleven, twelve.

We avoid any eye contact as we pass. The other swimmer in this 'fast' lane, a man about ten years younger than me powers up and down and we are careful to avoid hitting each other as we pass. But inevitably we do; our feet inadvertently kick each other. He says sorry simultaneously as I do. Oh, the politeness of the English. Fifteen, sixteen, only four to go and then I will be two thirds of the way. When I turn round, I realise that I have the lane to myself; the feeling of ownership of the whole lane is quite liberating. The man has left. There are only twenty minutes to the end of the session so that the chances of anyone else coming in now are remote. Great. Sometimes the water is a bit cloudy, but today it is pretty clear. When it is cloudy I do not like to dwell on the reasons for this. In fact I do not like to dwell on any aspect of the purity of the pool's water as a result of the state of people's bodies with whom I am swimming. Not a pleasant thought of mixing all those traces of body fluids or worse, notwithstanding the chemicals that are supposed to kill all the dangerous bugs. Nineteen, twenty. Have another breather.

The last ten lengths are always the easiest, because you can see the light at the end of the tunnel, if I can use such a metaphor. I seem to average a length a minute or thereabouts, possibly slightly less. Sometimes I go on and do more, forty, fifty and once sixty. I have been away

191

for a bit and haven't been swimming lately, but intend building up again to those sorts of figures.

I watch as people get in and out of the pool. Looking dispassionately at the human race, we are an odd shaped bunch, quite ungainly, in fact. I need another pee and I have got four more lengths to go. Wouldn't dream of peeing in the pool. Have peed in the sea many times, though. Last length, here we go. Then I clamber out and up the steps. I stagger to the shower, feeling my age and glad that I have done it, and say to myself that next time I will do forty lengths. People who are organised come to the shower with shampoo and conditioners and make a right meal of the whole business. I just rinse off all the chlorinated pool water and stand in somewhat of a daze as I watch the lifeguards rearrange the pool for a school session.

Shivering slightly, I make for my locker, walking on tip-toe, still needing to pee. Unlocking it, I notice the coin falling out of the mechanism onto the floor as it always does. Who designed these wretched things? Grabbing my towel and clothes, I bend down for the coin and realise that it has landed an inch or two away from a discarded sticky plaster with a small clump of hair attached. Yuk!

The business of drying oneself and dressing after swimming is a real chore. Shivering, wanting to get dressed as quickly as possible; whether to wring out one's trunks onto the floor or not. Not really drying oneself properly; being impatient to get dressed and the clothes not going on easily because your body is still partly wet. I can hear the school group beginning to arrive. A bossy teacher is telling them to get changed quickly and not to waste any time. "Come along now, we haven't got all day." Then I go to put my shoes and socks on at the bench by the door. The late-comers, who are coming through the swing doors, get a ticking-off for being late. "Come on you three, why are you so late? You'll have to see me after school. Now get a move on. Smithers, you were late last week as well. I am going to have to speak to Mr Paxton about you." I must remember to come in slip-on shoes next time. These laces are a bore. Anyway, now we are done. I wonder what's for lunch. Sardines on toast or will it be a cheese and salad sandwich?

Clutching my bundle of towel and trunks I go out past reception, wondering whether to get a hot chocolate from the machine. Today I think not; better for me not to, too much sugar, but it does taste nice. A penance for having had that Kit-Kat earlier. I can see through the tall glass walls that the sun is shining outside. It's going to be a lovely day. I'm free! I have forgotten to pee but cannot be bothered to go back, "Goodbye," I say cheerily to the grumpy-and-downright-rude lady on the desk. "Bye-bye, Mr Lewis, have a lovely day!" she says. So she does know my name and I think she is smiling.

In delicto flagrante

Since they had moved in, the shared drive had never really been a big problem. So long as no one parked on it for any length of time and everyone respected everyone's right of way, it was fine. Just occasionally he had had to go round knocking on the doors of the nearby houses to find out who the culprit was and tell them that they were blocking him in and that, anyway, they should not be parked there. Most people were perfectly polite about it, just occasionally they were a bit grumpy or even downright rude, but he took no notice of that. Just once he had had to call the police, when he was trying to go to work and he could not find the car's owner. When the police came, they said that they couldn't really do anything, but they did agree to help him bump the car out of the way. As the car had been parked across the double yellow lines by the end of the drive, the police slapped on a ticket for obstruction. But that was a really rare event and it had never happened again. Until now. It was evening and dark outside, he wanted to go out to get some wine for a meal they were having with some friends later on. When he went out to his car, he had noticed a small white Fiat parked in front of the gate and blocking his exit.

"Shit," he muttered under his breath. That day, a

Saturday, his wife had told him that a couple had moved in to the house but one along from them. The neighbour's neighbours, she had called it. It usually was the case that newcomers parked in the drive. Once they had been politely told not to, they were never any more trouble.

He decided that he would try them first; it was bound to be them as he didn't recognise the car. Walking the short way along to the house, he could see that the lights were all on and there were no curtains up in any of the windows yet. He could hear some classic rock music coming from the house, but it wasn't loud. As he came to the door he was right in front of a big window at right- angles to it. He looked in and noticed that the room had been redecorated and a new stripy carpet had been laid. And then he saw them, just to the right side of the room. A couple were lying entwined on the floor and they were making energetic love. In a split second, he took in the whole image. They were in the classic missionary position, with the heavily-built man on top. As he stared, he saw that the man was fully clothed, wearing a leather jacket with lots of leather strips dangling from the sleeves and across his back. There were silver metallic studs on it set out in a star pattern, just like a child's join-the-dots drawing; but his trousers and Calvin Klein boxer shorts were round his ankles. He hadn't even taken his boots off. The young woman, considerably shorter and smaller than him, was completely naked with her legs crossed behind the man's back as she clung to him tightly. It reminded James of the way a baby monkey clings on to his mother's chest as she leaps through the trees. The man's white buttocks were relentlessly pounding up and down, sort of in time with the music, and he could hear them both moaning loudly in rhythm to the thrusting and thumping of their frantically moving bodies. He instantly looked away, still wondering whether he should ring the bell or not, but immediately dismissed the idea. Of course he shouldn't. It would mean the couple looking up, and seeing him and massive embarrassment all round. He decided to leave straight away and to give them a few minutes and come back later. He went back to his house and told his wife what he had seen; they were both amused, but annoyed at the same time, although he wasn't in any hurry to get the wine. After what seemed like enough time for the couple to finish their lovemaking, he returned to the house. Gingerly he walked up to the window, they were still grinding away and in exactly the same position as when he had left them more than five minutes ago. Now he was tempted to bash on the window, and to hell with their embarrassment. He had had enough. But he did not know them and you never know how people might react. He estimated that the man was well over six feet tall, a bit of a gorilla, and he did not want to get off on the wrong foot with these new neighbours. He could be accused of being a peeping tom, that would be creepy, there would be a row, it could all get very, very unpleasant. He just stood there for a couple of seconds, mesmerised by the couple in this desperate act of procreation. They were completely absorbed in each other and oblivious to anything going on around them except for the thumping music. They were obviously extremely happy at moving in to their new place and were vigorously celebrating in time-honoured fashion.

He walked back to his house again and went inside, thinking that he would go back again in another five minutes or so. He put the kettle on and made a cup of coffee. Sometime later when he went out again, the car had gone and the lights in the house were all switched off. They had left. He went to get the wine.

When he got back from work the following evening, he went round to the house again and knocked on the door. It was answered by a smiling, fresh-faced young woman in her late teens or early twenties.

"Oh, hello. I just thought that I would come round and introduce myself. I live just two doors up there and we share the drive. My name's James."

The young woman stepped forward putting out her hand to shake hands and as she did so, she stepped onto the door's threshold. She was quite short and James realised that this discreet action gave her an extra couple of inches in height.

She looked back at him, still smiling and said, "Hello, that's nice of you, my name's Jane and I..." she hesitated. She was interrupted by the arrival of the man, her man, who grabbed her from behind proprietarily and clasped his hands together across her stomach holding her close to him.

He lowered his chin and rested his head on her shoulder and said, "Hi, my name's Guy. Is there a problem, boss?" David noticed the South African accent. It was a completely friendly and non-aggressive enquiry.

He must have been six foot three, and had a relaxed and pleasant manner.

"Oh, nothing really, just to say welcome and if there is anything you need, don't hesitate to ask. Oh and by the way, the shared drive, I hope you don't mind me mentioning it. It's important that no one ever parks for any length of time in the drive, because it's sod's law that that's exactly when one of us wants to get in or out. We can't know the times of each other's comings or goings, can we? And it's such a pain to come round banging on people's doors to find who's responsible." He paused for breath, he was trying to sound reasonable. Then he continued,"It's also very annoying for the person being knocked-up, if you understand what I mean, they might be busy, or otherwise occupied and not want to be disturbed. But they still would have to come out and move it. You see what I'm saying?"

They all stood staring at each other in a brief and pregnant silence.

James turned his head and, looking through the window, said. "Oh, that's nice. You've got a new carpet, did you get that laid or did you lay it yourself?"

James turned again to see the young woman staring back at him slightly colouring, her smile fixed as if the wind had changed. She turned her head and looked straight through the window. Her man stood up, let go of her and he was thinking hard. He was remembering that he had left his car in the drive last night and he was remembering what he and Jane had been doing on the newly laid carpet. Slowly he turned his head and he too looked through the window. The curtains were not yet up, the lights were all on and he had a full and uninterrupted view of the newly laid carpet in all its naked glory covering the floor of the empty, unfurnished room.

See you later

The light from the late afternoon sun cast long shadows across the uneven, litter-strewn cobbles. Few people were about. As the distance between us grew, we watched so very intently as the young couple moved away from us. What were we looking for? A sign or something? They were walking happily away from us, arm in arm, towards an uncertain, yet promising future. There was a spring in their step and they moved together in a rhythmic unison as one. What were they saying to each other? Where were they going? Back to the flat? To meet up with their friends? Catch a bus? It was their life, their business and all their tomorrows lay before them.

The small shops on either side of the lane were beginning to close. The news vendor picked up his boards scrawled with lurid headlines and carried them awkwardly into the dark interior of his shop. The fruit and veg man was desperately trying to sell off his remaining stock at rock bottom prices.

"Fifty pence a bag! Come on, ladies. Help yourselves! Lovely oranges, apples and bananas! It's all got to go! Get your five-a-day here!"

An old man rummaged through a pile of discarded veg boxes looking for something, anything to take home for his 'tea'.

Earlier that day, the graduation ceremony had passed happily and proudly. We had smiled, clapped and cheered as our dearest daughter had received her degree from the Chancellor of the University in a grand hall, along with all her peers. The scores of students wearing brightly coloured gowns and unfamiliar mortarboards had sat in rows and talked quietly, waiting for the ceremony to begin. Staff of the various faculties had processed to the stage. They were adorned in robes of a rainbow of colours and mediaeval style hats denoting their all-important status and subject areas. Once all were settled, there followed several long, worthy speeches. Honorary doctorates were awarded and then the moment for which we had all been waiting, arrived. In organised ranks the graduands lined up proudly in long lines to collect their scrolls. Some of the boldest students waved to family and friends in the crowd with shrieks of elation and relief, followed by nervous laughter. Others were more reserved in front of the hundreds of people and looked thoughtful and embarrassed.

It was the final official act in a process that had started some years before. During those intervening years, she had conscientiously worked hard, passed exams, filled in application forms and attended interviews. She had had to experience flat-sharing and being independent and coping with living away from home. This is a familiar rite of passage that so many young people must of necessity experience. Ever conscientious, she had worried a lot and had now finally achieved a successful outcome of which we were all, oh so very proud.

Afterwards, spilling out of the hall in a mass of emerald green robes, the students met up with families and friends. There were exuberant hugs and plenty of group photographs with brief and sometimes awkward introductions made to tutors and flat mates. Once photographed and de-robed, plans were quickly made for the rest of the day and for the evening's celebrations.

After a celebratory meal together, we knew that she was going off to start her new life with her boyfriend and we, of course, accepted that and were very happy for her and for them both.

" See you later!" they had each said. Life is to be lived and our job as parents is to try to prepare our children for coping with anything that life may throw at them, both the good times and the bad. We do not own our children and we want them to follow their own destinies. All any parent wants is for their offspring to lead a happy and fulfilled life, whatever it may be. By the same token, our children will always know that we are always here if they ever need us and that we will always love them unconditionally.

As they walked off into the evening light, we watched as they stopped, turned towards us and smiling, raised their arms and waved at us one last time, as we waved back and before they disappeared into a crowd of young people celebrating outside a pub.

Dear sweet Father Anselm

The "Lady" Maureen woke up with a start and stared upwards. She was lying beside her knight, the valiant "Sir" Don, who was quietly wheezing beside her. Two of the "gentry" lying side by side. It made her think of that tomb where she had seen a knight and his lady, hands in prayer, eyes shut, as they waited patiently for the Glorious Resurrection. She shuddered as she thought of their earthly remains, which would have slowly rotted to dust in the dry earth beneath. She shivered and immediately dismissed the unpleasant image. Her eyes followed the long crack in the ceiling as they had done a hundred times before and she sighed. It looked as if there two were more cracks. She must have a word with Don to put the ceiling right. She turned sideways to look at her husband who was now gently snoring. As she did so one of the dreams she had repeatedly been having lately came back to her. Over the weeks she had been making copious notes. She reached to her bedside table for the well-thumbed notebook and chose an already sharpened pencil. This time Father Anselm had been very specific, which was unusual for him. Settling herself against the pillows and her glasses onto her nose, she opened the book and flicked through the many pages of pencil scrawl until she came to the next empty page. She pursed her lips studiously, licked the end of the pencil, grimaced and began to write very quickly:

'My dear lady Maureen, greetings! Today in the Year of our Lord, fourteen hundred and thirty five, on the fifth of May. His Venerable Grace, Geoffroye de Burgh, the Abbott of the Priory in Earl's Colne, who alas languishes abed in his chambers, nobly suffering with the Great Sicknesse, and who awaits his Translation to Heaven with a fearful and trembling heart, has commanded me to establish a Chantry here in this town, so that he may be assured of his place in Heaven. God has chosen a site for this Great Enterprise next to the market place on Chipping Hill here in Meadstead. His Grace has generously provided me with a bag of gold sovereigns and I have commissioned a builder of repute, one John Snout, and a renowned architect, Julius Greatrex, to do this Holy Work. The building is to be constructed of oaken beams and wattle, lath and plaster with stone lintels and many glazed mullions and should be completed with all speed, preferably before his Grace's demise. God Save his Soul. And now I must depart to make preparations to begin the Greate Worke.'

And with that, the voice had disappeared from her head as quickly as it had arrived. Her heart was beating fast, for this was the conclusive proof. The proof they had been seeking ever since they had bought the old, partially-beamed building, which they had set about restoring with enthusiasm. The Lady Maureen could hardly contain her excitement. She tried to calm herself and reached for her beta-blockers and knocked one back with a sip of water.

She then turned to her sleeping husband and nudged his shoulder sharply.

"Don! Don!" she said. "Wake up! Oh, come on, do wake up!" She nudged him again.

Don farted loudly, opened his eyes and mumbled, "What, what are you doing. Oooh, that's a bad one." The stench of his fart assailed his nostrils as he struggled to sit up. The Lady Maureen moved her head diplomatically away.

Don groaned as he hauled himself up and lent against the pink, velveteen bed-head. "Now tell me, dear, but slowly, what has happened?" He said this in the patient voice of a long-suffering schoolmaster to a pupil who has something supposedly very important to say. Then he added, "I have had a terrible night, my urethra in my penis is sore again and I shall have to go and see the nurse." This was a recurrent problem for Don, who had had to make several trips recently to the clinic "because of the state of his waterworks".

"It's Father Anselm! He has told me! Now we have proof. He built a Chantry here, right here where we are now. I have written it all down." She read out to him exactly what she had written as he listened carefully.

They had bought the house some years ago and Don, a retired senior architectural technician, who had worked for the local council in the social housing department, had spent many hours renovating the building himself. The house had been converted into offices for a pharmaceutical company and he was now trying to convert it back into a single "historic" home. The building had a central core of a couple of rooms with walls and ceilings heavily timbered. The rest of the building consisted of a warren of brick-built rooms which had been added on at various times by the Victorians and others. Mysteriously there was no main original central fireplace. This had at first worried Don, but he put it down to the fact that in really early houses, there was no central fireplace constructed and the smoke found its own way out any way it could. If there had been a chimney it would probably have been removed by the Victorians for safety when they had converted the building into a house. The Victorians had constructed several other fireplaces in the adjoining rooms and he got over the problem of no fireplace in the main heavily-beamed sitting room – or lounge as he preferred to call it – by constructing a very convincing but fake chimney breast out of plaster board and studwork. He placed an electric artificial coal fire in the newly constructed hearth. There was a fireside set consisting of tongs, brush and poker all of which hung in a tasteful wrought iron stand beside the hearth. To complete the illusion he had hung over the fireplace a beaten copper shield depicting St George slaying the Dragon. He had found it in a large box of oddments which he had bought at a house clearance sale for a few pounds some years ago when he had worked as a part time "antiques" dealer. Even now he still regularly scoured local junk shops and auction rooms to acquire the kind of furniture for the house that would create the right sort of period atmosphere. Old habits die hard.

Wearing only an apron and a pair of pink fluffy slippers, the Lady Maureen was in the kitchen peeling some potatoes and yet keeping an eye on the time. Don had said he would come down for lunch when he had finished filling the cracks in the bedroom ceiling and she was worried that she would not get the lunch ready in time. She fondly remembered that before being swept off her feet by "Sir" Don, that she had worked as a humble lady's maid to the Countess of Essex in Hedingham Castle. She was recalling the time that the king came to visit and all the pageantry that went with it. She lit the stove and put a pan of water on to boil with the peeled potatoes and looked to see where she had put the sausages. Suddenly there was a knock at the back door. Wiping her hands on her apron she went to the door and opened it. A monk in a brown habit, and sandals and looking very like Friar Tuck, whom she had seen on TV in Robin Hood, was standing and smiling nervously back at her.

"Good Morrow, Mistress Maureen. Greetings. My name is Father Anselm. Prithee, my lady, would it be possible for an itinerant priest like myself to avail himself of a beaker of cool water ? It is fearful hot and I have come a long way and I would seek some respite in your barns, if I may."

Maureen stared back, dumbfounded.

"Why, of course, your holiness, come in, sit down and rest yourself. We cannot put you in the barns! We are honoured to have a holy man such as yourself gracing our humble abode. Come in to my kitchen." She held the door open and waved the priest to one of the kitchen chairs at the table.

"Why thank you, madam. I have come on urgent business to make report on the progress of the Chantry.

His Grace, Abbott Geffroye is failing fast. Why only two days ago his toes turned black and began to drop off and he suffers most dreadfully from the bloody flux. But forgive me, I am upsetting you."

Maureen placed a glass of water in front of Father Anselm, and turned back to check the potatoes. With her back to him, she poked them and strained them collecting the water into a jug which she mixed with some gravy powder. She began to mash the potatoes vigorously, before she turned the sausages which were sizzling in a frying pan. All this was done at arms' length, as she didn't want to get spattered, even if she was wearing just an apron. As she busied herself, she was chatting with Father Anselm about the lovely weather they were having at last and how good it was for the garden.

Don came in through the door from the hallway. All he was wearing was a hat that was splattered with plaster, which had also found its way, quite innocently, on to his chest and other parts of his anatomy, drawing some quite unnecessary attention to them.

"Hello love! Something smells good. I've finished filling the cracks."

He sat down at the kitchen table and started to drink the glass of water that he found there. It was a hot day and the water was cool and refreshing. He emptied the glass with a satisfied sigh and put it back on the table.

"That's better," he said, as Maureen turned back towards him bearing a steaming plate of sausages and mash drenched in thick brown gravy.

"Here you are, dear. But where's Father Anselm?"

"Father Anselm?" asked Don.

"Father Anselm was here a minute ago. I gave him a glass of water. Look he's drunk it all." And she turned back to the cooker to get her meal.

"That wasn't him. That was me. I drank it. Boy, was I thirsty. Tomorrow when the filler has set I'll sand it down and paint it. When I went to buy the plaster and paint I also bought some plastic tiles. They are embossed with small heraldic shields. I thought that if I stuck them on the ceiling and painted them white to match that it would look like authentic raised plasterwork. Stucco they call it in the trade. And anyway it'll cover up any traces of the cracks. What do you mean Father Anselm was here?"

Maureen hadn't been listening to any of this and didn't reply.

After lunch and a wash to get rid of the plaster from his body, Don went to have a read of the paper and a bit of a snooze in the lounge. As he dozed he remembered that every quarter he, "Sir" Don, always liked to go through the accounts himself. He did not trust his steward to do it properly. As he peered at the long columns of figures and tried to make sense of them, he was suddenly aware of someone else in the room. He looked up and there kneeling at a small prie-dieu chair was a monk praying. He was wearing a brown habit and he had a knotted rope tied round his waist. As he watched he saw the monk cross himself and he silently mouthed something. Don stared.

When the monk had finished his devotions he stood up, straightened his habit and turning to Don, said, "We must pray for his Reverence, the Blessed Abbott Geffroye, who passed away this morning. God rest his soul. I must now depart. Tonight there will be a candle-lit vigil in the priory and tomorrow we shall begin to sing a thousand masses here in the chantry in order to ensure that his blessed soul goes straight to Heaven." And with that he walked out of the room, but not by going through the door, but by passing right through the front wall into the street outside.

Don was astonished and he dropped his copy of the *Sun* open at the lists of football results, onto the floor and in a faltering voice, he called for his wife: "Lady Maureen, Lady Maureen, prithee, come hither, quickly!" Then, more urgently, "Oh for God's sake, old girl, where the bloomin' heck are you?"

Maureen who had been doing the washing up, came hurrying into the lounge still wearing her pink rubber gloves and clutching a dripping dish-mop.

Over the next few weeks both Don and Maureen had several sightings of the elusive monk, whom they had come to know well. He never appeared to them together, but only when they were on their own. Maureen filled several notebooks with closely written notes and observations. Sometimes she had to write so quickly that her writing became illegible, even to herself. But this only added to the mystery. Each of them had complete conversations and they gradually grew very fond of him, in fact he almost became one of the family. He was never threatening, but always benign and only too keen to tell them whatever they wanted to know about the house, the locality or anything else. He never commented on their lack of clothes and just accepted them as they were. There was no need to research in the local or district libraries; Father Anselm told them everything that they wanted to know. They would have complete conversations with him in a sort of stagey Elizabethan language with phrases such as: " 'Pon my word!" and "Prithee this and Prithee that!" and with a liberal scattering of "thee" and "thou". It was all very exciting. He only seemed to have one fault and that was his unpredictability. They never knew when he was going to appear. Sometimes it could be embarrassing, like the time when he walked into the bathroom, needless to say through the wall, when Don was on the lavatory battling with yet another dose of constipation and putting some ointment on his "problem". Maureen was forever plying Father Anselm with drinks, even tea and coffee, which were complete novelties to him. He liked three spoons of sugar in his tea and four in his coffee. Maureen unsuccessfully searched the local off-licence for mead, and they were happy to order some for her. Father Anselm was very grateful. He had a special penchant for sausage rolls, hot cross buns and Christmas cake, not to mention special cream teas, which Maureen did on High Days and Holidays. Both Maureen and Don had started to put on weight, but they didn't notice and it didn't seem to affect Father Anselm at all.

One day Maureen was browsing through the local *What's On* magazine when her attention was drawn to a small advertisement announcing the services of a clairvoyant, Madam Clarissa Spiggott. The advert proudly declared: *'Readings given, exorcisms conducted, investigations undertaken. Complete discretion guaranteed'* and then there was a phone number. Don and Maureen had told various friends and neighbours about the existence of Father Anselm. For some reason, they got the feeling that when they told some people, they were at best doubted and in some cases frankly just not believed. However, happily some of their closest friends were completely accepting of the whole idea and wanted to know more.

Without hesitation Maureen phoned Clarissa Spiggott and enquired if it was possible for her to come round to the house and see if she could call up the mysterious priest. Clarissa thought it would be a wonderful idea, and she came round the very next day and then regularly once a week. In doing so Clarissa familiarised herself with the atmosphere and found out all about Father Anselm. Don and Maureen showed her the notebooks, which Clarissa would borrow and take great care of. Don and Maureen decided that they were now ready to share Father Anselm with their friends and neighbours. About this time when Clarissa was visiting and happily after a couple of large gins and a good lunch, Clarissa fell into a trance and, speaking in pure Drama School Elizabethan Tudor, convinced Don and Maureen that she was a 'conduit' for Father Anselm. Although she had received several payments already, a larger fee was agreed for Clarissa to come and have a séance at home with their friends and neighbours, for cash only, of course, and of an amount which Don thought rather excessive. He calculated that he could rent one of the cheaper beach huts in Frinton-on-Sea for less, but said nothing for fear of upsetting Maureen. A date and time were fixed. Maureen planned to make some ham sandwiches and cold sausages for the event because by now she knew that they were some of Father Anselm's favourite foods. He had told her that he also liked venison, but Maureen baulked at that and thought that was too expensive. Anyway, since seeing the film *Bambi* as a child she had always thought of eating venison as repugnant. Verbal invitations were given to about fifteen friends and neighbours and then it was only a matter of waiting and preparing for the big day. And, of course, Don and Maureen would have to wear "textiles".

***

Clarissa Spiggott sat sprawled in a large, comfortably sagging armchair in the corner of the lounge to the left of the fireplace and was quietly wheezing. She was a large, breathless woman in her late seventies and she had high blood pressure and bad asthma. Her hair was done in a loose perm, and dyed a sort of camel-beige colour, which matched her beige cardigan and jumper set that hung in front of her like an overflowing, sticky toffee pudding as it tried to contain her ample bosom and bulging stomach. Her Dame Edna bifocal glasses, which needed a wipe, rested on the end of her thickly powdered nose, They had a gold-beaded chain affair hung from either side of the frame and round her neck and it gave her a faintly professorial air. She wore two strands of fake pearls and her asthma notwithstanding, she chain-smoked. She said to her friends that smoking helped her to "clear her tubes". She held her plastic cigarette holder between her stubby fingers. The nails had been painted bright red some days ago and they had begun to chip. She had bad legs that she concealed under a thick tweed skirt and thick lisle stockings and she wore comfortable shapeless boots lined in fake lambswool. On a small table beside her a large ashtray had been placed alongside a generous serving of gin and tonic in a club glass with ice and a slice of lemon. On the floor beside her lay an elderly, exhausted and overweight cairn terrier, which had seen and heard it all before and it would sleep throughout the evening's entertainment. Trixie was completely deaf to everything and everyone, except for her mistress when she announced that it would be time to go back to her damp, cluttered cottage beside the river.

The various guests arrived. They were introduced to one another and talked nervously. One or two bravely introduced themselves to Clarissa who discouraged any further conversation. Food and drinks were passed round. Clarissa ate extremely well and drank another gin and tonic. When the plates were being cleared away, people started to settle down. The younger folk could sit on the floor where some bean bags had been scattered. Almost automatically, everyone else moved their chairs into a sort of semi-circle and waited. A hush descended. Don turned out the lights, but left the one reading light next to Clarissa switched on. It suffused her in a warm orange glow which contrasted dramatically with the completely dark surroundings. Maureen then thanked everyone for coming and explained that Clarissa was a "conduit" and was going to try to summon Father Anselm and then people might be able to ask her questions. Clarissa forced a smile and said that she would see what she could do. And of course, eventually she did. Everybody had settled down to wait in a sort of polite and yet embarrassed silence. Clarissa, apparently without a care in the world, smoked her cigarette and sipped her drink. No one spoke. Maureen watched as the ash on Clarissa's cigarette grew longer and longer. When it fell, it landed on the sleeping dog's back and disappeared into its fur. If the dog felt anything it didn't show it.

It was as if that was the moment for Father Anselm to reveal himself. Suddenly and with her eyes clamped shut, Clarissa's chin dropped down to her chest, and it stayed there throughout the séance and although her mouth moved, the rest of her body stayed completely still.

She took a very deep breath and then in a man's deep base voice said, "Greetings to all of you, my friends! I am Father Anselm, chaplain in residence at the Chantry of Meadstead in the County of Essex, where I am come to say masses for the soul of the Abbott Geffroye, of Earl's Colne Priory, May he rest in peace. Prithee, dost any of the assembled folk here present have need of knowledge of the work of the Holy Priory and blessed chantry or indeed of anything which might pertain to my life in these parts?"

Everybody stared at her, open-mouthed. For some the hairs on the back of their necks and on their arms stood up. Although they knew it was Clarissa talking, it didn't sound anything like her. It sounded like a voice a long way away, as if it was coming from down a drainpipe. No one said anything. After what seemed an eternity to most, but which was in fact about a minute, Maureen, in a quavering voice that was half whisper, hesitantly said, "Father Anselm, thank you so much for coming. May I ask, can you tell me a bit about your life?"

"Why, of course, my lady Maureen. My mother was a poor scullery maid and she worked in the kitchens for a truly wicked man. He was Lord of the Manor of Great

Barstow, not far from here. Anyway, this wicked man took advantage of my mother, and she was got with child. That was me. Once her condition was obvious, she was cast out to fend for herself and to wander the lanes and byways. I do not know the circumstances of my birth, but my mother died soon after and, according to the priest who found me lying in the fields, I was brought up by the monks at the priory along with some other orphans, and they taught me my letters and the scriptures and so it was I became a Holy Priest."

"Oh, you poor thing!" sighed Maureen

"No, madam, I was blessed. I was brought up a true Christian to do God's work. There can be no better calling than that!"

And then there followed a string of questions from other people in the small audience such as, "When was the chantry finished?" to which the answer came, "It was finished two years after the death of Abbott Geoffroye, God rest his soul," and "Did you manage to carry out all the holy masses that had been commissioned?" "Why, yes of course," and so forth. All the while Father Anselm's accent wavered somewhere between BBC-standard-rustic-medieval and the sort of deep-base-and-breathy voice that one hears in trailers for horror films.

Everybody seemed to be completely in thrall to the proceedings and didn't really notice that all the answers were rather vague and lacking in any great detail. Or if they did doubt the veracity of the clairvoyant, then their sense of English politeness prevented them from saying so.

Don and Maureen, had not sat down but had hovered

at the back and now clung to each other, believing it all. In fact, Maureen was so overcome by the whole event that she could not help but quietly weep with joy and she had to keep wiping her tears and quietly blowing her nose on a little hanky which became completely sodden.

Then, as suddenly as she had started, Clarissa came out of the trance. Her head shot up and she opened her eyes, putting her free hand to her forehead in a classicly dramatic pose of thoughtfulness. Her other hand was still holding her cigarette, which had gone out and which had showered the sleeping dog and some of the carpet with more ash. The whole performance had lasted no more than five minutes.

Spontaneously there was a small ripple of applause from the onlookers. Clarissa blinked and shielded her eyes from the light of the reading lamp. Maureen wiped her eyes and smiled through her tears. Don stood behind with his hands on her shoulders. Suddenly, he felt very tired and needed to sit down.

With an air of complete innocence Clarissa asked, "Did anything happen? Did he come?"

Almost everyone murmured affirmatively in unison, so that it sounded like a verbal group hug.

Somebody said, "He sounded so real." Another agreed and said, "It was just like he was in the room with us."

Clarissa smiled weakly and seemed relieved. Then she said, "I'm tired I must go home now. Forgive me, everyone, I must go. "

Maureen said, "Why yes of course. Thank you so much for coming."

Don grunted incoherently, in agreement.

There was a murmur of understanding from the people

and another small ripple of applause. Clarissa struggled to her feet, and without further acknowledging any of the assembled company she grabbed her walking stick and with a snapped command of, "Come on, Trixie!" she moved slowly and painfully towards the door and into the hallway with Trixie close behind. Don followed her out of the room, shutting the lounge door behind them. They were alone in the hallway. He helped her into her coat, and without a word, slipped her a long, fat, brown manila envelope which disappeared instantly into her pocket. Clarissa looked up at him and silently mouthed "Thank you". Don opened the front door and let her out into the street. Her son, Colin, had been waiting all the while in an old brown Ford Cortina parkside outside. When his mother appeared at the opening front door, he ran round to open the passenger door for her and helped her in. He picked up the dog and put it on her lap. With a brief wave to Don he ran back round the car, jumped in and then drove off.

About six weeks later, Clarissa was sitting in her armchair, in her brand new, plastic customised "Heritage" conservatory with stained glass panels and ceiling vents, watching the birds skittering around outside on the feeders that Colin had hung up for her. The radio was burbling quietly in the background and Colin had made her a cup of tea before he had gone out to the football match. She had just stubbed her cigarette out and Trixie was asleep at her feet. *Damn and blast*, she thought. He had forgotten to bring out the custard creams. Suddenly she felt a strange, overwhelming surging feeling in her head, then there was a very bright light, right in her face.

She thought she could hear heavenly choirs singing and then everything went very dark and she had this weird sensation of falling backwards into a deep, black void.

Colin found her, stone cold, some hours later, when he came round to take Trixie out for her walk. When he had arrived, Trixie had been whining in the hallway and he immediately knew something was up. He went straight to the conservatory. Clarissa's head had flopped back onto the floral headrest on the rattan chair and she had a strangely quizzical look on her face. Her eyes were wide open and so was her mouth. It was exactly as if she was about to say something.

At that very same moment, some miles away, Maureen, was wearing just her apron and her pink fluffy slippers as usual. She was peeling some home-grown carrots for supper, and looking forward to next Friday when she and Don were going away on holiday. They were going to the Sunnyside Naturist Holiday Camp down in Hampshire, as they did every year, for a whole fortnight. As she did so she looked down on to the chopping board and gasped. The peelings had randomly fallen into the shape of two capital letters. They were plain to see. The letters F and A lay clearly in front of her.

"Oh my God! It's sweet old FA! Father Anselm! Would you believe it, he's here. He's here!" she said quietly to herself.

A moment later, Don who had been finishing off in the garden, arrived at the open kitchen door with just his gardening hat on and wearing his old wellington boots.

"Any chance of a cup of tea, love?" he asked.

Where have I come from?
Where am I going? Is this it?

Since waking that morning, they had spent the day indoors. They hadn't had to go out for anything. They could do that at their time of life. Enjoying the fact that it was better to stay in the warm than to go out into the sleet and snow of a grey overcast day and risk falling over on the icy paths, was one of life's little pleasures. It had snowed on and off for the last three days and sometime in the afternoon on this particular day, he had looked at her and she had looked at him and they decided mutually, telepathically almost, that they really ought to make the effort and go out and get some exercise and fresh air. It would be dark in a couple of hours, so if they wanted to have a decent walk then they ought to go soon. Right away, in fact. Now, even.

They quickly and half-heartedly tidied away the clutter of the morning, the breakfast things, the pile of ironing, the books and the newspaper with the unfinished crossword. Before putting on hats, scarves, gloves, jackets, waterproof trousers, thick socks and walking boots with an extra sweater under the jackets, they both remembered to have a pee. There's nothing worse than getting all dressed up and then to have to get all unbuttoned again. She took a bottle of water and her puffer; he took a bag of wine-gums and his phone, just in case.

When they left the house it had stopped snowing. There was not a breath of wind and the cloud cover was low. Everything was beautifully still, with hardly any traffic about and few people. They set off in a direction which they don't normally take, just to make a difference and they headed off gingerly down the hill through the town. Some of the pavements had been salted and cleared, others hadn't and these were covered in a lumpy layer of hard compacted snow that was icy and very slippery.

Going up the hill on the other side of the town, and getting a bit breathless, they stood and rested a while. Before them was an eighties housing development: rows of redbrick terraced houses with minimal front gardens and little or no hedges and shrubs. They moved carefully through a network of litter-strewn and dog-fouled paths with high wooden fences giving only brief glimpses as to what lay behind them; just gardens buried under snow, some sheds and dustbins. They crossed unsalted roads hoping that there was a footpath somewhere that would get them out to open country, but it had been a year or more since they had been this way. They passed cul-de-sacs with trampled,muddy patches of grass in between, with the occasional brightly-coloured tricycle or plastic toy wheelbarrow, abandoned or forgotten, lying on its side because no one was about. In one garden stood a broken trampoline with a foot or more of snow on it forming a strange white cake-like sculpture. Parked cars were everywhere, covered in more snow, empty, dark and abandoned for the duration of the snowy weather, no doubt. Occasional glimpses at passing houses showed that almost everyone, or so it might have seemed, was sitting in overheated living rooms on large leather settees with steamed up windows. Most curtains were half closed and large areas of glass were streaming with condensation. The inhabitants had probably been holed up there all day. There was one family watching a game show on a wide screen television while they ate their chicken nuggets and fries and sucked on cartons of chocolate milk. The voices on the television were muffled by the large tightly-closed window.

Leaving the houses behind and crossing another bit of muddy grass, they saw the small signpost leaning dramatically , indicating the footpath leading off through a gap in the fence. Crossing through the straggly hawthorns and emerging on the other side, it was as if they were entering another world. Before them lay two vast, silent, snow-covered fields divided by a straight path. Only a few walkers had used it that day; they could see that there were not many footprints in the snow. The fields were untouched areas of silent pristine snow under a lowering sky. Way in the distance to where the path was taking them, there were blackened spidery outlines of naked, bare trees. Beyond them indistinct and darkened shapes suggested thick woodland, and way beyond that, in the gaps, were more snow-covered fields disappearing into an indigo-tinted mist. The late afternoon light was fading, and the temperature was falling slowly.

Quite suddenly they were immediately aware of a loud twittering, clattering and tinkling cacophony coming from the large hawthorn bush that followed the line of the path across the field. They stood and listened in awe; hundreds, possibly thousands, of small birds had returned to their traditional roosting spot. They were all completely out of sight within the enormous hedgerow. Were they sparrows or starlings? It was hard to say. Were they just clamouring for space, to assert their territorial rights amongst each other? Or were they gossiping and telling those who bothered to listen about their day; how they had survived being chased by a cat, or had had stones thrown at them, or how they had found a well-stocked bird table complete with seeds, nuts and bacon rind. Or were they just pleased to see each other and rejoicing in each others' company, huddling together for warmth and security through the long, dark, cold night ahead?

They left the birds to settle.

As they trudged on up the path, careful where they put their feet, they were aware that it was in a direct line to the nearby village; the distant church spire was the thing to aim for. And they talked and wondered how long the path had been here; centuries possibly, being the only route for the workers – men, women and children – to get to the town's mill, to work the long hours before returning in the dark to their village. And there would have been people coming to town for the markets, to visit friends, to meet a lover or to visit a sick or dying relative. This would all have happened over centuries perhaps. Hundreds and hundreds of footprints, an endless stream of them over the years. The path was so muddy and wet. And as it followed a ditch, which separated the two large fields, it was more important than ever not to lose one's footing and fall in to the muddy and freezing water at the bottom. As they walked they could see across the surrounding snow the footprints of all the birds and other animals that had been this way; the tracks of creatures desperately looking for food to survive this unforgiving weather.

It reminded them of a walk that they had taken the other day, up by the rabbit warrens above the water meadows on the other side of the town. They had walked through thick snow and the watery afternoon sun was low in the sky and they had noticed in several places where there were small patches of pink. They had realised that it was evidence of a mortal struggle for survival. Miraculously they had seen the delicate ghostly imprint of the owl's wings in the snow on either side where it had landed, talons extended to snatch its prey, before it could run to the safety of its burrow. Across the warren they had seen several of these sets of imprints of wings, as delicate as the wings of angels. These particular "angels" had brought instant death with their sharp talons and beaks. And there was something so magical and ethereal about these marks, and yes, they were beautiful even though they were made at the moment of a painful yet mercifully quick slaughter.

The light wasn't the same here. It was too overcast for any setting sun. Suddenly, the stillness was broken. They could hear voices in the distance. They could just make out a couple of figures coming the other way towards them. They had dogs with them which were running about, back and forth, relishing the freedom, the sense

224

of space and the excitement of the snow. The two women were talking about their day, about their work, and not really watching the dogs. Suddenly, the dogs saw the couple and started to run towards them. Their owners called out for them to come back, but they ignored them and continued running. Their tails were wagging and they were friendly and they greeted the couple like long-lost friends; they jumped up and put muddy paw prints on their jackets, but the couple didn't mind and they welcomed the dogs as if they were their own, rubbing their ears and patting them. The owners shouted impotently for the dogs to get down and to return to them. The dogs continued to ignore their cries and ran in circles round the couple, who laughed and clapped and spoke kindly to them and gradually their owners got nearer and the dogs became a fraction more obedient. The women, after much dancing about and laughing and apologising, put leads on them. One of the dogs then ran round and round its owner and her legs became bound together and she was in danger of falling over. Her friend, laughing, grabbed her and then the dog, knowing full well what it was doing, turned round and ran back round its victim and unbound her. Everybody sighed with relief and they laughed and apologised again; they moved off down the muddy track, the dogs bouncing around their rightful owners, and they were soon swallowed up in the murk of the distance.

By this time the couple had reached a muddy ditch and it seemed as good a place as any to turn back for the light was fading fast. And anyway, a quick calculation of the effort needed to get across the yawning gap without slipping and the risk of landing in the freezing churned-up mud at the bottom of the ditch was too great. They were getting cold and the mists were coming up from the valley and threatening to envelop them. So they turned round and retraced their steps back along the slippery paths that followed the hedges and ditches which bordered the field.

When they passed the hedge where all the roosting birds had been chattering, all was now quiet. The sun, what there was of it, had gone behind the darkening trees in the west and night was falling. With some sense of relief they slithered out of the field and were back in the estate. Walking along the pavement, they noticed a small snowman, no more than two or three feet high, a yard or so from the path up ahead. They hadn't seen it earlier, but now it attracted their attention for some reason. It had been crudely made, and yet, unwittingly, whoever had made it – probably a young child with the help of a parent or sibling, perhaps – had produced an object of some extreme poignancy, or at least that is how it seemed at the time. The little squat legless figure with two spindly twigs for arms hanging down either side, seemed to be leaning slightly backwards, his head tilted so that he could look up to the darkening turquoise sky trying to ignore the orange glow of a streetlamp nearby. His piercing eyes were mere stones pressed in to the upper part of his face. His nose was just a stubby carrot and his sad downturned mouth which had been made with a curved twig, gave him such an air of sadness and bitterness. He looked as if he had lost everything; he was searching for something, somewhere up in the sky.

226

Was he staring back at the beautiful place that he had come from? Could he be trying to get just one glimpse of his ancestral home? Did he yearn to return to its empty spaces? Down here he was surrounded by muddy trampled snow and dirty slushy roads, with plastic toys abandoned, bits of litter and dog mess. And he was alone, no one else was around, no one cared; everyone had gone into their houses and shut the door and he was forgotten. Only by looking up to the vastness of the darkening sky could he feel any sense of hope. But is this it? Yes ,this is it. After all, that's where he had come from, with no possibility of returning. It was all as it was meant to be. Matters completely beyond his control. He would not be here in a day or two, but did he know that? He probably guessed. He was going to melt and the water would trickle back down into the ground and into the river, And was it not too fanciful might one wonder, to think that once in the river it could all make its way to the sea out to the ocean and then be sucked up again into the beautiful sky, together? Yes, of course it was. Really? The millions of water droplets would be scattered in every direction and would never, could never, ever, ever be reunited again… Get over it. This is your time, your one moment and that's it. There's nothing you can do about it. Nothing at all. You have to make do with now. At least you became a snowman, some of your cousins had salt thrown on them the minute they landed and God knows where they will end up. Others are just lying about doing nothing, or causing accidents. You've been an actual snowman! You were photographed with the little girl and her Dad. He only got out of prison two days ago and he's promising to go straight. The photograph of him and his little girl and you the snowman which they made together which will sit on his mantelpiece, will remind him of that. You've done really well, you have, not everyone can say that. Looking back up into the sky with self-pity might give you some kind of bittersweet pleasure, but in the end, it won't achieve anything.

"Your table's over here"

"What a lovely view," one of them murmured, as they stood hesitating in the entrance to the busy dining room. The group of three adults were wondering where to sit.

A smiling waitress looked up from what she was doing at the sideboard and putting down a handful of cutlery, she approached them.

"Hello," said David and his wife Geraldine in unison. Then, Geraldine said, "We are staying in room 220."

"Ah, yes. Good evening. Your table's over here."

There was the strong hint of an East European accent from Reina, the waitress with pale skin, tired eyes and bright red lipstick. Walking sideways, with one hand forward and the other behind her in the manner of an ancient Egyptian and smiling simultaneously, she led the three of them to their table.

"Here it is, it's number five. You can see everything from here." She pulled back the chair to give its occupant the best view. She indicated, by just looking at her and forcing a smile, that it was for Jean, the oldest of the group, who, having handed her walking stick to her daughter, sat down gratefully on its slightly sagging upholstered seat. The waitress, smiling all the while, then tried and failed to push the chair and its occupant nearer to the table. Giving up on that and leaning forward, with one arm either side of Jean, she shuffled the whole table itself nearer, causing the cutlery to clink and the glassware to wobble ominously. The other two in the party, Geraldine and David, her daughter and son-in-law, had sat down and now looked about themselves, feeling very relaxed and noticing that, in terms of the view, they really did have one of the best tables in the restaurant. They felt very pleased. Jean, from her side of the table, just looked straight ahead and Geraldine only had to turn her head to the right, but David, with his back to the view, just joined in with the murmurings of agreement that there was no doubt that it was truly lovely.

David and Geraldine had brought Jean, a sprightly eighty-seven-year-old widow, to the hotel for a short break, and they had had a long drive. Now they were here at last. The view from the big window was truly spectacular; it encompassed the wide sweep of the bay with, on the left hand or southern side, a huge rocky headland, which provided shelter from the worst of the English Channel's weather. On the right-hand or north-eastern side, you could see down into the village, which consisted of a slipway leading up to a terrace of small, brightly painted houses and a scattering of thatched cottages and a central village square. This was framed by yet another bay beyond and a high line of rocky cliffs that faded into the misty distance where it was possible to see Cornwall on a clear day, or so said the locals.

From where they sat, mother and daughter could not help but be drawn to the view. Someone remarked on the sunset. David twisted round in his seat. There was hardly a breath of wind; the surface of the water was flat and calm. The sun, a fiery orange ball, was setting and was just about touching the horizon. It was dazzling to look at and strong shafts of bright, white light powered into the dining room and lit up everything with the power of a searchlight. As they watched, mesmerised, it had began to dip behind the horizon. Someone at a nearby table started talking about the phenomenon of the green flash that would appear for a very brief moment as the sun disappeared below the horizon. The man added that it was not easy to stare directly at the sun because of the glare and also to do so was potentially very dangerous.

"Would you like to see ze menu?" said the young waiter, interrupting their thoughts. Pierre was a pallid, shy young man, who spent most of the time looking at the floor. He had suddenly appeared beside them as if from thin air. He was flourishing a clutch of green, leather-bound menus embossed with the word 'Menu' in gold lettering on the front of each. And without waiting for a reply, he handed one to each of the guests, two of whom were momentarily blinded by the bright light from the sun and were blinking their eyes and trying to focus. As he turned to escape to allow the guests to make their choices, David asked to see the wine list.

"I will get ze wine waiter to come to you." And with that he disappeared through the swing doors into the kitchens with a bap-bap-bap of rubber on wood. For this was silver service, and everyone had their allotted roles; the wine waiter or sommelier would deal with the wine, and would, of course, come as soon as he possibly could.

From out of the kitchens, another waitress, Anna, appeared with a basket of bread rolls. After asking who would like one, she nervously but dextrously served them using a spoon and a fork as tongs, held crablike in one hand. "White or brown?"

The decor of the long, aisled restaurant was typical of the hotel style of forty, fifty or even more years ago. It was comfortably familiar with its well worn patterned carpets, mirrored alcoves with dried-flower arrangements, pastel-coloured curtains and wallpaper. The layout of the room consisted of two long rows of tables for two, four or six diners. The row of better tables, allocated to the sea-view rooms with balconies had the advantage of being by the windows. Each table was laid with a full range of the usual paraphernalia: traditional hotel "silver" cutlery, glasses, condiments, a small arrangement of flowers and such like. Most of the diners talked in hushed tones with each other, discussing their day and what they had done, their plans for the next day and so forth. Some who were with those who were hard of hearing had to raise their voices above the general hubbub. "What did you say, dear? Can't hear a word," and "Would you like the soup or the fish, dear? You won't want any of the meat dishes, remember your indigestion."

Others sat in thoughtful or watchful silence, a bit like lizards, eyes either immobile, blank and staring or darting from side to side in panic or complete misunderstanding. The only other voices that could be heard clearly were those of the ever cheerful sommelier "working the room" with bonhomie and his well worn jokes and that of the well-built Czech waitress in charge of the sweet trolley. The majority of the clientele were mainly retired folk chattering happily, aimlessly or even mindlessly. Some couples were eating silently opposite one another, each lost in their own miasma of memories and regret or, who knew, even loathing and spite, or they were concerned and caring middle-aged sons and daughters taking their elderly parents on holiday, for the sea air and a change of scene. There were also some younger couples, bringing complete sets of grandparents and children for a "family holiday by the sea", who were determined to have a good time, come what may and would bury any feelings of resentment at the imposition and plain dislike of each other out of consideration for the greater good. One such family was trying to get organised for their journey home. Having had supper, the children were running up and down the dining room and going in and out of the sitting room pretending to be dive bombers, while one set of grandparents were trying to round the children up, without much success. The other set of grandparents, confused, didn't really know what to do, so were waiting by the door as the bossy daughter came to collect everyone together and who was obviously annoyed, "Come along you lot. Jeremy's got the car by the door, he's blocking someone who is trying to get out so we must hurry!" She looked at Malcolm and Astrid, the confused couple, her in-laws and sighed, "Do come along!" and as they turned to go, sotto voce she murmured, "Get a bloody move on, why don't you!"

At table four, a couple from Derbyshire, determined to get their money's worth, had had their starter; they had both chosen the pâté, which consisted of two thick slices of liver pâté, one chicken and one duck, resting one on top of the other like two paperback books, on a rocket and herb salad, drizzled with a balsamic vinegar and French mustard dressing. They had also had the locally-made lemon sorbet (described vicariously as a palette cleanser as if the palette was somehow dirty) and were now purposefully working their way through the roast loin of pork, with sage stuffing, apple sauce and rich gravy with aromatic herbs including rosemary and thyme, with an assortment of fresh vegetables and roast potatoes, locally grown of course. He was a semi-retired tenant farmer, with large hands and a weather-beaten face. He had left the dairy farm in the hands of his somewhat worrying son, about whose abilities to run it in his absence he had serious doubts. He was constantly anxious, and had visions of returning to a farm in chaos. His dutiful wife sitting opposite him, with her own worries about her weight and trapped wind, was having problems with the heat in the room, which seemed to envelope her. She frequently mopped her forehead and upper lip with her napkin and constantly pulled at her jumper, which clung to her body uncomfortably, especially where it creased round her bulging midriff. She said to herself, more than to her husband who wasn't listening anyway, "I think I ought to finish with the crème caramel, but I do so like the chocolate brownies!" And then she quietly belched behind her hand.

Across the way, a foursome of two couples from the Midlands were eating their lemon sorbets, the second course and palette cleanser, which were made locally. As the two perma-tanned women, one in a frock of electric blue and turquoise splodges on a white background, the other in a bright orange blouse and leopard-skin leggings, listened, feigning interest and understanding to their husbands loudly discussing the game of golf which they had enjoyed that afternoon out on the links in the neighbouring bay. The two men, also perfectly tanned, Barry and Clive, were business partners in a chain of sports shops, which specialised in golfing equipment back in Solihull. Whether it was playing golf together or running the business, they were always fiercely competitive. Always looking to "get one over the other". Their wives, with dyed bouffant hair and heavily made up, who were also good friends, just let them get on with it and as occasion required rolled their eyes, giggled or ooh-hed and aah-hed appropriately and flashed their manicured nails dramatically for effect. They had enjoyed their retail therapy in Plymouth that day and "had splashed the cash" on stuff for themselves as they would happily tell their husbands later when the time was right. Today they had found some gorgeous costume jewellery made from a purple semi-precious stone just like the ones they had seen on the shopping channel on TV and some amazing beachwear printed with bright geometric patterns and designed by someone with an unpronounceable name.

"You should have chosen a number nine iron on the fourteenth, Baz. The ball wouldn't have ended up in the pond. Things could have turned out quite differently for you. I did warn you, but you wouldn't listen." Baz, or Barry as he preferred to be called, smiled weakly and sipped his warming lager through gritted teeth. Clive looked past him and couldn't help but notice the size of the waitress's backside, with her black skirt stretched to its absolute limit as she bent down to pick up someone's napkin that had fallen from another table.

"Get a load of that. You wouldn't get many of them to the pound!" he muttered under his breath. His wife, who had noticed everything, flicked at him with her napkin coquettishly, but with unsmiling eyes.

"Clive! What are you like?" she hissed.

"Oh, that's all right," said Barry weakly, who hadn't heard what Clive had said, and was unaware of the waitress bending down. "He doesn't get to me. It's only because he knows I've won more games than him."

By one of the mirrored alcoves, Helen was sitting opposite her ninety-year-old widowed mother, Georgina, Lady Barford, whose head hung so low it looked as if her chin was going to dip into the soup-of-the-day at any minute. They had been coming to this same hotel on and off every summer since the 1950s. Lady Barford's husband, an impecunious baronet, had died of a heart attack, some twenty years ago, and yet still they came. Helen, their only child, had never married and so Lady Barford had long ago resigned herself to not having any grandchildren. Helen lived with her partner, Mary, in West Hampstead; they were both retired PE Teachers and kept five cats. Mary conveniently used the cats as a pretext to stay at home for these regular trips to the south west. They were so particular in their needs and didn't take kindly to strangers, she always said. Lady Barford didn't mind and was secretly relieved. She had taken many years to accept her daughter's choice of life partner, and had always found conversation with Mary difficult, anyway.

"Are you enjoying your soup-of-the-day, mother?" asked Helen, trying to sound caring and interested.

"Wha-a-at?" asked Lady Barford, staring at her blurred

daughter. She had momentarily forgotten where she was and she had left her glasses in her room.

"I said, are you enjoying your soup?" repeated Helen, this time trying not to sound annoyed.

"No I don't want any fruit, dear," said Lady Barford.

Helen gave up and smiled at her mother, who shakily scooped up another spoonful of silty sage-green soup and sucked it into her mouth, wondering why they were here.

***

"Would you like to see the wine list, sir?" asked the cheery wine waiter, and opening it at the front page, he thrust it enthusiastically at David.

"I'll be back in a minute for your order, sir. Is everything alright so far? Have you settled in to your rooms, sir?" Barely waiting for an answer, he turned and immediately went across the aisle, to table number 7, to help an old man who was trying to stand up, but who looked as if he was about to fall over at any minute and pull the tablecloth with him as his poor wife looked on helplessly. Gently guiding him by his forearm, he asked, "Now, sir, are we going to the lounge for coffee?"

"No! I'm off for a bloody leak!" came the honest and blunt reply, as he tried to wrench his arm free from the helpful embrace of mein host.

The man's stoical, straight-backed wife, who had been helplessly watching her husband and who was sitting, resigned and patient, at their table, looked utterly exhausted. "I'm so sorry," she said. But the sommelier had moved off.

The sweet trolley had arrived at the table of the tenant farmer and his wife. With practised enthusiasm and with a flourish of her hands in showgirl fashion, as if introducing a magician pulling a rabbit out of a hat, she recited her oft repeated lines.

"Good evening, sir and madam. Would you like to make selection from the sweet trolley?" She paused for dramatic effect and continued, "Here is the chocolate gateau, we also have the toffee caramel cheesecake, the strawberries and vipped cream in meringue nests, the summer pooding, the strawberry cheesecake, the crème caramel and finally, everyone's favourite, the choc-o-late brownies." She paused to take a breath and tried to look pleasant. "We also have the selection of the cheeses and the biscuits, if you are wishing it, some." At the end of the recitation she stood demurely, with her hands clasped together and a fixed smile on her face, waiting for choices to be made as her guests marvelled and pointed hesitantly at the display set out artfully on the heavy mahogany trolley.

The farmer chose toffee caramel cheesecake, something sweet and filling, comfort food to end the meal. Throwing caution to the wind and not to be outdone, so did his wife. What her husband was thinking was difficult to tell. He hadn't told her that that morning he had phoned their son to be told that three of his prize herd of Friesians had mastitis. He didn't want to worry her. She would regret her choice later, but by then it would be too late. She would have chronic indigestion, terrible trapped wind and yet another sleepless night.

Pierre, the waiter, re-appeared at table number five and

took the order for the meal. Geraldine chose to start with the chickpea fritter and mango chutney, and to follow she opted for the mild lamb curry with the cumin flavoured rice. David decided to start with the locally caught sardines on a bed of cucumber and red onion salad and chose to follow with the locally caught plaice. Jean chose to forego any starter and picked the roast loin of pork and asked that it be served with the others' starters, as she was a slow eater and didn't want to hold everyone up.

The cheery wine waiter followed on closely behind and the wine was ordered. When he delivered the bottle and showed David the label, he deftly unscrewed the cap and poured out a small amount to be tasted. Once this was done, he produced a chit of paper.

"And now, sir, I need your autograph for my collection," he grinned triumphantly, and David duly signed it.

Pierre the waiter arrived and changed David's place setting; removing the knives and forks and replacing them with fish knives and forks.

The meal arrived and was efficiently served. It was good, unfussy, home-cooked fare. They ate in happy silence with the occasional appreciative comment. They all declined the sorbet course and eventually, Magda arrived with the dessert trolley.

Almost word for word she repeated her now familiar announcement, "Good evening, sir and madams, would you like to make the selections from the sweet trolley? Here is the chocolate gateau, we also have the toffee caramel cheesecake, the strawberries and vipped cream in meringue nests, the summer pooding, the strawberry cheesecake, the crèmes caramels and finally everyone's favourite, the choc-o-late brownies." She giggled nervously, "Also, we have the cream or the crème fraiche as accompaniments. We also have the cheeses and the biscuits, if you are wishing it, them, it."

***

Sometime later, feeling replete, most of the guests were sitting comfortably in the lounge, where they had gone for their coffee. This was a large wood panelled room with clusters of armchairs and sofas in a variety of styles and upholstered in various flocks and brocades and varying colours of fabrics and chintz arranged around different shaped coffee tables. There were artificial coal-effect fires in each of the two redbrick, Art Deco fireplaces. Bizarrely the fires looked just like piles of clear plastic blocks masquerading as large ice cubes under-lit by watery pink and orange lights.

As they relaxed in their burnt-orange velveteen armchairs they chatted quietly about their day and what they had done. The waiter arrived with their order of two coffees and one Earl Grey tea.

"Have you had a good day?" he asked solicitously.

"Lovely, thank you. We have and we have been very lucky with the weather," replied Jean. Geraldine and David murmured their agreement

"That is good," replied the waiter. "Last week it rained all week, dogs and cats." And, having set everything out on the table, he went off to see to the other guests.

"I think that tomorrow we'll go to Dartmouth," said David. " You'll like that. It's at the mouth of the estuary,

240

where the river Dart reaches the sea, and Geraldine has found out that there is a nautical museum there, which specialises in ships in bottles. We could go there, and perhaps find somewhere nice for lunch."

"That would be lovely!" said Jean, wishing that she could have just one cigarette.

Ultramarine (Oltramarinos)

1.adj. Situated beyond the sea.
2.n. Blue pigment got from lapis lazuli.

He picked up the small parcel which was made up from a piece of thick, folded, hand-made paper that was tied up with some brown hempen string. Written across it on the top fold, it read '*Lapis Lazuli for JMWT from JMWM 1795*' in a shaky, inky scrawl. He weighed it in his hands and marvelled at what he had been given; he also felt a bit daunted at what he was going to do with it. Setting the small packet on the table, he carefully untied the simple knot that was holding it together and for a moment gazed in awe at the contents. It was a handful of small pieces of broken rock, lumps of a mysterious blue stone. They looked like broken bits of marble and they twinkled as they caught the morning sunlight pouring through the grimy window of the workshop. Looking closer he noticed that each piece of rock was veined with white and gold streaks of coloured crystals. He had been told that the Italians of the Renaissance had called it '*oltramarinos*', meaning 'beyond the seas', and the name alluded to the fact that it came from a place of mystery on the other side of the oceans, on the other side of the world. It was just so mysterious and for a moment it made him catch his breath. Was it not too fanciful to think that they looked just like tiny pieces of an actual dark blue sky that by some chance had fallen from the heavens and he had caught them in his hands? He also knew that this lapis lazuli was very precious and more expensive than gold. It had been a very generous present to him from his dear old uncle, Joseph Marshall who was a baker and his erstwhile guardian. He had mentioned to him that he needed to make some quantities of blue paint for his first submission of an oil painting to the Royal Academy; up until this moment he had only ever exhibited watercolour paintings in the Summer Exhibitions during his time at the Academy Schools there. Watercolour was a cheaper and some would foolishly say an easier medium to use than oil paints. He wanted to challenge himself and planned to paint a night sky over water. But where would he find it? The trouble also was that good quality blue pigment was so expensive. His uncle Joseph had then gone and ordered him some. He could only wonder at how many dozens of currant buns or loaves of bread that he had had to sell to pay for it.

He let his mind wander, knowing that these small, exquisite pieces of blue rock had been carried all the way from the wild mountainous regions of a far distant country beyond the Persian Empire. The valuable cargo would have been transported by donkey and then camel caravan, hidden amongst other cheaper goods, travelling westwards on ancient tracks for many days. Sometimes the merchants would, of necessity have to navigate by night across remote deserts and over unnamed mountains using the stars to guide them, possibly along the famed Silk Road itself. Changing hands many times and with some luck, it would eventually have arrived in Constantinople to be bartered for again with traders from the West; then carried on by ship across the Mediterranean, perhaps to Genoa. From there it would be hauled by packhorse over the Alps to northern France and finally by the packet boat to the dealers in London. Its journey would have taken anything up to two or three years. His uncle had proudly bought it for him from a business friend, who had trading interests in the Far East. And now he actually held it in his hands. What good fortune was that? He was now impatient to begin his project. He knew that first it needed to be turned into a fine powder; he would take it this very day to the old colourman in Cheapside who would use his skills to prepare it for him so that he could at last make up his precious ultramarine paint.

***

Some weeks earlier, in early March, he had gone to the Isle of Wight to paint and draw his favourite subject matter : the sea and the sky in all its manifestations. He had gone with some fellow students from the Academy Schools where he was studying; they had just wanted to drink and carouse with the locals. He had not produced anything worthwhile. This time he had gone on his own. He had needed to concentrate in order to prepare for his submission for the Royal Academy's annual exhibition. On the first night, asleep in his lodging house, he had been woken while it was still dark by the gusting wind rattling the windows. He could then not get back to sleep. He had restlessly tossed and turned on the uncomfortable, lumpy bed, worrying about his current plans for the painting and not knowing where to start. It was a full moon and it seemed too bright to be able to sleep. As he lay there listening to the wind, he heard the church clock chime twice. His mind was full of ideas for what to do, but so many different ideas were all muddled up that he couldn't think clearly. So he had got up, shivering in his nightgown, and he had gone to the window and had held back the flimsy curtain to look out at the churning sea. He was both amazed and delighted by what he had seen. Dark, almost black clouds were scudding across the sky. Every so often they broke up just long enough for him to see the moon shining so very brightly and bathing everything in its gaze with a ghostly yellow pallor; then they closed up again and all was dark and indistinguishable once more. The clouds would then part again and immediately below them the surface of the sea shone like the brightest polished silver. Wrapping himself in a blanket and settling into a chair with his sketchbook open on his lap, he set to work. He grabbed chalks and charcoal and made some preliminary sketches of the way the light appeared to dominate the scene. It was only once he had started that he noticed two small fishing vessels way out in the bay being tossed about by the choppy seas. They were drifters, joined together by a trawl net and struggling with the elements. Who were they and why were they fishing so late at night, and in such terrible conditions? He watched as the weather deteriorated and the wind seemed to throw the boats about just like toys on a child's blanket. He could just make out the small figures crouching on the decking of the nearer boat. They were huddled round a lantern and he could see its warm glow amongst them, but they were too far away to see any detail. The comforting light of the lantern contrasted so dramatically with the cold harsh light from the moon. Two other figures in the boat seemed to be keeping an eye on the net as the boat rolled about, and yet it seemed that at any moment the boat might founder and that they would all be swept to their doom. The other boat was further away and he could only just make out its presence; he saw no light on board except for the reflected light from the moon. So insignificant were the figures in such tiny boats against the vastness of the roiling seas and sky that he had suddenly and inexplicably felt moved to witness such a thing. *What brave souls!* He thought. *They are driven to this, because of their povery just to catch fish for somebody's supper*! Man's epic struggle to survive in the vastness of creation was revealed in this simple but dramatic scene. And then it came to him, he realised that this would make a wonderful subject for an oil painting for the Summer Exhibition. After a few more glimpses, the clouds closed up and any more light on the scene was obliterated. But then as he watched they broke apart again, just like curtains being pulled away on a stage. Thus he spent the rest of the night making more drawings of the scene when the light allowed and from memory when it was dark; eventually he must have fallen asleep in the chair. He awoke as the dawn broke, and was disappointed, but not surprised, to see that the little boats had gone. Drawings and chalks fell from his lap and he had a terribly stiff neck. The bay seemed so empty without the boats and the fisher folk. But then he thought how selfish he was to think such a thing; they had toiled all night in very difficult circumstances and he was so much warmer in his room. The patchy early morning sunlight played on the powerful sea, which was a mass of greys and blues and ochres, as the big waves crashed in a slow ponderous rhythm on the shore below.

After a quick breakfast of tea and bread, he gathered up his sketching things, and wearing his thick coat and muffler he struggled against the wind as he walked along the shoreline. He had decided to go to the place where he knew that all the fishing boats would be dragged up on to the beach. Last night's storm was all but abated, but the wind was keen and the sea, even now, was very choppy. Bent to the wind, he nearly lost his hat a couple of times so he had to keep one hand on his head to stop it from blowing away. His bag of pencils, paints and sketchbooks hung heavily on his shoulder and he was looking forward to setting it down. It wasn't long before he got to the boats. Breathing hard, he stood there and let his eyes just take it all in, but he delighted at what he was witnessing. A few boats had been dragged up onto the beach above the high tide line, but what amazed him was that two other boats were actually trying to go out to sea and were being pushed off by groups of fishermen on the shore. *Why would they do this in such unsettled weather? They must be desperate fellows, in need of a catch.* There was much shouting and calling but from where he was he could not make out a single word. The men were trying to point the boat out to sea and seemed to be waiting for a lull, counting the waves. It was said that every seventh was the biggest, or so tradition would have it. Then he watched aghast as the boat went broadside to a wave and tipped one of its crew out and the poor soul disappeared into the foam. Eager arms bent down to grab him as he emerged, spluttering and cursing everyone and everything. He was hauled back onto the boat, shivering, and was immediately wrapped in an old sail. Eventually both boats got off after a couple more false starts and the men on board rowed them out to where the waves weren't breaking before they each raised their jib sails and reefed their mainsails. They were traditional wooden fishing smacks, of a shape and build that had changed little over the last three or four hundred years, made from English oak, elm or ash or any other timber that they could get hold of. The boats were tough and compact and they could survive most things that the weather threw at them if they were in the hands of experienced sailors. By contrast, the boats on the beach lay like cats asleep in the sun, their blood-red sails had been furled and tied down and their anchors had been pushed into the shingle higher up the beach.

He looked for a vantage point from where he could see, but not too conspicuously. He decided to sit on a lobster pot on the shingle in the lee of one of the bigger boats and where he was sheltered from the wind. For a long time he just sat and watched. He watched how the sky and the clouds gradually changed colour. He noticed how the light played on the boats out in the bay, both near and far, riding the waves like corks from a bottle, and how the circling, screeching gulls flashed white when lit by the sun. After several minutes he took out his sketchbook and began to draw. He made quick studies of the boats on the beach and was fascinated by their structures and complexities and he made sketches of a few of the fishermen who were mending some nets. He drew rapidly as some of the women were sorting and gutting the fish while others in groups or alone were shading their eyes and trying to get a glimpse of their men-folk out at sea. Yet others were just standing around talking while their children and a dog played at the water's edge. He shut his eyes and breathed in the air; he smelt the salt tang of fish and listened to the wind in the rigging as the boat halyards knocked in the wind. He was so engaged that he spent much of the day there and produced several drawings and some quick watercolours, only stopping as the light began to go. At some point during the day two of the fishermen came up to him and quietly watched him as he worked. They muttered quietly, but he could not hear what they were saying. After a while, he turned to the older man and, surprising himself, he expressed a wish to go out on a boat with them to experience what they had to go through and to better understand the nature of their work. At first the old sea-dog hesitated, but then, after some persuasion and a handful of coins he agreed, on one proviso: if the weather was bad, he would be allowed to tie the artist to the mast of the boat for fear of him being swept away. He had little choice but to agree. And so it had happened the next day; he was bundled on to the boat by two of the fishermen and they went off at dawn on the full tide. It was a much calmer day and luckily there was no need to be tied to the mast.

What he saw delighted him and he was dazzled by the brilliance of the light from the rising sun, which bathed everything in gold. As they got out into the Solent it was absolutely spectacular. They spent a full day out fishing round the island and he made many sketches. He was particularly taken with the famous Needles, a line of grey, chalk pinnacles of various sizes that looked exactly like a set of the fearsome, giant teeth of some long dead monster from the deep and he made many drawings of them. When he got back to his lodgings that night he slept like a baby for he was so exhausted.

On his return home he had immediately gone to collect his precious ultramarine, which was ready for him. It had been reduced to a rich blue chalky powder with no sign of the twinkling stars, which was disappointing. Nevertheless, it was a haunting and beautiful colour that seemed to hint at other worlds and places where we as humans could only go in our imagination. Using an old, bent metal spoon he carefully scooped up some of the rich blue powder and formed a small pyramid of it in the centre of the pristine white marble slab on his workbench. Next, he took down a bottle of linseed oil from the shelf above and picked up a palette knife. He pushed down the top of the pyramid with the knife and made a small well in its centre. Taking up the bottle of linseed oil he carefully poured some into the small depression and started to mix it all together with the palette knife. The whiteness of the marble slab dramatically enhanced the strength of colour of the rich ultramarine paint which was forming. Piling the mixture together into a heap, he then took the stone grinder and, pressing down onto the blue sticky paste that was now coming together, he slowly started to grind the mixture together. In doing so, the two ingredients began to form into a rich, smooth syrup with the consistency of warmed honey. In grinding it in a circular figure of eight motion, it spread out on to the marble slab so that every so often he would have to scrape up the mixture and pile it back into the centre again and again. Gradually, the mixture gained a more and more lustrous sheen and he worked the grinder faster so impatient was he to arrive at the perfect finish. All this while his excitement and anticipation grew for the painting with which he was planning to use it. And at the end of the process, when he was happy with the glossy smoothness, he really felt quite tired. Taking up a small, cleaned piglet's bladder and using an old teaspoon he scooped up all the finished paint, spoonful by spoonful, slowly, and with some difficulty, filled the bladder and then closed the opening tightly with some string.

***

Surrounded by a gilded frame with a minimum of ornament upon it, the watery contents of the picture now being carried across the room seemed to actually be moving! One or two of the eminent and not so eminent Academicians of the selection committee, as they watched the painting's progress, were regretting having drunk so much port and eaten too much turbot at the luncheon held in their honour that they had enjoyed earlier. They tried to focus on the images that were emerging from the vigorous dark blue-black brushstrokes on the moving

251

canvas, from which was emerging the moon or 'Luna' as they would have it. The mistress of the tides who hung like a bright jewel in the heavens, was gazing down mysteriously yet benignly on her night's handiwork. She watched as the dark, oily waters far below rose up in iridescent swirls of blue and brown and grey, as if to swallow the two small wooden fishing boats as they bucked and rolled on the ever-moving surface. They were at the mercy of the elements poor souls. The red ochre sails had been furled and, in the nearer boat, some of its tired and bedraggled crew were lightly depicted huddled round the warm comforting glow of a lantern amidships. No such luck for the other boat. A rogue wave must have extinguished the lantern and probably drenched the crew. Their only light was the reflected ghostly glare from the diamond-hard regal moon. She appeared as a small, yet perfectly formed, crystal-delicate sphere of the brightest opalescent light and was surrounded by her attendant clouds, glittering in incandescent white lace. She gazed down coldly – some might say harshly – on the struggling mortals below. Appearing aloof and yet with an air of superior majesty, she watched the developments with great interest. The small boats looked perilously close to a line of jagged rocks, which together looked just like the open jaws of a sea monster where the poor sailors may soon be wrecked and consumed. Unmoved, the moon, in the exquisiteness of her appearance, gave not even the slightest hint of any concern she might have for the poor wretches. Her phenomenal power over the seething dark waters and even the life and death of the miserable wretches toiling below was invisible and absolute. Ironically, however, she struggled impotently to assert herself against the menacing and ever-encroaching soot-black ragged clouds that tried again and again like pestering hands to obliterate and completely smother her radiant influence. In the event they only allowed her to partially illuminate the heaving mass of sea far below for just a few moments, being as they were all and every one – Goddess above and mortals below – at the capricious whim of the Zephyrs of a cold, biting and vengeful northerly wind that rampaged across the heavens.

The two tired porters then rested the painting in its heavy gilded frame on a box for the esteemed gentlemen of the selection committee to study and to adjudicate upon. It was just one more of the many hopeful submissions to the annual exhibition that year. It was a large painting and the porters were grateful to have the box on which to rest it. Someone coughed and then the assembled company went quiet.

"And what have we here?" asked the important-looking gentleman, with just a hint of a colonial accent. For this was Benjamin West originally from America and the revered President of the Royal Academy. He was sitting a few feet away in the gilded presidential throne, upholstered in crimson velvet, facing the painting. He was speaking to no one in particular. He had an air of self-important authority and was sitting up straight-backed. Traditionally and somewhat incongruously he was the only gentleman in the room to be wearing a hat. It was a black bicorne.

"Tis a submission from the young Turner, Mr West. He attends the Academy Schools. It is called, 'Fishermen at

Sea'. It is his first ever oil painting submission," explained the President's secretary, sitting to one side of the gilded chair as he fussily shuffled through his papers.

"Not a very imaginative title, if I may say so," drawled Mr. West.

On seeing the painting, some of the members of the committee had moved nearer towards it and then such a crowd gathered round it that it soon blocked the view of the chairman himself.

"Can't see a damn thing now," he said, standing up. "Make way, gentlemen. It would appear that I need to get closer."

The group, without any of them taking their eyes off the painting, parted like the Red Sea and the President, moving forward, adjusted his monocle and peered closely at the work. As he did so, he could smell the familiar smells of fresh turpentine and oil paint.

"Quite astonishing. Remarkable, don't you think? Such power." he muttered out loud.

The assembled gentlemen mumbled their assent and seemed to be in agreement.

"His control of colour is quite outstanding for someone so young," said a famous society portraitist. "And his sense of movement within the composition is sublime."

"I do so agree with you, Sir Thomas. The light of the moon, it is so cold. The moon itself is so bright; see the warm light of the lantern in the boat on the left? So beautiful!" said Paul Sandby, the landscape artist and sometime map maker. Sir Thomas Lawrence smiled and nodded in agreement.

"It all looks so drenched in sea water," murmured James Barry, a renowned figure painter. "The boy has a real talent. I met him the other day; such an earnest and serious young man and so dedicated to his work. We must accept this for the exhibition."

"Well, let's see," said the President, as he straightened up and looked to left and right. "All those in favour?"

There was a hush and slowly at first, and then more quickly, every single member of the august committee raised a hand.

At this point, the two porters struggled to peer round from behind the painting to see what all the fuss was about.

Murder in the vicarage

The front door banged shut, allowing in a gust of cold January air that made him open his eyes. Martyn lay flat on his back, quite still, with his head awkwardly lolling to his right side and resting on the hard wooden floor. His breathing was quick and shallow. He tried to focus on the parquet tiles, arranged in a herringbone pattern, which spread out like ripples in the sand before him. They had been the first thing he had seen when he had walked into the house just six months ago. He had worried that it all looked a bit too big for a bachelor village priest and he had wondered if he could justify moving in to such a place. He smiled to himself at the memory, yet the features of his face remained unmoved. He could not feel anything distinctly; in parts his body felt numb yet in other places it felt as if it was on fire, particularly his hands and chest and he began to feel very frightened. He tried to move and found that he couldn't and anyway, it made the pain worse. He must have momentarily blacked out. He felt so tired, exhausted even, so it was actually quite comforting to lay there immobile, staring across the hall floor, drifting in and out of – what? A dream? Or was it a nightmare? It all seemed so unreal, but frighteningly real at the same time. He could see the lurid colours of an open magazine. It looked like some kind of pornography; a man's naked body covered the whole page and yet it was splattered with blood, reminding him of that painting by, oh, who was it? The martyrdom of St Sebastian, but where were the arrows? And then he saw – *oh God, no* – there were things scattered all over the floor and what was that? *For pity's sake, God have mercy... I must clear everything up before Mrs Canterbury gets here tomorrow morning. Whatever would she think? When he had rested he would clear all this mess up and chuck it all in the bin.*

He had noticed that something was moving in front of him not two feet away and somehow he knew that it was changing everything. A large dark pool was slowly growing before him. *Just like the tide coming in*, he thought, *across sand*. After all the shouting and the yelling and the pain, it was so peaceful. Now this tide coming in would spoil everything. Just then he heard his sisters' laughter. He shut his eyes. He was playing on the beach with them, oh so many years ago now. Three innocent children splashing about in the shallows: he in his dark blue, itchy woollen bathing trunks, they in their frilly costumes with smocking on the front. They had made a huge sandcastle,with Daddy's help. They had decorated it with seaweed and shells and paper flags and everything. They had watched excitedly as the tide came in. His sisters squealed with excitement as the first little wavelets covered their feet and washed against the castle sides, scooping out the sand from its base . The sand seemed to disappear as if by magic. He furiously shovelled more sand into the breech. "Come on, Sissies," he yelled. "Help me, help me!" But it was no good. Despite their efforts, the sea gradually, inevitably, wore away the castle. Then suddenly, the remaining heap of sand collapsed all at once into the churning waters, leaving the little coloured paper flags with the red dragons on floating away like leaves on a lake in autumn ; the castle was now no more than a memory.

**

A couple of months earlier...

A motley group of men and women of various ages from the village were sitting in armchairs, dining chairs and a sofa in a sort of circle in the priest's sparsely-furnished sitting room. Martyn, for he was the priest, was leading the final read-through of a play that the villagers were going to put on in the church. He had wanted to do something that would bring people together and putting on a play had seemed a good idea.

"Right then." He wanted to draw the meeting to a close. He had been up early that morning and he had an early start tomorrow, it being the week before Christmas, so he knew he was going to be busy, very busy. "You all know who you are now, and I want you to go away and start learning your lines. We start rehearsals in the village hall, on the first Monday after New Year's Day at 7.30. pm sharp. You don't all have to be there. I'm going to work out a timetable for rehearsals and will give you all a copy first thing after Christmas. Are there any pressing questions before we draw the meeting to a close?"

"I know that you are planning to do the play in the church but whereabouts exactly in the building is the play going to be performed?" said the man who was going to be playing the Third Knight.

"Well," said Martyn, patiently, "the church committee has agreed in principle and Sid has said that he would be happy to build it, with some help of course. We are going to be putting up a stage right in the middle of the church, in the transept. It will be a proper stage, three feet off the ground, with wings and scenery and proper lighting. It's going to be wonderful." He pursed his lips and smiled at them. He was feeling rather proud of himself for having got this far with the arrangements. There was an audible gasp from the group and murmurings of "wow" and the man who was going to play Thomas said, "Really? That's amazing," but he couldn't quite visualise it.

Christmas came and went. Rehearsals began, some lines were learnt, and costumes were thought of, designed and made up or adapted from clothes bought in charity shops. Props were scavenged; a bishop's mitre was made from good quality cardboard. Scenery was designed, built and painted. The wooden stage, which had gradually emerged in the centre of the church, dominated everything. To build it Sid had acquired a mass of timber of all shapes and sizes from a friend in the timber trade who wanted shot of it. It was all off-cuts and cancelled orders, but it did the job.

***

A couple of weeks later...

"I've managed to borrow some armour from a friend of mine at the National. Could a couple of you come and help me unload it from the car?" said Martyn, breathlessly. The Bishop of Canterbury, four knights and several priests had been waiting for Martyn in the pews of the chilly and badly lit church, staring at the half-built stage and talking quietly. As they had talked, their breath had formed clouds of vapour. They had all turned in unison as the huge, ancient door had opened noisily; the noise from the heavy mediaeval wrought iron latch banging loudly and echoing round the church. They could just make out the familiar figure of Martyn, their priest, walking into the nave and clutching a bundle of some swords and a couple of helmets in his arms.

"I've got them just in time for the rehearsal tonight, quite appropriate as we are going to do the murder scene. You won't have to use the walking sticks and broom handles tonight!"

"At last!" said the First Knight, Reginald Fitz Urse. "I can't wait to get to do this properly."

When laid out on the side tables, it was a truly amazing collection of realistic-looking armour and weaponry and it made everyone realise that now it really was all going to happen. For any waverers, there could be no going back.

After trying on the breastplates, they then chose their swords – authentic-looking replicas – and marvelled when feeling the weight and balance of them in their hands. They practised drawing them from their scabbards and got themselves accustomed to holding them and waving them about. "They are so much bigger than I thought," said Thomas, quietly.

"Steady on, chaps," said Martyn, somewhat ironically. "You don't want to hurt anyone. I wouldn't want any mishaps."

An involved discussion ensued about what everyone was going to do and then they went through it again to check that everyone remembered their moves. In their quieter moments, they had all reflected on what a brutal way it would be to die if one is attacked by someone wielding a sword or a knife; however, the thought was so horrible that none of them had brooded on the reality for too long.

"Now," said Martyn, calling things to order, "we'll just run through this very, very slowly at first. As we become familiar with the moves, it will be less dangerous and you will have more chance of remembering exactly what you have to do. Think of it as a very slow dance – a ballet if you like – and remember the moves just as if they were choreographed for a dance. It is not necessarily naturalistic and it doesn't have to be. It is more like a sacrificial dance or ceremony, a sacrifice to God. After all it is the centrepiece of the whole play. Becket is giving himself to God as a sacrifice. It is both real and unreal," and then he paused and, looking directly at them, added, "But I don't want anyone getting hurt. Right, let's do it!"

The four knights enter the cathedral from the main west door, accompanied by a clerk.

Thomas is standing beside a pillar, centre stage left. One arm is round the pillar as if for support. The knights surround him, two on each side. They all point towards him. They look at each other nervously. Will they remember their moves? Four priests are standing back at some distance near the edge of the stage, centre stage left, they have been telling Thomas to flee. They cling to each other in fear, whispering nervously to each other. They have failed to persuade Thomas. Thomas patiently explains that he is in God's hands now and he cannot run away from God's will.

Then, as if in slow motion, the four knights demand in unison that he absolve all those that he had excommunicated. Becket looks up to the ceiling, raises his free arm to heaven, shakes his head and refuses.

The four knights, then lunge for Thomas, and try to pull him away from the pillar, which he has clung to as a child clings to its mother. They back off when Thomas tells them to unhand him (which they grudgingly do) and to show the respect his office deserves. Reginald Fitz Urse, the first knight, leans in again and single-handedly tries to drag him from the pillar with both hands, but Thomas hangs on, and orders him not to touch him. Reginald lets go of him and, not taking his eyes off Thomas, he slowly and menacingly draws his sword. As he does so, the other three knights all follow suit, metal grating on metal. They each point their swords at Thomas so they are like the spokes on a wheel with Thomas at the hub. Thomas, realising that he is about to die, raises his eyes to heaven and quietly commends his cause to the Church of God, St Mary and St Denis. Then William de Traci, the second knight, raises his sword and swings it at Thomas's head, slicing through his flesh and skull, taking him from searing pain to blessed sleep. Thomas instantly is dying a martyr's death and falling to the ground, the other three knights weigh in to the melee, stabbing and slashing mercilessly as his body crumples at the base of the pillar.

Blood splatters in all directions and pools on the floor One knight hacks at his head for the second time and then another for a third. Then Reginald Fitz Urse turns to face the horrified priests, in case they should try to intervene, and intercepts one, a clerk, Edward Grim, who comes forward, arms outstretched. Fitz Urse hacks at the clerk's arm, which is nearly severed from his body. The clerk falls to his knees, moaning loudly and staring at his butchered limb. Thomas is on the ground and surely he is dead when the third knight, Hugh de Morville, plunges his sword into Thomas's side, cutting him most terribly. He puts his foot on the body to extract his sword, the tip of which has broken off with the force of it hitting the floor. With the sword extracted Thomas's body rolls over and the top part of his head which had been hacked at so cruelly separates from his body, spilling his blood, brains and earthly life on to the floor. The four priests can stand it no longer and one of them helps raise the wounded clerk who is clutching his mutilated arm and they all run off crying and wailing into the enveloping darkness of the cathedral.

Then there is silence. The lights dim. One spotlight remains on Thomas who lies at the base of the pillar.

The knights stand over Thomas's lifeless body, each with his own thoughts, they are breathing deeply and their faces shine with sweat. They are inwardly extremely shocked by what has happened. After a few moments, they exit slowly, together walking backwards as if in the presence of royalty, as they near the open door, they suddenly turn and run.

The remaining actors stand around sheepishly in silence, some looking from one to another, others just looking at the ground. No one says anything. Thomas's corpse lies on the cold stone floor, his face is ashen white and yet there is the hint of a smile on his face. His blood is seeping across the paved floor and running into the cracks and into the very earth beneath.

From somewhere in the dark behind the stage, the chorus begins to curse the day and the season and the very earth upon which a saint has died and they bewail his tragic death. They call for the air and sky to be cleaned and the stone and the bone, brain and soul to be washed and washed and washed and washed for evermore.

Then as the chorus's words fade away, the blackout is made complete.

Then silence, a blessed silence, and oblivion.

"Erm... Well done, everyone!" After what had seemed like an eternity, Martyn's disembodied and quavering voice cut through the silence from the darkened back of the church. He had been silently weeping throughout this action and he was overcome with emotion, but he tried to hide it from the cast.

There were only four more weeks to the three performances.

***

Later that evening, some of the cast and Martyn had gone to the local pub and were relaxing together over some drinks

The Second Priest said, "Imagine dying like that, it looked awful. Luckily he must have been knocked out by the first blow."

"He might not have been, he could still be conscious after a head wound like that, but not for very long, I would have thought," said the Third Priest. "All he had to do was to do what the king wanted and everything would have been fine."

"But," said the Third Tempter, "that's the whole point. Once he had become a priest and Archbishop of Canterbury, he was a servant of God, bound by his sacred oath. It was his pleasure to do God's will and if God wanted him to die for his faith, then he was happy to do that, too. That transcends anything, anyone, even a king, might command him to do."

"People have died for their beliefs for thousands of years," said Martyn. "I suppose that it's part of the test of one's faith that all those of us who profess one might have to confront a real test at some point in our lives. After all it's the finest thing that a person of faith can do. But at least nowadays we don't burn Catholics. And thank God for that!"

"I suppose in your work you don't really meet much violence, at least not here in our little village!" said Thomas.

"You never know what's around the corner," said Martyn, thoughtfully. "I get all sorts knocking on my door at any time of day or night. Some are really desperate for help; single mothers and the like, and there are some really heart-rending cases. Others sometimes just want to chat for advice, so I give them a number to ring like the Citizens Advice Bureau or Social Services. Some just want someone to listen to them or to have a shoulder to cry on. No two visitors are ever the same.

But you must understand that I have to answer the door and see if I can help them. Usually I am the last resort; when people are at the end of their tether they turn to the church, even if they are not churchgoers. We have to be there for them and without wishing to sound melodramatic, we are submitting ourselves to the will of God, otherwise how on earth can we truly say that we do His work? I had a chap a couple of months ago who was in a really bad way. Trouble was, I realised pretty quickly that there was something not quite right about him. He had a teardrop tattoo on his face which unnerved me. Anyway, very troubled he was, talking to himself all the time. I fed him, but he scared me quite a bit by his aggressive manner. He started to say some vile things about the church. How he had been abused as a boy by priests, albeit Roman Catholics. When I told him that I was a Church of England priest he got very angry, saying that all priests were the same. Luckily the builders turned up to discuss my plans for the alterations so I was very relieved when he suddenly said that he had to go. And he just left muttering obscenities much to the amusement of the builders."

"You know what teardrop tattoos mean?" said the second Tempter.

"Not specifically, no." admitted Martyn.

"It's a sign that someone has killed someone, or intends to do so. It's usually done in prison. But it can also mean lots of different things as well." continued the second Tempter.

"There has to be a better way," said Tom, the First Tempter. "By opening your door to anyone, at any time

266

of day or night, you are laying yourself wide open to any maniac or nutter. Anything could happen! For God's sake, Martyn. Beg pardon, but you need to be really careful, mate. You really do. There was a vicar attacked recently somewhere in the Midlands. It was terrible what happened. It was in all the papers."

Martyn smiled calmly. "Don't worry," he said. "I'll be careful. Now I think we should adjourn this pleasant meeting and all get an early night. Don't forget we are doing a run-through of the whole of the first half at the next rehearsal and some of you need to learn your lines, not mentioning any names."

Not many people knew that Martyn had joined the priesthood because of a car accident in which he had been badly injured. He had broken an arm which would never be a hundred percent right again. He had also cracked a few ribs in the accident which resulted in some livid bruising. How would they know? He never discussed it with any but his closest confidants. It wasn't in his nature to discuss his private life. It was irrelevant to his work in the parish. During his convalescence he had had an overpowering religious experience that left him shaken. When he had recovered, and to the surprise and disappointment of his colleagues in chambers, he had abandoned his career as a barrister and had trained to be a priest. He had dedicated the rest of his life to God and the Church and chosen to manifest this by making it his sole purpose to help the needy, the helpless and the flotsam and jetsam of life, no matter what the cost to himself.

***

Billy D Tray-Zee woke up in his cramped bed with a cracking headache and a familiar pressure and ache in his groin. He had had one of his very vivid bad dreams and he was breathless, confused and disorientated. What day was it? Where was he? He had dreamt that he had been hunting down a priest, a weasel of a man, wrapped in black robes that flapped about and became snagged on brambles. He had been chasing him through a dark wood. Eventually he caught up with him and had started hacking at him with a hand-held crucifix as if it were an axe and he remembered the terror in the man's eyes and his scream and the flecks of spittle that flew out of his contorted mouth.

His headache was getting worse and one of his voices was repeating, over and over again, "Crucify! Crucify!" then, another voice screamed, "Kill the priest! Kill the priest!" and yet a third voice yelled, "Do it now, do it now!"

As he lay there in his turmoil, he knew like he had never known before that his mission in life was to seek revenge for what had happened to him as a child at the hands of those filthy priests all those years ago. At first he hadn't told anyone; he was so ashamed and felt so dirty. How could he possibly tell anyone? On one occasion, as a young adult, he had told a therapist who had asked him where he thought all his anger came from. He told him about what the priests had done to him all those years ago. The therapist couldn't believe why he hadn't told anyone at the time and said that he was probably making it all up as an attention-seeking excuse for his weird behaviour and for effect. That had resulted in Billy

D attacking the therapist and eventually being sectioned and incarcerated.

Now it was clear: he must clear the air, clean the sky! Make everything fresh and clean. He must kill a priest or two, or three. Throw them in the bin, get rid of them. Then he must wash all the blood away. And he knew which priest. He had stumbled into that village when he had been thrown off the bus for threatening another traveller on one of his aimless journeys, and by chance he had seen the priest and had followed him. He saw him going into his house and he had knocked on the door and then those sodding builders had turned up. All he needed was to get the same bus and then–

The small grimy room closed in on him, with his voices screaming louder and ever louder, he felt he was losing control. He felt utterly claustrophobic and had to get up. He caught a glimpse of himself in the mirror. His face looked tired and drawn and much older than his years. The teardrop tattoo on his right cheek now seemed to mock him and he smashed the mirror with his bare hand, causing it to bleed. It was a shallow cut which in a way calmed him and he welcomed the pain. So he just wiped it on the grimy curtain and then ignored it. In an effort to calm down and in an attempt to ignore the voices, he thought he would have a shower in the small cubicle in his room, but the water was cold and came out in just a trickle; so he gave up the idea and urinated into it instead. He was supposed to be meeting his doctor that afternoon to review his medication, but he had already decided that he wouldn't bother. He'd had enough of this shithole of a town and was going to move on, today, now, and get the hell out of here. One of the conditions of his release from the secure unit where he had spent so much of his life, was that he was going to be trusted to self-administer his drugs to handle his psychosis and would have to report to the doctor every week. If he didn't, he would have to come back. The overworked staff in the hostel were supposed to monitor him, but had failed to do so properly. He hadn't taken his medication for some time now; in fact, he had flushed it down the toilet. It had made him feel sick and exhausted and, if he went to the doctor today, the doctor would know and then it would start all over again. The bloody nagging and the bloody moaning never seemed to stop. "Crucify! Crucify! Kill the priest!" The voices were stridently insistent. God, these fuckers had no fucking idea what he was going through. He dressed in yesterday's clothes. It had been a good day, yesterday. He had been out, stealing a few items. Things that he was certain that he was going to need; although, at that moment, he was not sure why. It just seemed to be what he wanted. The items lay scattered about on the table and bed and some had ended up on the floor. With a rising sense of panic and with his voices eating into his brain, he scrabbled around, stuffing everything into a large cotton bag, emblazoned with the logo of the local supermarket. There was a hammer, a bible, a gay porn magazine, a picture of Jesus and a hand mirror and two carving knives. Everything except the knives, was stuffed in haphazardly. He put the knives into a pocket on the inside of his coat. Most of his other stuff was in carrier bags and black sacks stuffed under his bed. He wasn't sure of his plans but he knew he had to make one so that he could feel better and, having nicked all the stuff, he felt like the plan was already half-formed.

Feeling hungry and very thirsty he went down to the canteen to see what he could get to eat and drink. He had spent most of his adult life drifting from one dead-end job to another and one grimy hostel to another. He had been put in to care when his mother had died of a drug overdose after his father had left them some years before. Billy D couldn't really remember his father, and remembering his mother only brought a bitterness to his mind; it always made him angry and then sad. His parents had never married. His mother seemed to resent his very existence and only just tolerated him. There was little or no maternal love, no cuddles, no terms of endearment, just coldness and distance. His father had been a petty criminal and not a very good one at that, and had frequently hit his mother. Billy D was the end result of a violently ugly drink and drug fuelled copulation on a filthy carpet littered with drug taking paraphernalia, discarded beer cans and take-away packaging. However his mother could never say with any certainty who his father was. She was so disoriented at the time that it could have been her dealer to whom she owed money or it could have been her violent partner, supposed his father. To be honest, she probably didn't even care. As he grew up his only way of surviving was to withdraw into his own imagined world, and that was when the voices had started. At first they were comforting in a strange sort of way and he welcomed them, but then, as he grew older, they became threatening and more and more angry; now, they were incandescent with rage. One of the first angry ones was a dwarf who would creep up on him and give him a fright and then just laugh at him. It started to tell him to do things and, if he didn't, the dwarf would tell him that he would be eaten by wolves, and then he would just laugh at him again. His misery continued in the children's home where the abuse was of a different kind. With his mother, the abuse had primarily been that of neglect and the lack of any meaningful emotional contact, with occasional bouts of violence from his father or his mothers men-friends.. The visiting priests, always alone, used to make him do stuff that made him feel dirty and uncomfortable; when he went and told the housemother, she would tell him to go away and to stop making up silly stories and say that she wasn't going to believe his terrible lies. She said that he was a nasty, evil-minded, ungrateful little boy and he should be ashamed of himself, and sometimes she slapped him. She said that the priests were very good people and would never, ever be capable of doing such things. How dare he say such filthy things! As he grew up, he sought the friendship of other boys and sometimes girls in the home and confided in them. As a young adult, he had a confused and brutalised attitude towards sex and he had been with both men and women. It was always a disaster and completely unsatisfactory, he was totally incapable of forming any kind of meaningful relationship and his voices always saw to it that any relationship ended violently anyway. The voices were several characters and over time became more and more judgemental and strident. When he tried to talk to them or argue with them, they wouldn't listen and they always ruined everything. Any people listening to him would stare at him and move away.

His life had been one long string of disasters and he had had enough of it all; he wanted to do some damage, he wanted to put it right, he wanted to find a fucking priest and do him in good and proper and make him pay for all the misery he had suffered.

***

The play was a great success in the town and for all three nights there was a full house. The parish magazine proclaimed that:*'It was an excellent example of how to bring a community together .Well done to Father Martyn and his team of actors and backstage helpers. We look forward to the next production.*

Martyn was a self-effacing man and was embarrassed by the praise and adulation and yet he was pleased that it was a success. He was the youngest of three children and the only boy. His father had been a bank manager in the local high street, a remote figure who had little involvement with his son's upbringing other than occasionally giving him random bits of paternal advice such as, "If you work hard, you will reap the benefits, my boy!" or, "The devil finds work for idle hands", and "Keep away from any smut, I don't want you falling into the wrong company". If truth be told, Martyn was a bit of a mummy's boy; he was his mother's youngest child and she doted on him. His mother was a stay-at-home housewife, a member of the WI and she kept a very well ordered and tidy household. His two sisters also mothered him and their games, when he was young, tended to cast him in the role of "little-orphan-lost" to their role as missionaries, having seen Ingrid Bergman as Gladys Aylward in the film *The Inn of the Sixth Happiness*. They decided that he needed to be taught how to pray to Jesus and to be fed disgusting homemade medicine. Martyn tolerated this as long as he could. As he grew older and he brought home one or two of his more bookish friends from school who wanted to play highwaymen and to rob the girls at musket-point and shout, "Money or your life!", the girls' missionary zeal cooled somewhat. When the boys were older still and taller than the girls, spotty, with cracking voices and a weird sense of humour, the sisters did not know how to react and left Martyn and his few friends well alone.

He was not a rebellious boy by nature. His adolescence was quite scary and he was embarrassed to the very roots of his being by the way his body changed and changed again. He sat blushing scarlet in biology lessons when being told about what happened to teenage boys and girls and how he came into the world. How could his parents possibly do that? He assiduously avoided any smutty talk behind the bike sheds and remained an innocent to many aspects of teenage life; trying to ignore the more gross aspects of adolescence which assailed him. He couldn't help but overhear of the exploits of other boys with regard to what they did with girls or by themselves, and preferred to plan his train layout or help out backstage with his local amateur dramatic group. He never grew his hair long or smoked cigarettes stolen from grown-ups, let alone ask girls out for a date.

To the eternal joy and pride of his parents he won a

scholarship to Oxford to read law, which set him on the path of emulating his uncle who was an eminent barrister that specialised in criminal law. Martyn was a hardworking and dedicated student and didn't really involve himself with the more rowdy aspects of student life. He liked a drink, but never to excess, and he chose his friends carefully, preferring to mix with the more studious undergraduates who took their work very seriously. No one was surprised when he graduated with a first-class honours degree and was instantly snapped up by one of the more prestigious sets of chambers at the Inner Temple, where he successfully completed his pupillage and was subsequently called to the Bar soon afterwards. When he started paid employment, he worked on prosecutions and specialised in criminal law, which he at first, found challenging and entirely satisfying. After three or four years, however, his work had lost its lustre and he had become disillusioned; it seemed to him that his work consisted of mainly prosecuting mankind's lost causes. On the one hand, were the hardened criminals who were really some of the most unpleasant people he had ever come across and were nearly always mostly repeat offenders, and on the other hand, were the pathetic individuals who had no control over their lives and had just been swept along on a tide of greed, mindless violence or just pure, cold- blooded murder. Ultimately, he didn't feel that the law helped to rehabilitate the criminals; in fact, it just led them into some kind of cul-de-sac. As for the victims of crime, their fate was to have to rebuild their shattered lives or not. It was up to them and with help from underfunded and understaffed agencies they just had to make the best of it.

He had needed a break, to get away, to blow away some cobwebs. And so it was that, while motoring up to Northumberland with a couple of work colleagues to walk the length of Hadrian's Wall, the car that he was driving became involved in a rather nasty accident with a lorry that was driven by a very tired driver who had fallen asleep at the wheel. The upshot was that Martyn and both his passengers ended up in hospital. Martyn had suffered serious injuries and spent time in traction and subsequent physiotherapy. He was in hospital for two months. His two passengers, who had both been asleep at the time, had miraculously got away with it quite lightly, only suffering some rather painful cuts and bruises and a possible concussion; they were kept in overnight for observation. It was while convalescing one night that it suddenly dawned on Martyn that something in his life was missing. There was a great big black hole in the middle of everything. The more he thought about it, the bigger the hole got. At first he couldn't think what it was that was missing. He wasn't lonely. It wasn't the fact that, unlike most of his friends and acquaintances, he hadn't got a girlfriend or partner. Sex had never played a huge part in his life and where it had, it had usually left him confused and at sea. As he had grown up, he had realised that he actually didn't like any aspect of sex at all. He wasn't attracted to either sex and didn't feel the need to search for what he didn't need or even like. His life up to this point had been all about him – his education, his achievements and his career – and yet at this very moment, the feeling that he still needed something else grew stronger than ever. Only that morning the hospital chaplain had been round the wards and had given him bread and wine and they had said prayers together and he had drawn great strength and a feeling of well-being from this. And now it dawned on him, in a truly Damascene moment. It was a completely shattering feeling. He suddenly knew what he wanted to do with the rest of his life: he was going to leave the law and become a priest! He wanted to spread the Gospel and to work with people; helping them, caring for them, guiding them and teaching them to love God and the church. He looked at the clock on the wall, 4.30am, the gentle pink light of dawn was beginning to seep past the blinds in the hospital windows. He wanted to remember this moment forever. Tears rolled down his face and yet he was feeling deliriously happy. He had not felt as excited as that since he had been a small child anticipating Christmas morning.

***

Martyn loved the quiet, especially after all the clamour of the day, and particularly after the Parish council meeting that evening. Lady Camberworth, whose family had lived in the big house for generations, had been particularly unpleasant about the new plan to get landowners to clear all the footpaths that adjoined or were on their land in the parish. He was looking forward to a hot bath, putting his feet up and reading his new book: a biography of Cardinal Newman. He wasn't one for Radio 4 burbling in the background, let alone a television blaring. He did sometimes listen to Radio 3 if there was a particular concert he wanted to hear. He had just cleared away his supper things. He was used to eating alone and in silence. He enjoyed the quiet and it gave him time to think. Supper had been a gift from a grateful parishioner and neighbour who had come round yesterday with a fish pie that she had made, saying how she thought he needed a proper meal in the evenings and she wanted to thank him for doing such a lovely christening for her grand-daughter last week. He was just plugging in the kettle to make a coffee when the doorbell rang several times in quick succession. It was one of those old-fashioned bells and sounded quite discordant. As he walked towards the door, wondering who it could be, he made a mental note that the noisy bell was one of the things that he wanted to change in the house.

He opened the door and was confronted by an unshaven man in his fifties. He must have been standing very close to the door for the light from the porch shone down on him, accentuating his pallor and emphasising the blackness of the night behind him. With a jolt, Martyn saw a teardrop tattoo on his right cheek. Martyn gasped and as he did so he caught a waft of the man's stale breath and unwashed clothing. He was carrying a cotton bag, emblazoned with the logo of a local supermarket. Martyn also noticed how unusually still he seemed. He felt that he had seen him somewhere before; then he remembered and instantly felt uncomfortable.

Trying to sound calm, he said, "Hello, can I help you?"

The man just stood there, staring at him coldly, without responding.

278

"Are you alright?" Martyn tried again. Still there was no response.

Suddenly, the man pushed Martyn backwards into the hallway and, following after him, slammed the front door shut behind them.

Martyn stumbled backwards and just managed to stop himself from falling against the banisters.

"What on earth…?" he managed to gasp.

"I've come to crucify you," said the man quite calmly, and then yelled "Crucify! Crucify!" Flecks of spittle flew out of his mouth.

Martyn stood there aghast. His legs felt as if they were going to give way underneath him and his stomach turned to water. He staggered back a step to stop himself from toppling over.

The intruder threw his bag to the ground. From his coat pockets, he produced two carving knives and, holding one in each hand, he started slashing and stabbing and kicking and spitting in a piteous and frenzied attack. As he crumpled to the floor, Martyn's mouth was opening and closing, but no sound came out other than several loud gasps. As if some kind of reflex had kicked in, he began to urgently whisper a prayer; "Now to Almighty God, to the blessed Mary ever Virgin, to the blessed John the Baptist, the holy apostles Peter and Paul, to the blessed martyr Denis and to all the Saints, I commend my cause, and that of the church. Amen."

The pain was like a fire across his body. His vital organs were being punctured and sliced and irreparably damaged. Martyn slipped into unconsciousness. The man was screaming abuse about "You fucking priests!", as the hurt and shame he had felt all his life, the confusion and the hate, the need to kill and to kill again, and to destroy anyone to do with the church overwhelmed him. He stopped as suddenly as he had started and he stood, legs apart, panting and sweating, staring down at Martyn, who lay there unmoving and unseeing with his eyes open. The man picked up the bag and shook it violently and tipped the contents onto Martyn's bleeding body and everything scattered about him: the hammer, the bible, the picture of Jesus, the gay pornographic magazine and finally the mirror. "Here you go," he said. "Thought you might like some company." Calmly he carefully placed the items on and around the body. He bent down and picked up the mirror and held it to Martyn's face, and said, "This it was it looks like to die, you bastard," and then he flung it across the hallway and it shattered into a thousand pieces, some of which rebounded and skittered across the floor.

Martyn was lying on his back in bed and he complained of a burning feeling all over his body; his mother was saying what a lovely day they had had and how he and his sisters had made such a lovely sandcastle and how he had caught the sun and had probably overdone it. She smiled as she took off his pyjama jacket and, taking up a brown glass bottle, she liberally applied a cooling, chalky liquid to his chest and back. Martyn flinched and said how cold it felt and she gently said, "Don't be such a baby, your sisters didn't make nearly such a fuss." She smiled down at him. "Now, let's do the rest of you." Afterwards she put his pyjama jacket back on him and buttoned it up. She tucked him up in bed and kissed him on the forehead. Turning back to him as she shut the door, she said, "Good night, darling, God bless!" and switched off the light.

***

When Mrs Canterbury opened the front door, the first thing she noticed was that Martyn seemed to be looking straight at her and smiling, and then she fainted.

It was noted in the coroner's report that Martyn had been laid on his back, arms stretched out as if on a cross, and each hand had been pinioned through his palms with a knife hammered in to the parquet floor. A picture of Jesus lay on his chest and a pornographic magazine, opened at the centre page, had been laid on his groin. His feet had been tucked side by side into a cotton shopping bag with a garishly printed slogan which proclaimed that *'This bag-for-life will last forever and ever and ever. Amen.'*

Searching for a broken promise

She is in her eighties and lives alone in a chaotic and run-down little terraced cottage. She has no friends and the locals tend to leave her alone. She sleeps on the ground floor in her cluttered sitting room. The lace curtains are grey and limply hang behind smeared windows. She doesn't go upstairs any more, there's no point.

Every morning when she wakes up, the first thing she always looks at is a small photo on her bedside table. It is propped up there between the detritus of her life. She always reaches out and pats the frame gently with her pale, boney hand and says something in a soothing tone, almost like a prayer. Sometimes she smiles, sometimes she can't. The black and white unmounted photo is only the size of a matchbox and held in a cheap, tarnished metal frame. It is a close-up shot of a fresh-faced young man who is smiling into sunlight. One eye is almost shut as he blinks into the brightness of the moment. He is laughing and his fair, spiky hair is cut short, he has a cowlick that gives him a cheeky, boyish air. It is an honest face with clearly defined features, inherited from his Anglo-Saxon ancestors. His mouth is slightly open in a broad grin, revealing a set of good, straight teeth. He is, in fact, a picture of health and wholesomeness, like a face on a cereal packet, a real happy-go-lucky sort of fellow, the sort of person who seems never to worry about anything. She took the photo on his eighteenth birthday many, many long years ago.

Whatever the time of year, her alarm clock always gets her up at six and her daily routine never changes. She briefly washes in cold water, dresses herself – typically in a grey blouse, an old grey skirt, pale green jumper and wellington boots. She gets all her clothes from jumble sales or local charity shops. She makes herself a cup of tea and has a couple of plain biscuits while she sits at the kitchen table and scans the free newspapers or junk-mail that regularly pours through her letterbox. Then she puts on her coat and a headscarf, picks up her bag and her stick. She walks through the town and always finds it full of the usual ghosts going about their business. She tries to avoid them. They are always there and such a nuisance. She always goes the same way. She is alone, but never lonely, there are too many people in her head. All the while when she is walking she prefers to look down in order to search. For her eyes are scanning every nook and cranny of every pavement and path she walks on. When she does look up there is always someone who wants to talk to her or tell her something. It may be her mother's friend who is asking after her, sometimes it is the vicar on his way to yet another funeral, she doesn't like him, but she doesn't know why. And there are always the same people whom she tries to avoid. Why can't they leave her alone and mind their own business? She will mutter brief excuses and keeps moving, always scanning the ground. She is a busy person with a purpose. She has not got time to stand about chattering. She might talk to them as she walks along. Some people look round at her when they hear someone talking to no one in particular. When she finds something, she bends down and picks it up, she is so quick that people rarely see her do it. She once found something that was worth a lot but then she lost it.

For now she is always searching. She is looking and she hopes to find it. It all started quite by chance, when she found a ten pound note in the car park, with its inscription, '*I promise to pay the bearer on demand the sum...*' She didn't finish reading it, she had found a promise! In her sadness and solitary existence she had found proof of a promise made. So you *can* find a promise if you look hard enough, she reasoned. When she gets to the car park her work really begins in earnest. This is the main place for her searches. At that time in the morning the car park is usually empty except for one or two vehicles left by partygoers or forgetful people. She always says to herself, if anyone would listen, that she is just having a wander, enjoying the morning air. She is not some daft old lady with an obsessive compulsion! The very idea! Her walking stick is used for poking at things, turning litter over like a blackbird looking for snails. Effecting an air of nonchalance, she slyly moves up and down every single white-painted space in every single row looking at the ground. In winter she has a small torch. After she has done the painted rows she then makes a special point of always walking round each of the ticket machines. This is where she will most likely find what she is looking for. If anybody does notice her she just looks as if she has lost something and has returned to the car park to find

284

it, a rather forlorn figure maybe, but invisible to many. The one or two commuters waiting in the bus shelter are too engrossed in their tablets or mobile phones to even notice her. By the time the first shoppers come to park their cars her job is done and she is on her way to the library to read the local paper and to finally catch up with any of the other lost souls who might be there.

She took the photo of that dear boy all those years ago. They had spent a very happy day together on the beach at Great Yarmouth. They had gone there on his new motorbike; she had clung to him so tightly, riding pillion and she loved the feeling of the breeze blowing in her face and of him so close to her. She felt like a movie star in an advertisement. He had bought her candyfloss and a strawberry ice cream. They had sat on their towels on the sand, together, their bodies just touching. They had talked about all sorts of things. He had changed into his trunks while hiding himself in a towel and standing on one foot with his head sticking out of the top. She laughed so much and took photos of him with her new Box Brownie and he laughed too. She didn't have to do all that hopping about in a towel, as she had put her costume on at home under her clothes.

He had then said, "Last one in the water is a scaredy-cat!" He had grabbed her hand and they had run down the beach. They ran past people eating sandwiches who were annoyed by the flying sand and the two girls who were smearing themselves with sun cream and watching them and smiling at them as they ran. When they got to the water it was cold, so very cold, and she had screamed, "No!" He had turned and looked back at her and with just a hint of sadness he had let go of her. He had continued running into the water and had dived in under a wave and he had come up for air and swam out further. He had turned again and briefly called to her, but she couldn't hear what he said. And then he had disappeared into the sparkling bright lights of the reflected sun on the water. She began to panic, a terrible feeling arose in her and after a while she saw him again and he turned and swam back and then walked through the shallow waters towards her. He thought she looked like a goddess standing there waiting for him, she had such a fantastic figure! She admired his lean body and at first she thought that he looked naked, but it was a silly trick of the bright sunlight. His body was beautiful, shining gold, and he was saying, "Why didn't you come in?"

She said, "It's freezing!"

Then he said, "I missed you. I wanted you with me."

He took her in his arms and tried to kiss her right there in front of all those people. At first, his body was too cold and wet and she struggled against him. Then she felt his body, warmer now, against hers and they kissed and they clung together and he said, "I love you." It was such a happy day, the happiest ever.

Soon after that he got his call-up papers for his National Service. He would have to go away up north. When he told her, they hugged and she wept. So they went and got a special licence and were married in the local registry office the next day. On his last evening with her, he promised to return on his first leave, which would be in a month's time. She wept as she waved him off and he roared down the road on his bike. She could not see his tears, which were lost in the wind. But she knew that she would see him again in just four weeks because he had promised.

That night, the first on her own, she dreamt of him running towards the sea and of them laughing.He had turned round with that sad look on his face and then had run away from her and had dived into the foam and disappeared into the golden waves.

In the morning, two policemen, looking sad and worried, came knocking on her door.

He hadn't stood a chance.

Travellers

Sitting in the car, he first noticed the two ponies in his rear-view mirror. Their heads, which were looking in his direction, were very close together and they seemed agitated, but it all seemed somewhat out of context.

He was in the car with his elderly mother-in-law next to him in the passenger seat and his wife was on the backseat handing out a picnic. They had parked facing the river and were enjoying watching the boats coming and going up and down the marked channel between the moorings. It was a very pleasant place; there was a pub nearby and it was a sunny day, as English as you could get, with a clear blue sky and few clouds. Other people were out in the fresh air enjoying themselves on this September weekend, when summer is really over and autumn on its way, when the chill winds from the North East will soon change everything. Looking across the river, it was a tranquil enough scene, slowly changing, but there were some occasions that entertained them; such as the time when a large boat was coming in to tie up to a mooring buoy and the person who was trying to catch it with the boat hook, failed badly and missed his target. Even though they couldn't hear anything, they knew from the excited body language of the man at the helm and from the poor individual with the limply-hanging boathook that strong language was being bandied about and spoiling a nice day for a father and his teenage son.

He turned his head to get a better view of the ponies in the rear-view mirror; a matched pair of geldings, possibly siblings; handsome, lively things. They were a rich chestnut brown with huge white flashes on their faces, and they had long flowing manes and tails, as is the fashion among travellers. He guessed that they stood about twelve hands high. He could see the ancient Arab heritage in their delicately featured heads and pricked-up ears. He opened the door of the car and got out to have a closer look. Together and quite surprisingly, the two ponies had been tied to an enormous and familiar old sea anchor that stood higher than them and which had been abandoned many years ago by some forgotten sailing ship and now lay sideways on the grass, unnoticed and un-remarked by many.

He could sense that the ponies were unhappy. Being tied so closely together, their movements were restricted and they didn't like it. They raised and lowered their heads in forced unison, nostrils flaring and showing the whites of their eyes. They were still harnessed to a small two-seated trotting cart which moved awkwardly behind them. They had been attached together with a very short rope and every so often one pulled away from the other and inevitably pulled the other one with it. They couldn't reach the grass and they skittered and whinnied and pulled against each other impatiently with what can only have been utter frustration and some irritation. He walked towards them holding out his hand, intending to try to calm them down. As one, they reared up their heads and stared at him wildly and seemed to pull harder against the restraining rope. He imagined the leather bridles breaking, so he immediately stepped backwards, not wanting to alarm them any further. It was then that he noticed that, further up the green, were several other ponies, some piebald, some chestnut and some greys. They were all harnessed to trotting carts. They must have all arrived as they were having their picnic in the car and watching the boats in the river. Some had been tethered in the shade of a group of large sycamore trees and others were tied to bushes in the full sun, grazing peacefully amongst the blackberry briars and scrub that fringed the large open green. They were minded by hard-faced young girls with ponytails of bleach blonde hair, wearing large hooped ear-rings and who looked about them with a bored sense of superiority, or by weather-beaten brown-faced boys some with scarred and tattooed forearms in sleeveless t-shirts, wielding sticks and who occasionally called out commands harshly to their ponies just like they had heard their fathers do.

The two chestnut ponies continued their restless fidgeting and couldn't settle. He stood there not sure as to what to do. He did not know how he could relieve their discomfort. They weren't his. He would never have tied up two ponies so tightly. Where was their owner? Was he in that crowd of noisy drinkers in the pub garden? Then, with a sense of relief, he noticed a short stocky man in a blue striped shirt coming from the pub towards them and then talking to them. The way he greeted them and the way they reacted to him immediately signified his ownership of these animals

He spoke firmly to them, with familiarity and rubbed their faces and patted their withers.

"Steady on now, steady! You've got to settle down, good boys. We're going in five minutes!" He spoke firmly but quietly to them, with a parent's authority, as if speaking to a pair of naughty children. Then, after one last tousle of a forelock, he turned on his heels and walked away. As he did so, he called to all the others standing around with the ponies, "We're going in five minutes, so be ready."

Remarkably, for the next five minutes, the ponies just stood there calmly, they seem to have heeded the words of their master and they stood quietly side by side, looking expectantly in the direction of the pub garden to where he had gone to rejoin his family to finish his drink.

After exactly five minutes, the short stocky man in the striped blue shirt returned and freed his two ponies from the ropes that had kept them tied to the large anchor. They whinnied a greeting and were obviously excited at the prospect of moving off. Other members of the group calmly prepared to leave and climbed up onto their trotting carts. No two carts were the same. They were sturdy enough and well constructed, but they all seem to have been tailor-made for the size of each pony, matching them perfectly. Some of the bigger carts carried whole families of six or seven souls; others carried just one or two. Without being directed by anybody they just seemed to fall in behind each other into some kind of pecking order along the length of the track that wound its way up the steep hill and away into the trees. Smarter-looking, more recently painted carts went to the front of the line, with the leading pair of chestnut ponies happy to be free of the anchor. At the back of the line came the last of the carts with a family of five or six children on board. All sat perched on it and hung on to each other, silently staring at the few day-trippers who stood about watching them. As the line of carts began to move off, their mother took up the reins and with a couple of clicks of her tongue and a command of, "Gid-on! Me beauties!" they started to move slowly up the hill. The two stocky ponies snorted and strained at the shafts of the cart as uncomplaining and loyal as ever they were.

While the carts had been getting ready to depart David had hurried back to the car and picked up his camera. He wanted some good shots so he ran up to the top of the hill, past the leading pair of ponies and stood waiting and readied the camera in the shade of a large sycamore. The ponies strained at the heavy loads; the familiar tapping and scraping of hooves and the snorting and whinnying came from them and David started taking photographs. First he tried to fit the whole group into a couple of long shots, and then he photographed each cart and its pony as it went past. As the leader went by, David called out, "Thank you!" without really knowing why. The short stocky man in the blue striped shirt waved and smiled and said, "It's a grand day, so it is." David stood there photographing the passing carts. The rest of the drivers and passengers now ignored him and looked directly ahead, steadfastly up the hill, in the manner of pioneers out to conquer the wilderness. Some of the younger ones, took sneaking sidelong glances at him, shyly.

As the last cart passed by, he suddenly caught his breath. A feeling of great emotion came over him, and it completely surprised him, his eyes began to prickle and he realised he had a lump in his throat. He didn't know these people from Adam. Why should he feel like this watching a few travelling folk trot away with their ponies? He stood there staring as the last heavily laden cart disappeared into the darkness of the shaded trees at the top of the hill. He realised that the sounds and smells of ponies on a warm summer's day was taking him straight back to distant days in his own childhood, half a century ago now. He remembered his family's ponies; and harnessing up the trap and ranging round the lanes and villages with his sister and brothers. He heard the familiar sound of hooves on tarmac and the tinkling of the bridles and the ponies chewing snatched mouthfuls of grass and snorting in the sunlight. And he saw the clouds of pollen falling from the tall cow parsley as they brushed past the overgrown hedgerows.

A weird tale

Edmund is lying in bed. Without opening his eyes he knows it is dawn, that special time of day between the darkness of night and the light of day. He relishes the warmth and comfort of his bed. The sounds inside the house of his family moving about and outside of sporadic traffic and a dog barking, all tell him to get up. The world, his world is slowly getting going. He can hear a siren in the distance and nearby some contrasting birdsong. He opens his eyes and gazes at the ceiling. He follows the spidery cracks overhead. It's an old house; his family have lived there as long as he can remember. It's Saturday at last, no school. Edmund turns on his side and looks towards the window. He needs to pee, but he doesn't want to have to get out of bed just yet. He wants to stay in the warm, and try to ignore the pressure in his bladder, but he knows that he is going to have to get up soon. He wonders what the time is. He tries to recall the dream that he was having just before he woke. Something about endlessly looking for something, he tried to remember the crazy kaleidoscopic mess of images. He had been looking for books in a chaotic library, and he had kept on opening the books to see what was inside; myriad pictures of everything imaginable. Images of crowds, babies crying, a dead cat lying in the road, an old man sitting on a bench drinking from a can and horses stampeding had filled his vision. He never quite found what he was looking for. What *was* he looking for?

Now he hears someone moving along the corridor outside. Whoever it is, they are trying to go quietly but the old floorboards will not allow this. He hears the bathroom door open; it makes the familiar creaking sound that he has heard so many times before and then it is shut firmly, the bolt is slid home. It is either his older brother, who has moved back home, or his mum's new boyfriend. He can hear the muffled but distinct sound of someone peeing, and farting and the flush, and then the door being opened again and the footsteps come back past his door, and then stop right outside. Waiting. Listening. It feels quite menacing. He holds his breath and listens back, intently, a floorboard creaks and then the sound of the footsteps continues along the corridor until he can hear them no longer. He decides that he really has to pee and he gets out of bed. As he comes out into the corridor, he quickly looks both ways. His mother's boyfriend, Dan, is standing at the far end of the passage-way in just his boxers, watching him. "I can see you," he says. Without either of them saying anything else, Edmund hurries along to the bathroom and closes the door.

As he pees with a great sense of relief, he decides that he had had a good day yesterday. In fact, to celebrate, he would have a bath! Those bully boys. He'd sorted them out alright. The two in particular who had so annoyed him and had really got to him.

It had all begun a couple of days ago on Thursday. As he had watched from his bedroom window, he had seen two boys he vaguely knew from school, ambling along the lane that ran round behind his house. The smaller of the two, Arnie, was wheeling his bike beside a bigger, taller boy, Tyler.

He turns both taps on full pelt and looks through the bathroom cabinet for some bubble bath to add to his treat. He loves bubble bath.

They had been talking loudly, most likely boasting to each other about something – to do with football, probably – he couldn't really tell what and as they walked they were carelessly eating chips. Greedily shoving them into their mouths and chewing them like industrial cement mixers, stuffing more and more in. There was a ginger cat, dozing on top of the wall nearby. He instantly recognised it as Miffie, his family's cat. Tyler saw it too and suddenly stopped. The cat noticed the boys as well and stiffened; her ears pricked up as she stared intently at them. Moving in a strange, mesmeric kind of slow-motion action and in one continuous movement, Tyler handed his chips to the other lad, bent down, selected a stone the size of a golf ball and hurled it as hard as he could at the cat, at the same time as yelling, "Fucking ginger twat!" The stone glanced off the cat's back end, just as Miffie was in mid-air, leaping from the wall to safety. Miffie had yowled and had disappeared into the undergrowth.

After rummaging in the bathroom cupboard he finds what he is looking for. It is called essence of 'Mango and Ginger', that will do. Oddly appropriate he thinks.

The two boys had laughed together, a vicious, cynical laugh and had high-fived in some kind of evil bond.

Arnie yelled, "Fucking brilliant, Tyler! That fucking showed the ginger flea-bag!" And he had handed back the chips.

Angrily Edmund squirts a large dollop of the bath essence into the water and undresses. He avoids looking at himself in front of the tall mirror on the end wall, which his Mum had asked Dan to put up for her when she had started that diet, for he knows that he is skinny, physically immature for his age and bone thin. He adjusts the temperature of the bath to exactly how he likes it. He climbs in and fluffs up the bubbles. He lies back so that only his head protrudes above the luxuriant foam. As he wallows there he relives the events of the last couple of days.

Poor Miffie! That had really annoyed him, really, really angered him and he had had to do something about it. He had quickly run down the stairs and cautiously peered over the hedge. The two boys were disappearing round the corner of the lane. He had decided to follow them, to find out where they lived. They were shambling down the lane to the road. He had kept his distance. The two had been so wrapped up in their own world, that there was no fear of them seeing him from so far back. They crossed the big road and disappeared into the estate. He quickly ran down the lane, crossed the road and from about a hundred yards away, was just in time to see the bigger of the two boys about to go into his own house. It was a cliché of the scruffy redbrick council house: flaking paintwork, broken window stuck with tape, overgrown grass, scattered litter and a muddy path leading to the bright red front door, which was badly scratched at the bottom. The marks looked distinctly like those of a dog which regularly pushed at the door to get in. As the front door was opened, a crossbreed, a sort of Rottweiler, bounced outside, jumped up and welcomed him and they went inside together. He could hear someone, an older voice say, "Shut the fucking…" but the rest of the sentence was muffled by the dull thud of the door as it was slammed shut. The other boy had given the house a wide berth and was presumably making for his home. Edmund hoped that he would not be spotted and tried to look as if he was just wandering down the road. But the other boy did not turn round and carried on and went into a slightly better kept house just a few doors along on the same side. He threw his bike down on the path and opened the front door. As he did so, Edmund could hear a woman inside say, "Is that you, Arnie?" and just as the door closed he heard the reply, "Yes, Mum."

Edmund had then carried on down the lane into town and had gone into the supermarket. He had bought two multipacks of fun-size mini caramel chocolate bars. He had felt lucky as it was a buy-one-get-one-free special offer.

His head slips under the very warm soapy water and as he surfaces he luxuriates in the sheer pleasure of the silky bubbles, inwardly smiling and congratulating himself.

When he had made it back home and into the sanctuary of his room. He had put his plan into action. From under a loose floorboard he had taken out a scalpel. He had "borrowed" it from science some time ago. He always knew that it would come in handy someday; that day had arrived sooner than he had thought it would. The whole class had been kept behind when Mr Newton had counted the scalpels up after the science lesson and had found one missing. Everyone's bags had been searched by the two science technicians, and despite the teacher's threats and pleas, no one had owned up. The scalpel was missing. Everyone then had to turn out their pockets and all that had been found was fat Lorna's cigarettes, but no scalpel. The deputy head had been summoned and said that if the scalpel was not produced, then there would be no more experiments until further notice. Eventually they were dismissed, with warnings of "dire consequences". He had heard that some parents had phoned in to complain that their children had been kept behind for no good reason. When he had got home that night he had carefully removed the scalpel from inside the long handle strap of his school bag and had slipped it under the loose floorboard in the corner of his bedroom. He had thought that he would test it. He had held up an old comic with one hand and sliced it with the scalpel. It had cut through the cheap paper like a proverbial hot knife through butter. He had rummaged in his bedside drawer and had found the miniature roll of clear sticky tape, which he had won in a cracker last Christmas. He had then selected eight of his favourite mini chocolate bars from each bag and very, very carefully had slit their packaging open along the little seam at the back of each one. His heart had been racing and he could hardly breathe. He had found it hard to stop his hands shaking, but he had carefully extracted the selected chocolates one by one, trying not to tear the packaging. He had then eaten them all in one go, all sixteen of them, savouring every last scrap. As he did so he had idly read the list of ingredients on the package: sugar, cocoa butter, milk powder, cocoa mass, lactose, vegetable fat, skimmed milk powder, emulsifier, soya, lecithin, malt extract, milk fat, flavourings (various), acidity regulator, potassium carbonate, and vanilla. It had contained at least sixteen different ingredients. He was now going to change all that. He had immediately regretted scoffing so much chocolate, because, not surprisingly, he had felt sick. To take his mind off this, he had gone to his computer and had found the perfect picture that he needed, and, adding a suitably menacing message, he had printed off two postcard-sized images. He had also printed off two labels with a festive greeting on each and then he had added another picture, which he had found on-line, onto each one. His Mum had given him the computer and printer when his Dad had walked out. He knew that it was to distract him. It didn't really do that, but he had loved having it and had found it very useful.

Later that day, when he had got back from school, when his brother was at work and his Mum and boyfriend had gone shopping, he had gone out into the garden to find Miffie. She was lying stretched out on the decking, enjoying the sunshine. When he had seen her, she had uncharacteristically jumped up and had run away to the far end of the lawn and warily laid down again, keeping her distance. She was obviously unsettled and not her usual relaxed self. Talking gently and trying to sound as unthreatening as he could, he had slowly walked up to her, getting down on to his hands and knees as he got near. He had taken his time and he had been relieved and thankful that she had allowed him to pick her up. The stone hadn't broken the skin, but he could clearly see the bruising on the pale skin under the light ginger fur. He had stroked the back of her head and had reassured her by speaking soothingly to her saying that the boys who had hurt her were going to pay for it. He would see to it. When his hand had got too near to her bruise she yowled and jumped out of his arms, scratching him as she did so and she had disappeared into some bushes at the bottom of the garden.

He had wandered round the garden looking in nooks and crannies and amongst a patch of weeds and nettles in the dry and sandy soil. This was Miffie's midden. She was a tidy and scrupulous cat and she always went in the same area to do her " business". Scratching around with a trowel he had found several well-formed cat turds. Some were desiccated and had turned grey but there were plenty of fresher ones. Selecting one of the oldest and driest looking, he had scooped it up with a trowel and had put it into a small plastic tray, the kind that his dad used to buy when full of small seedlings. His perfect plan was coming together nicely. Next, inside the shed he had found a load of cobwebs and, in amongst one particularly large clump, he had found an enormous dead spider. He had put the spider into his seed tray. He had also scooped up others and had added them to his collection. In the garden he had put a couple of empty snail shells into the little tray, and a beautiful, dead dragonfly. At the other end of the garden he had picked some pieces of dried fungus clinging to a branch on the apple tree, and under a rotting log he had found several woodlice and a load of red centipedes. The woodlice had been a bit tricky to catch but once in the tray the movement had kept them rolled up, and anyway if they had started to crawl about they would have never been able to make it up the sides. Finally, best of all, he had found a couple of brown leatherjacket larvae in the potato patch. In total he had collected exactly sixteen items.

He had only just managed to get it all back to his bedroom without anyone stopping him. As he had gone back into the empty house, his mother and boyfriend had come in the front door, carrying shopping bags and walking unsteadily. They had obviously been to the pub and had had a few drinks. He had been halfway up the front stairs and had managed to shield the small plastic tray with his body as he had continued upwards.

"Hi, Ed. Are you alright, love?" His mother giggled. "I'm just going to make a cup of tea, would you like one?" He had looked down at her and noticed that her red lipstick was smeared on her mouth. He had also noticed that there were traces of lipstick smeared on Dan's cheek and it looked as if he had tried to wipe them off.

Edmund had just muttered, "No thanks, Mum," and had moved quickly into the safety and security of his room.

Before he had shut the door, he had heard Dan say, "That boy's completely, fucking weird. I tell you he's not normal. He should be out with other lads kicking a ball about, not creeping about the house like that."

His mother had replied, "He's OK, Dan, and you should leave him alone."

"That's his bloody problem. He's always alone."

Edmund had shut the door silently.

***

That night he had waited in bed till everyone was asleep and the house was quiet. He had dressed quietly in his darkest clothes; black jeans, black T-shirt, black trainers, and black woollen balaclava. Picking up the two bags of chocolate caramels, now all safely resealed with their "replacement" contents, which noisily crackled, he had slipped them into his school bag. He knew where all the noisy floorboards in the corridors and on the stairs were and he had glided down the stairs like a shadow. His heart was racing. It was a full moon and shafts of moonlight were filtering through the stained glass windows in the porch, which had added a weirdly kaleidoscopic aura of coloured beams across the hall floor. On the bottom step, he had suddenly frozen. He could hear his brother's voice coming up the front steps and could see movement through the glass panels of the front door. He could vaguely make out his silhouette and that of his girlfriend staggering behind him. They were obviously drunk and he had heard Mickey fumbling with the key in the lock. As he did so he could see an eerie orange halo around his head, coming from the street light on the pavement outside.

"Can't get the fucking thing in!" His voice had slurred.

"Oooh! That's not normally your problem, Mickey," his girlfriend Tricia, had said and she had squealed and giggled. "Get that door unlocked, I'm freezing and I'm going to wet meself!"

Edmund had quickly moved back into the darkened rear of the hallway and had melted into the army of random coats and jackets that hung on a row of pegs, burying himself and becoming completely invisible. Standing flat against the cold plaster of the wall, his feet among the shoes and wellingtons which cluttered the floor, he had tried to calm his breathing. He had stood stock still and had let the bag of sweets hang from his hand. He could smell the musty stink of old sweat, beer and nicotine that came from the coats.

Eventually they had got the door open and propping each other up, Mickey and Tricia staggered and stumbled into the hallway, shushing each other.

He had heard his brother say to her, "Come on, love, give us a kiss."

He had heard Tricia trying to whisper, "Oooh, not now, Mickey, not here. Someone might be listening, your little brother's bedroom is just up there."

"Don't worry about that little creep. He'll be fast asleep, dreaming of fairyland."

Edmund had then heard a moan as their lips met. There had been some obvious fumbling and what could only have been minimal resistance from Tricia. He had heard something rip and then Tricia had said, "Steady on, love, that was new on tonight."

And then he had felt a great pressure on him. Both of the drunken lovers were breathing heavily, they were leaning up against the coats and were squashing him. They began moving about. Yuk! They were snogging! He had thought that he was going to be sick. He was being pressed right up against the wall. Lucky for him that there were so many coats. He hoped that they would not realise that he was there.

As he had stood stock still, he heard Mickey say, "You're gorgeous, Trish, you know that, don't you? I'll always love you."

It all felt completely sickening. He had to get away, but he couldn't move, he would just have to grit his teeth and let them get on with it. Suddenly there was a dreadful ripping sound, followed by a couple of dull thuds and then a muffled moan, followed by silence. The hapless pair had collapsed on the floor, taking several coats with them. He had stared down at them in horror. Tricia with her skirt rucked up, was on top of his brother and he was gently snoring. Tricia was not moving at all, she was lying completely still, momentarily unconscious from having hit her head on the newel post of the staircase as she fell. As he had looked on, she slowly started to come round. Edmund had to get away fast. He had run straight to the front door and as silently as he could he had let himself out. The last thing he had heard, was Tricia saying, "Oh Gord, get away Mickey you blinking great lump, I've wet meself!"

He had flown down the steps to the pavement and with a sense of relief, had disappeared into the fresh air and freedom of the night.

***

Tyler is going to be late for his paper round unless he gets a move on. He crawls out of bed and dresses himself in yesterday's clothes. He then stands in front of the bathroom mirror and squeezes a couple of spots on his chin, which pop satisfactorily. Without washing or stopping for anything to eat, he lets himself out of the house and noisily shuts the door behind him. As he walks down the garden path, he sees a carrier bag hanging on the inside of the gate. He cannot help but notice that there was something bulky in it. He goes up to it and sees that there is a sticker fixed to the side of the bag. *'From the Easter Bunny. To Tyler'* Underneath this, there is a picture of an orange cartoon rabbit. Peering into the bag he sees a multipack of his favourite fun-size caramel chocolate bars. He can't believe his luck and wonders who has done this. Probably his grand-dad, he was always dropping round with surprises for him. He quickly stuffs the bag into the front of his bomber jacket, conscious of the fact that if anyone sees him with chocolate they would all want a piece and he wants to enjoy these all on his own later. He is a bulky lad and the extra load in his jacket would be unnoticeable.

A few doors down the road, Arnie's Dad is leaving for work. As he comes out of the house he sees that his son's bike is leaning up against the wall of the house. *That's a first*, he thinks. It was usually left in the middle of the path for him to trip over.

Some ten minutes later Arnie emerges from the front door and, without noticing that someone has picked his bike up, he walks towards it. As he gets near he notices that there is the handle of a carrier bag sticking out from under the lid of the side pannier which hangs on the back wheel. He pulls the bag out and reads a label that had been stuck to it, "From the Easter Bunny. To Arnie."

With a drawing of an orange cartoon rabbit underneath. *Good old Dad*, he thinks, he never forgets. And he stuffs the bag back into the pannier, with a warm gooey feeling of being wanted and loved.

Tyler, with the chocolates stuffed into his jacket, finishes his paper round and then he has decided to go to the park for a smoke with some cigarettes which he has just stolen from the newsagent. On the way there he meets his mate, Jonno, and they cycle together across the huge expanse of grass towards a bench on the far side under the trees where they usually go to smoke when they are bunking off school. No one is about this early except for a couple of old ladies walking their dogs but they are a long way off, beyond the defunct ornamental pond. The old ladies are talking to each other and pretending not to notice as the dogs run around and foul the grass.

The two boys sit on the bench and Jonno produces a crumpled pack of cigarettes and offers one to Tyler. Tyler takes it and is then offered a light. As they are self-consciously puffing on their cigarettes and spitting the bitter taste on the ground, Tyler remembers his bag of chocolates still stuffed in his jacket. At the thought, he cannot help himself as his hunger makes him take it out and he proudly shows it to Jonno, whose eyes light up.

"Look what me granddad gave me!" he says, as he holds it up.

"Give us one, go on. Go on, Tyler, I'm starving," whines Jonno. "I gave you a fag."

Neither of them have had any breakfast and Tyler was planning to scoff the lot himself, but now that he had showed them to Jonno he has no choice but to give him one. Carelessly, he rips the bag open and takes one out and hands it to Jonno who takes it, bites the end of the wrapping paper off and sucks the chocolate into his mouth. He chews on it greedily as Tyler takes one out of the bag and rips open the wrapper, sucks it into his mouth.

"Mmm, that's great, give us another." Jonno holds out his hand for another one, Tyler hesitates, but Jonno is bigger than him and he knows from past experience that he has a vicious and unpredictable temper. Jonno suddenly reaches forward and grabs the whole bag. Tyler holds onto it and it rips open spilling the contents onto the ground.

"Oh, fucking hell. Look what you've done now, you fucking idiot!" splutters Tyler as he chews his chocolate and bits fly out of his mouth.

They both bend down and start to pick up as many of the chocolates as they can and stuff them into their pockets.

When they are all picked up, they stand facing each other, breathless. Jonno is obviously not going to give any back and there is no way Tyler can make him.

Jonno suddenly turns, runs to his bike, jumps on it and cycles off across the grass chanting, "Loser! Loser! Tyler is a lo-o-oser!" at the top of his voice.

Totally demoralised, Tyler sits back on the bench, and taking the chocolates out of his pockets he counts them out on to the wooden arm. Only five are left, he might as well finish them. He begins to open another of the chocolates when he notices something lying on the ground at his feet, mostly concealed by the remains of the bag. He bends down and picks it up. It is about postcard-sized and it must have fallen out of the ripped bag. It is a picture of a snarling tiger leaping towards the viewer. Underneath it is printed, in thick black letters, '*Ginger Twat's Revenge!*'. As he is trying to dredge up in his mind what this was about, he absent-mindedly puts the chocolate into his mouth. It is dry and powdery and tastes vaguely of fish, he chews it some more and it tastes disgusting just like shit. It has sort of crunchy bits in it and he immediately spits it out. He looks at what he had spat out on the ground. It stinks! He retches violently, again and again. And as he does so he has a blinding flash of insight into what the message on the card means.

"What the fuck?!" he says out loud. "How could it…?"

One of the dog walkers has by now come close. She has noticed the commotion from afar and so she walks up to the boy who seems somewhat distressed.

"Are you alright, dear?" she asks, helpfully. Tyler keeps spitting and spitting on the ground. He wipes his mouth with his hand and distinctly smells shit. He retches again. He is desperate for some water or anything with which to wash out his mouth. He stands up.

"Oh piss off, lady!"

As he picks up his bike and rides away to find some water, the dog walker says, "There's no need for that language, young man. I was only trying to help," and then trying a bit louder, "Now come back and pick up this litter. Look at the mess you've left!" and then to herself, "Honestly, young people these days."

Sighing as she did so she picks up the remains of the bag and the post card of the tiger, but she doesn't bother to read it. She puts this rubbish in the bin by the bench and as she does so she sees the four remaining chocolates on the bench. She stares at them. She lives very frugally and she loves chocolate and she thought, what could be the harm? Her friend is approaching fast and she will not be able to get them into in her pocket quick enough.

"What have you got there, Ida?" asks Gill, as she approaches with Pippa, the dog bouncing at her side.

"That boy has left some chocolates behind." Ida points at them lined up on the bench.

"Do you think you ought to?" says Ida.

"They'll be alright. Look, there's four." She is resigned to having to share them and she isn't ungenerous. She picks two of them off the bench and hands one to her friend, "One for you, one for me, and those other two for Pippa and Mac!"

Some moments later Ida bites into a brown leatherjacket larvae and gags on the bitter taste. She has been distracted by Pippa, a large red setter, who is hoovering up the two remaining chocolates from the bench, taking in wrappers and all. Unbeknownst to anyone, one of them contains a family of several live woodlice, curled up and oblivious to their fate and the other a snail shell with a comatose centipede resting inside. The dog doesn't notice and merrily crunches them all up and swallows them all in one go. As Ida is spitting out the disgusting muck in her mouth, Gill, who has wandered off a bit, is embarrassed to be seen eating a chocolate which she has found in a public park. She opens the wrapper to expose a dead spider wrapped neatly in cobwebs and she gives a muffled scream. Her dog Mac is sniffing the legs of the bench and deciding which one to leave his mark on.

Jonno, cycling along the lane, reaches into his pocket

and takes out a chocolate and rips it open with his mouth, tosses the wrapper over his shoulder and sucks in a decent-sized chunk of moist fungus. By chance this particular fungus is not edible and should be avoided at all costs, but after a couple of chews on it, Jonno's mouth goes numb and he tries to spit it out, but can't; his ability to spit has been temporarily affected by the toxins in the fungus. In a panic, with a mouth full of half-chewed fungus, he rides his bike straight into a ditch containing an unpleasant mixture of filthy water, brambles, marsh weed and stinging nettles, all hiding a broken concrete post or two. When the emergency services come to rescue the unconscious boy they find a brown sticky mess in his mouth, which after analysis will prove to be a noxious, yet ultimately harmless fungus. The doctors will naturally assume that the teenager had thought he had been experimenting with magic mushrooms. The boy will feebly claim that it was in the chocolates, but when the rest of them in his pockets are checked they are, quite by chance, all found to be un-tampered with and perfectly all right.

**

Arnie is on his way to see his Gran; he goes to see her most Saturdays. He is just padlocking his bike to the railings of the alms houses where she lives. He doesn't want to leave his bag of chocolates in his bicycle pannier so he surreptitiously slips it back into the carrier bag as quickly as he can. Before doing so he scans the area about him to make sure that he isn't being watched and he tries to do it as naturally as possible. He walks across the courtyard, he has to go past the bins. When he goes round the corner of the building he is confronted by three older boys who he immediately recognises from school. They are all well known bullies.

"Well, well, well! What have we here?" says the oldest boy in the middle, with a smirk. He is known as Roach, and has several ASBOs. He has long greasy hair and a sheen of sweat covers his blotchy, spotted face.

One of his sidekicks says, "Another little second year, just ripe for plucking don't you think?"

Arnie freezes and looks at the ground. "What do you want?" He says, trying to sound normal.

"What have you got in your bag? We're hungry, aren't we lads?" says the boy in the middle.

"Nothing, er… just nothing," says Arnie, trying not to sound nervous. "Just some shopping for my Nan."

"That's nice, so you won't mind if we have a quick look then? Will you?"

And with that, the two sidekicks move towards Arnie and grab the bag. One of them gets hold of it and wrenches it from him. It stings Arnie's hands as it is pulled away so quickly.

"Give it back!" yells Arnie, but the other boy has grabbed his arms from behind as the bag is opened and its contents tipped onto the ground. Out comes the unopened bag of fun-size chocolate bars and some of his dirty PE kit from school.

"Bingo!" shouts the leader as he bends down to pick up the sweets. "Thanks lads!"

Arnie is still being held by one of the boys. He tries to break free and reach the bag. "Give it back! They're mine!"

The bigger boy holds them up out of his reach and replies, "You lied. You said there was nothing in your bag. Shopping for your Nan? You little shit. So it's nothing. You said you had nothing in your bag."

Arnie is pushed to the ground and lands in a puddle by his muddy PE kit.

The three boys run off down the street to consume their prize of chocolates behind some builders' skips where some flats are being refurbished. A notice says: "Keep Out ! Contractors only." Ripping the bag open they greedily try to eat them all as quickly as they can. They don't notice that the packaging has been tampered with, but are shocked and sickened to find that some the wrappers contain wood lice, a couple has centipedes in them and one lucky boy gets a whole dead dragonfly.

"What's all this? Some kind of fucking joke?"

"What the fu…! That's revolting. Who…?"

They throw the rest onto the ground in disgust. As they are leaving the area, quite by chance they are caught by a zealous local police constable on patrol who knows them all very well. He has heard the commotion and swearing and has come to investigate. He tells them to pick up the litter, including the bag of sweets. He takes their names. Their parents will be informed. The boys will be fined for littering. Letters telling their parents of their crime will be sent home, which will result in further punishments. So distracted were they by all this that they completely forgot about Arnie and the contaminated chocolates. The policeman puts the bag of sweets into his pocket to enjoy later, on his way home.

***

As Edmund luxuriates in the bubbles, he realises that the water is cooling and he decides to get out.

Suddenly the bathroom door bursts open. He had stupidly forgotten to lock it. It was his brother, Mickey.

He is standing there in his boxer shorts. He looks annoyed.

"Oh, it's you!" he said. "I've got a pissing headache and I want a bath."

Edmund slides down into what was left of the bubbles and says,

"I'm getting out in a minute."

His brother walks towards the lavatory, which is right beside the bath and starts to pee, Edmund tries to ignore him. He hopes that he will leave and then he can get out of the bath.

Suddenly, Mickey turns towards him as he is peeing and aims towards Edmund, he sprays the foam and Edmund as he lay in the bath. " Look at you in your poncy bubbles! Maybe this'll hurry you up!" He jeers.

Edmund leaps up trying to avoid the shower of piss that seems to be going everywhere and yells at his brother, "You fucking creep!" And grabbing a towel, he runs out of the room and down the corridor to the safety of his bedroom as Mickey laughs and turns back towards the lavatory.

Sometime later, still angry and upset by his vile treatment, Edmund is lying on the sofa in the living room, eating some cereal and pretending to watch a TV show, *Dr Why?*, a science programme for school kids, when his Mum's boyfriend, Dan, comes into the room.

"Are you still here?" he asks. "Aren't you going out, haven't you got any mates?"

Edmund doesn't answer; he just carries on eating his cereal. No, he isn't going out. And yes he does have mates. If he replies, it would be something sarcastic, and he doesn't want to rile Dan any further. He has a reputation for having a quick temper, and Edmund could do without the aggro at present. He is secretly plotting his revenge on all of them.

"Do we have to watch this crap?" Dan demands. "There's football on the other side. Where's the remote?"

"Mum said that I should watch this," said Edmund, bluntly.

"*Mum said that I should watch this*," Dan imitates him in a high pitched whiney voice and then mutters under his breath, "For Christ's sake," and gets up to leave as Edmund's Mum comes in to the sitting room, with a tray bearing three cups of tea.

"Thought we would all like a cuppa together. Just like a proper family." Dan helps himself from the proffered tray and sits down again. Edmund takes his tea, and smiling at his mum, says, "Thanks, Mum, the programme's great. It's going to help me with my school work."

Behind her back Dan silently mouths, "*This is going to help me with my school work*," and waggles his head from side to side in some kind of grotesque parody of Edmund.

His mother says, "You should watch this, Dan. It's really good. You might learn something."

Edmund can't help noticing that Dan looks distinctly nauseous as he pretends to read the football results on the back of the paper. Edmund feels a minor victory has been won.

After the programme finishes, Edmund leaves Dan and his mother to watch the football. He isn't very interested in the game and anyway, he has things he needs to do. As he goes along the landing and passes his brother's room; the door is open and he can hear him moaning. He stands in the open doorway and stares inside. His brother is sitting on the edge of his bed with his head in his hands and is looking as if he doesn't know what to do. Tricia is propped up in bed with several pillows and looking very pale.

"Oooh, Mickey, my head, it hurts." She wails. "Whatever happened? One minute we're in the hall having a lovely time and the next thing I know I'm sitting up in bed with a cup of tea. What day is it?"

"Saturday," says Mickey.

"I'm supposed to be at work by nine, what's the time?"

"Dunno," says Mickey feebly.

"It's just past eleven o'clock," says Edmund from the open door.

Both Danny and Tricia look up at Edmund.

"Whaaaat!!" cries Tricia. "I'm supposed to be at work." She clutches her head and struggles to get out of bed, forgetting that she is completely naked and giving Edmund an instant view of her whole, generously proportioned body, cascading off the bed and moving to the chair to look for her clothes. He is transfixed by her large, pendulous breasts and some trailing roses that are tattooed from her right shoulder down over her stomach and down her left thigh; he notices that each breast plays host to two or three butterflies. He is unaware that his eyes are popping out of his head and his mouth is open in shock and surprise.

"What are you fucking staring at? You fucking little pervert!" Mickey picks up one of Tricia's red stilettos and hurls it at Edmund, who ducks as it flies past him and smashes into his mother's painting of a sunny beach in Bournemouth, for which she had won first prize at her local art club.

The glass shatters as the painting frees itself from the inadequate hook that Dan had put up and crashes onto the floor, making the frame explode into its four separate pieces of faux gilded moulding, covering everything near it in shards of glass and bits of wood.

Edmund quickly runs to his room and shuts the door. For the next forty-five minutes all hell is let loose outside. He hears his Mum rush upstairs, he hears shouting and weeping. He hears doors slamming and arguing and then when he looks out of the window he sees Tricia hobbling down the garden path, half dressed. She is wearing one shoe and holding the other as she runs to catch a bus to get her to work. Once there she is going to get the sack for being late three times that month. He feels it best to not get too involved with the rumpus as, after all, none of it had anything to do with him.

***

That evening the local police constable is rushed to hospital with suspected appendicitis.

Once in bed, Edmund begins to hatch a plan of revenge on his brother and Dan. It would prove to be his best ever.

In a muddy puddle

The new boy, just eleven years old, shy of nature and with narrow drooping shoulders, is dropped at the bus stop by his dad. He doesn't turn to say or wave goodbye as he shuts the passenger door, and his father drives off without acknowledging him. He is in his new school uniform, one size too big for him, and he struggles to put his schoolbag on his back. It is nearly half past seven in the morning on a damp autumnal day, a Wednesday. There is a slight chill in the air and the sun has yet to break through the clouds.

As the family car disappears down the road and round the corner, he stands alone, unsure what to do. Not far away, beside the bus shelter, at just a few paces, he is aware of a group of three boys in black blazers wearing the same uniform as him. They stare at the boy blankly but say nothing. One of them whispers something to another, trying not to move his lips and without moving his head and they carry on staring. The boy then looks at the ground, his arms by his side, his school bag hanging heavily on his back. He feels anxious and tries to think of something else. He thinks of home but then has to fight the urge to cry.

A bit further away another group of slightly bigger boys in purple blazers is also waiting for the bus. One or two of them look round at the new arrival, but with little interest, a quick glance and then they turn back to their more urgent conversation, something about a new teacher in one of yesterday's lessons. One of them laughs. They all laugh loudly.

The boy quickly looks up and towards them and is relieved to realise that they are not laughing at him.

He looks down again and sees a stone lying on the ground just by his feet. It stands out from the rest of the gravel that lies there. It is a sort of burnt orange and has a distinctive shape. It is flat with the diameter of a golf ball. It has a bulbous middle and jagged edges. It looks like a little sun. He focuses on it intently, noticing its shape and colour.

Suddenly the boy gently kicks it along the ground in the direction of the middle boy in the group of black blazers.

The middle boy blocks it, hesitates and then gently kicks it back. The boy kicks it towards another of the black blazers, who kicks it towards the boy beside him, who smiles. And it is then passed back and forth between all four of them in turn, crisscross, back and forth. No one is left out. No one says a word. They are imagining it is a football and that they are playing at Wembley in the cup final. For a few precious seconds they are not at the dreary bus stop waiting for the bus that will take them to the noisy clattering school with its echoing stone corridors, the maths test, the threatening PE teacher, the hurried lunch, the smelly toilets and all the latent aggression.

The bus pulls up and stops. All the boys cluster round the opening door. The purple blazers push to the front, the black blazers give way, the new boy gets on last, and the bus drives away.

The burnt orange stone lies submerged in a muddy puddle.